THE
RISING

A NOVEL

THE
RISING

A NOVEL

BAIRBRE TÓIBÍN

**NEW
ISLAND**

THE RISING
First published October 2001
by New Island Books
2 Brookside
Dundrum Road
Dublin 14

ISBN 1 902602 65 X

British Library Cataloguing in Publication Data.
A catalogue record for this book is available
from the British Library.

The author has asserted her moral rights.

The Arts Council
An Chomhairle Ealaíon

New Island received financial assistance from The Arts Council
(An Chomhairle Ealaíon), Dublin, Ireland.

*The author wishes to acknowledge the support of the Tyrone Guthrie
Centre at Annaghmakerrig where some of this book was written.*

Cover design: Slick Fish Design
Printed in Ireland by Colour Books Ltd.

For Brendan, Nuala, Colm and Niall

Chapter 1

October 1891

Michael Carty walked across the muddy yard and up the narrow lane. He was going towards the village of Ballyduff hoping to meet his father who had been in Dublin at Parnell's funeral. It was beginning to get dark. There had been a lot of rain, and the ditches were lush with long wet grass and nettles. Brambles stretched along the sandy ground in front of him. He was sixteen years of age, but he had been lonely in the house on his own while his father was at the funeral.

He came out on to the open road of the townsland of Kilbride, and walked quickly uphill past Grogans' house and the marl pond. A water hen skimmed across the pond and disappeared into bushes. He walked down the hill and turned on to the low road. He couldn't stop thinking about Parnell who had died of a broken heart because the Irish people had betrayed him. They had called him their Chief, the Uncrowned King of Ireland, but then they had voted against him to please Gladstone and the bishops.

There was one star in the sky and when he came to the cross he was delighted to see his father coming slowly towards him on the road from the village.

"I was thinking you'd come to meet me," his father said. There were two or three days' growth of beard on his face.

They walked back towards home.

"What was the funeral like?" Michael asked.

"I never saw such a big crowd. The people of Dublin stood by Parnell. The whole city came out to walk past his coffin," his father said. He was moving slowly, and Michael walked slowly too.

"How did you get on without me? Were you lonely?" His father was short of breath and stopped on the road to ask the question.

"I went down to Mrs Murphy every day for my dinner, and I went to Murphys' at night as well," Michael said. He had been going in and out to Murphys' since he was a child. Mrs Murphy had been friendly with his mother who had died when he was young. He couldn't remember his mother. His father never talked about her, but Mrs Murphy sometimes did. His brother Jim who had gone to England would never spend as much time in Murphys', and used often give out to Michael about going there so often.

"Mrs Murphy has always been like a mother to you," his father said.

The wind was rustling through the trees. Michael was a step or two ahead as they turned to go up the hill. He waited so that he would be beside his father. Suddenly his father shouted in pain. "Aaaaaaaa." He staggered sideways and arched towards the ditch. "Michael," he shouted as he slumped down. His head banged off the road.

"What's wrong? Are you all right?" Michael bent down over his father and then knelt beside him. "Are you all right?"

His father didn't answer. His eyes and his mouth were closed. His right arm was lying on his stomach.

"Are you all right? We're nearly halfway up the hill. We'll go very slowly," he said, moving along the ground on his knees until he was kneeling close to his father's head which was propped up a little by a rise in the road. "Have a rest for a while and we'll walk very slowly. There's no hurry."

His father didn't move but Michael knew that he could hear him. He was probably very tired after the long journey from Dublin and all those days away. He looked as if he had fallen asleep. The best thing was to get him home. He shouldn't be lying out here in the cold.

"Wake up. We're nearly home." He lifted his father's arm. It felt limp. He put it down gently. He knelt there for a while, looking at his father, not sure what to do. There was a stone digging into his knee, hurting him. He looked up and down the hill, hoping to see somebody. He wished his brother Jim was there with them. He wished Jim had never gone to England. The sky was pink and a dull yellow around the setting sun.

"Will I go for Joe Grogan? Joe could bring you home on the cart." He knew his father could hear him. His face was moving a little as if he was smiling. "Answer me. Say something. I'll go for Joe." He stood up. He saw his father's hat on the grass at the edge of the road. "I'll be back in a minute."

He could hear his own voice. It was strange to be talking like that out on the hill in the dusk with his father not answering. He stood looking down at him. It didn't seem right to leave him, but Grogans' house was only a short distance away, over the top of the hill. The wind was whining, and the ash trees were swaying. He wouldn't be a minute. He ran up the hill but when he got near the top he knew that he shouldn't have left his father. If his father was dying someone should say an Act of Contrition into his ear. He turned and ran back down the hill. He slowed down when he got close to him. He must be cold lying there on the damp ground. He told himself that his father wasn't dying. He knelt beside him and touched his hand. It was warm, and his mouth was moving. All the colour was gone from his face. He wasn't dead. He wasn't going to die.

"Are you all right?" He tried to sound calm. He didn't want his father to know that he was afraid. He gripped his arm. "We'll go home in a minute."

His father's face was peaceful but suddenly his mouth opened to let out a strange sound. It came from somewhere deep within him, out through his mouth. His eyes flickered but stayed closed. Michael knew that the sound was the sound of his father dying. He looked around him. The ditches on both sides of the road looked terribly dark. He touched his father's forehead and head. He bent down close to him and began to whisper. "O, my God, I am heartily sorry for having sinned against Thee …" But he knew that his father was dead and couldn't hear him.

"What am I going to do? I'll get Joe Grogan. We'll bring you home."

He stood up and walked away. He was on his own in the world now, completely alone. His father was dead. Jim had cleared off to England. He didn't know how he would manage on his own, or what would happen to him, but he didn't care. He turned to look back at his father. There was just a dark shape, lying on the road close to the ditch. But he could see his father, still alive. He could see himself and his father, a few minutes before, walking along the low road coming towards the bottom of the hill. They were walking along the road talking. It was as if he was above them both, or walking towards them, as if he wasn't just himself but another person as well, watching himself. He could see the two figures coming along the road towards the bottom of the hill, walking slowly, hunched down against the cold.

He ran up over the top of the hill and into Grogans' yard. His father was dead. He would have to get Joe Grogan to bring down the cart. The sheepdog barked loudly and Joe opened the door before Michael knocked on it.

"It's my father. He's after falling. He's down the hill. Will you bring the horse and cart?"

He couldn't look at Joe. He turned and ran out of the yard. He knew that he shouldn't have left his father for so long. He ran down the hill.

"Michael. Wait for me." It was Joe's wife, Nora. He stood on the road as she ran towards him.

"Joe is getting the horse out." She put her arm around him.

He ran and she ran after him.

He was still lying there, awkwardly sprawled out on the hard road. Nora knelt down and touched his father's face and lifted his arm.

"Kneel down beside me, Michael, and we'll pray," she said, blessing herself. "He's dead, Michael. You know that your father is dead, don't you?"

She gripped his arm so tightly that it hurt. He nodded and turning away from her he began to cry. He wanted his father to open his eyes and to talk. He wanted him to get up and to walk home. He could go to bed and he would be all right in the morning.

The cart came rattling and banging down the hill. Nora got up and walked over and began whispering to Joe. He knew that his father was dead but he wanted to stay here beside him for as long as he could. He wanted Nora and Joe to stay whispering at the cart. He didn't want anyone to come near him.

Joe came over. "We'll bring him home, Michael," he said. "We'll lift him up on the cart and we'll bring him home."

*

The neighbours gathered in the house as soon as word spread that his father had died.

He sat at the fire while the women laid his father out in the bedroom.

"This is terrible, Michael," Mrs Murphy said, bending down and shaking his hand. There were tears in her eyes. "You're on your own now but you'll come often to visit us, won't you?"

The house was full of smoke. Nora Grogan had lit the fire and she had put too much turf on it. Joe Grogan had gone into the village to get the priest.

"I can't believe that he's dead," Mrs Murphy said to Nora. "He was in our house two or three nights ago and he was in the best of good form. You know how funny he could be. You'd never know what he'd say. I always had to listen very carefully to make sure I kept him on the straight and narrow."

He went into the bedroom to see his father. There was a candle and a crucifix on a chair at the head of the bed, and a bowl of holy water and a leaf. He stood at the side of the bed and looked down at his father. The colour was gone from his face. It was pale now, the colour of mud dried by days of summer sun. He was wearing a brown shroud. A heavy cream sheet covered his body. His hands were joined as if he was praying, and there was a rosary beads entwined around his fingers. He touched his father's hand but he was afraid of touching his forehead in case he would hurt his father although he knew that he was dead and nothing could hurt him.

People came in and took up the leaf and sprinkled holy water on his father. They blessed themselves and stood with their heads bowed, praying. One of the women gave out the sorrowful mysteries of the rosary. Two of the men carried a bench in from the kitchen and leaned it against the wall. He sat on the bench when the rosary was over. People sat with him and he told the story of his father's death again and again.

He could hear laughing in the kitchen. There was a huge crowd at the wake. The women started to pray again taking it in turns to give out the different mysteries of the rosary. Then he noticed that the talk in the kitchen had stopped. He could hear whispering. Maybe Father Roche had arrived.

He went to the door. He couldn't see Father Roche, but Joe Grogan was back, standing close to the fire talking to Nora and Mrs Murphy. The people in the kitchen were watching him as he went over to Joe.

"Father Roche won't come out," Joe said. "He says that your father was a Fenian, and that he was excommunicated from the Catholic Church. He had plenty of chances to recant but he never did. He won't allow your father to be brought to the church nor to be buried in the cemetery. It will be a lesson to all Fenians, he says."

"It's ridiculous," Nora said, "but you've heard Father Roche yourself lambasting the Fenians from the altar. Hell is not hot enough, nor eternity long enough to punish them for not accepting the law of the land and the authority of the Catholic Church. Your father never got on with Father Roche."

"God will be my father's judge, not Father Roche. I think priests should stay out of politics. My father never harmed anyone," Michael said angrily.

"I won't hear a word said against poor Father Roche," Mrs Murphy said. "He has to do what the bishop tells him. Father Roche is a good man. It's all this talk about politics that caused the trouble." Mrs Murphy always supported the clergy.

"Maybe Father Roche will change his mind," Nora Grogan said. "If you went into him in the morning, Michael, and asked him, he might change his mind."

"That's the best thing to do," Mrs Murphy said. "We'll go into him in the morning. He's a good man. He might see things differently in the light of day."

Michael was shaking with anger but he knew that it was best to say nothing. He didn't want to annoy Mrs Murphy by attacking the clergy, but there was no doubt that the bishops and priests were wrong, not the Fenians. How could it be wrong to fight for freedom and justice? Father Roche was siding with the British against his own people. He had refused his father absolution unless he renounced the Fenians and his father couldn't do that.

"We'll go with you in the morning, Michael," Joe said. "Maybe he'll change his mind."

He nodded at Joe but he didn't think Father Roche would change his mind. He had deprived Michael's father of Communion and confession for years.

"Sit down at the table, Michael," Mrs Murphy said. "You'd want to eat something." There were two plates of brown bread on the table and dishes of blackberry jam. Over near the hearth there was plenty of turf and big blocks of wood. People always brought things to a wake. Mrs Murphy cut some apple tart and put it in front of him.

"Forget about the funeral until the morning," she said. "The less said about all that the better."

"Where …" Michael began, but then he decided not to ask the question that was in his mind. He didn't want to hear the answer. Where would his father be buried if not in the cemetery? Would they dig a hole in a ditch, or on some boggy land, and throw him into it, like an old dog?

The people around him were talking and laughing. Joe Grogan was pouring whiskey. Michael had taken money from the rent-box and told Joe to buy whiskey in the village. His father would have wanted a proper wake.

Suddenly he needed to get away from everyone. It was

too hot in the kitchen. He slipped out into the yard. The wind had died down and the moon was high in the sky. He felt a huge surge of anger towards his brother Jim. Jim was five years older than him. It was Jim who should be here to deal with all of this.

He walked across the yard to the top of the lane. There were puddles here and there, and the ground was muddy. There was a bank of grey cloud, low in the sky. He could see part of the road, and then blackness. The trees on the lane looked unreal, like shadows in the darkness. He could hear a buzz of talk from the house. He would have to go back inside or it would look as if he didn't care that his father was dead. He went slowly back across the yard although he wanted to walk and walk, to walk anywhere away from the house where his father was being waked.

*

Clouds raced across the sky and smoke from Father Roche's chimney billowed down towards the village. Michael was walking behind Mrs Murphy and Joe Grogan when his father's death hit him again, taking him over, filling him with hopelessness and a kind of rage. During the night of the wake he had almost forgotten at times that his father was dead, and when he had remembered he had kept the thought of it away from him, at arm's length, out of his head. But sometimes without warning the horror of it came rushing through him. As he walked past the oak front door of Father Roche's house he wanted to howl out loud because his father was dead.

They walked around the side of the big two-storied house. The greyhounds in the outhouses began to bark ferociously. Father Roche's greyhounds were well-known all over County Wexford. They often won prizes at coursing meetings in Enniscorthy. The back door scraped along the kitchen floor and Father Roche came out into the yard.

"Go away down," he shouted at the greyhounds, turning around to face the outhouses. He was wearing a black soutane which was blowing in the wind. "Go down." The saplings quietened but the pups in the outhouse nearest to them continued their squealy barking. "Shut up. G'up." His voice was hoarse and rough. They heard the thump of the saplings landing on the timber bed. The barking stopped as Father Roche walked towards them.

"I'm sorry for your trouble," he said, shaking Michael's hand. His face looked red and almost scalded as if he had got a bad burning from the sun. "I've been praying for you. I remembered you this morning when I was saying Mass." He gripped Michael's arm but his bright blue eyes moved their gaze from Mrs Murphy to Joe, and back again. "It's hard to understand why your mother was taken from you first when you were young, and now your father, but God's ways are not our ways. These good people here are helping you. God often shows His love for us by giving us good neighbours."

"We came to ask you could the funeral come to the church tonight, Father," Mrs Murphy said. Her voice was gentle and quiet. She held her head sideways. There was a slight smile on her face.

"But I told you about that last night, Joe," Father Roche said, frowning. "The funeral can't come to the church. I'm sorry but I'm only following instructions. I have to do what the bishop says."

Michael wanted to walk away and never see Father Roche again.

"It's very hard on young Michael, Father," Mrs Murphy said.

"It is indeed." Father Roche nodded. He bustled forward and then backwards. He was getting cross with them for challenging him so much. "But I'm sure God will give Michael the grace to be strong at this time. I know the difficult time he's going through. I offered up the Holy Sacrifice of the Mass for him this morning."

"You're very good Father," Mrs Murphy said.

She was different when she was talking to the priest. There was no one else that she would give in to like that. Father Roche wasn't good. He was getting his revenge for all those Sundays in the churchyard when Michael's father had refused to acknowledge him. Father Roche walked among the people after Mass on Sunday. Everybody wanted to talk to him. The women would bow their heads as they saluted him, and the men would doff their hats and caps as they wished him good day, but everybody knew that Sunday after Sunday Jim Carty walked proudly past as if the priest was a man of no importance. Michael had seen the anger on Father Roche's face after he was shunned like this in front of everybody and he had asked his father would he not speak to the priest, would he not pretend that he liked him?

"No. I won't," his father had said laughing. He laughed every Sunday as he talked about how much he loved ignoring Father Roche.

"Shut up." Father Roche had turned his head towards the outhouse where the greyhound pups had begun to bark again. "Fenians cannot be buried in consecrated ground," he said, jutting his mouth and jaw out in determination. "I'll have a hole dug in that patch up past the cemetery between the two parishes where the unbaptised babies are buried. He can be buried there whenever ye like. Good day to ye, now."

It was as if his father was a dead dog, lying out on the road, in the middle of everyone's way.

"He could have pretended he didn't know my father was a Fenian," Michael said as they got back on the cart at the top of the village. "That's what the priests in Enniscorthy do.

The Fenians in Enniscorthy are given absolution and they receive Communion."

"I felt sorry for poor Father Roche," Mrs Murphy said. "He's only following orders. Surely you don't expect priests to tell lies."

"They'd tell lies quickly enough if it suited them," Michael said.

He was worried about what the Fenians who had been gathering all the morning at his father's wake would do when they heard that Father Roche was still refusing his father a Christian burial. Ten or twelve of the Fenians were standing beside the ditch under the bushes when they arrived back in the yard in Kilbride. Charlie Walsh, a Fenian from Ballyduff was among them.

"Will you look at those Fenians," Mrs Murphy said. "They're terrible troublemakers. Standing out in the yard, making a show of themselves."

The Fenians came over to the cart.

"What did Father Roche say?" Charlie asked.

"He said that we can't bring him to the church or bury him with …" Michael hesitated. He couldn't say the words "my mother". He never did say those words out loud. Sometimes he said them to himself, and tried to imagine having a mother. But he didn't remember her, and saying the words would be as if he was laying claim to something that wasn't his. "He says Fenians can't have a Christian burial. My father can't be buried in the cemetery." He got out of the cart.

"God blast him," one of the men shouted. He had a pale complexion and extraordinary bags of flesh under his eyes, like small extra cheeks. "Why can't the clergy deal with religion and leave politics to us?"

Mrs Murphy sighed as she got down off the cart and went

inside, without looking towards the Fenians. Joe turned the horse over to the corner of the yard.

"May the priest roast in hell," the tall man said. There was a strong smell of whiskey off him. "May he never see the face of God."

The Fenians all shouted loudly and angrily against the priest. Michael nodded in agreement at a small man with brown-rimmed glasses who said that it was a sad day for Ireland when the Catholic clergy had turned on her.

"That tall man," Charlie whispered, turning his back on the group and facing Michael, "is Mogue McCabe, the centre of the Fenians in Enniscorthy."

Michael had often heard his father talking about McCabe. He had been involved in the Fenian movement from the beginning. He knew all the top men, and had suffered like them in English jails. McCabe, still talking loudly, began to walk towards the ditch and the others followed him. Michael thought about McCabe being tortured, then shackled to the wall of a damp dungeon, shivering in the cold and dark, a diet of bread and water, no one to talk to. McCabe turned around, and it was his eyes that Michael looked at. They were intense and alive, like the spirit of the Fenians. The British could never break the spirit of a Fenian. Michael hoped that he too would be strong enough to suffer like that for Ireland.

"I don't give a tinker's curse about priests or bishops," McCabe was saying, shaking his clenched fist. "We'll go in after dark and give that blackguard a right fright. We'll get Jim Carty a Christian burial. The clergy have betrayed the Irish people before and they will betray them again. We will fight the British with or without the Catholic Church and we will win," McCabe continued. The anger and excitement of his talk lifted Michael's mood and he wanted this speech to go on forever. "Our struggle against the British has gone on for centuries, but the day is coming when the Fenians will drive them, like you'd drive a herd of cattle, out of this land, and Ireland will take her rightful place among the nations of the world."

He stopped abruptly and moved on towards the ditch. Michael looked after him. He wished McCabe would keep on talking. He felt let down after the speech ended as if there was something in him, or in his life, suddenly gone missing. He wanted to cry. The sun was shining behind the trees and some of the leaves looked yellow in the sunlight. A few leaves fell twirling slowly to the ground. The Fenians had followed McCabe and they were all talking again, standing under the ash-trees. He was on his own in the middle of the yard when he remembered that his father was dead. He pictured dead fingers but he didn't let his father's dead face come into his mind. He leaned one foot heavily on the ground and pushed it forward so that the mud squished out on either side of his shoe. He wanted to be in the middle of the Fenians again, listening to them, forgetting about himself.

He heard horses coming down the lane. Two men on horseback came into the yard. It was Doctor Guilfoyle from the village but the man on the second horse was a stranger to Michael.

"That's Willie Redmond, MP," Mogue McCabe said as the two men got down off their horses and tethered them to a tree in the ditch. "What's he doing here?"

"Willie Redmond often comes to visit Doctor Guilfoyle," Charlie Walsh said. "The two of them are friendly for years. They were in school together, in a big college up near Dublin."

Doctor Guilfoyle and the stranger went into the house.

"Those MPs should stay over in Westminster, licking Gladstone's arse, and let us bury our own dead," an old

Fenian said. "What's he coming down here for? He wants to have his finger in every pie."

"Don't take any notice of Willie Redmond," McCabe said. "Let him go in there and say his prayers. We'll deal with Roche. We'll pick a few of the younger lads and send them in after dark with sticks to get him to change his mind."

"But we couldn't violate the body of an anointed man of God. The priest's body is consecrated to God. It would be a mortal sin to hit a priest," one of the Fenians said quietly.

"When priests interfere in politics they lose the protection they usually have," McCabe shouted angrily.

Other voices were raised in argument and Michael turned away and moved slowly towards the house. He couldn't bear to listen to an argument and Willie Redmond might want to say something to him. He didn't want the Fenians to beat up Father Roche. Mrs Murphy would go mad, and nobody in Kilbride would like it.

There was the smell of tobacco in the kitchen. Willie Redmond and Doctor Guilfoyle had gone into the wake room where they were talking to Aunt Mary, Michael's father's sister, who had come from Enniscorthy to the wake. Michael stood looking around him. He knew where he was, inside the kitchen of his own house, but in a strange way he felt he wasn't there. He could see Mrs Murphy fixing the fire. There were men sitting around the kitchen but they were strangers to him, Fenians probably, or Parnellites. Some of them were very drunk. But everything seemed very far away from him although he was standing close to it. He didn't feel he was inside his own body or head. It was as if most of him was gone off somewhere else. He wished he could get back to normal, that whatever was gone from him would come back.

Most of the people from Kilbride had gone home. They had stayed through the night but as soon as the house began to fill up with Fenians they had left. As he moved towards the wake-room one of the Fenians who was drunk grabbed his arm and said something to him which he couldn't understand. Willie Redmond was kneeling at the bottom of the bed with brown rosary beads in his hands. Doctor Guilfoyle tapped Redmond on the shoulder and whispered something to him. Blessing himself, and kissing the crucifix of the beads, Redmond stood up and came over to him. He was tall and broad, like Doctor Guilfoyle.

"I'm sorry for your trouble," he said, shaking Michael's hand, and gazing intently down at him. "I met your father once or twice at meetings. What were they saying in the kitchen about the priest not letting the funeral go to the church?"

"Father Roche won't let him be brought to the church or be buried in consecrated ground because he was a Fenian and all Fenians are excommunicated," Michael said.

Willie Redmond shook his head in disbelief. "That seems a bit harsh." He turned around to Doctor Guilfoyle. "I met Father Roche once in your house, didn't I?"

"You did," Doctor Guilfoyle said. "He sometimes comes to us for dinner."

"Maybe I'll go in and have a word with him." Redmond said, gripping Michael's arm. "It would be a terrible pity if a great Irishman like your father couldn't get a Catholic burial."

"Father Roche's nephews are in school in Clongowes Wood College," Doctor Guilfoyle said. "I often tell him stories about my time there. He loves talking about Clongowes and the Jesuits."

"We'll talk about Clongowes," Redmond said, "and would you invite him to dinner tonight? That's what we'll do first – invite him to dinner."

Doctor Guilfoyle laughed.

Michael sat down on the bench and listened to Willie
Redmond announcing to the people in the kitchen what he
and Doctor Guilfoyle were going to do. He was worried in
case the Fenians would blame him for allowing Redmond to
go in to the priest. Most of them wanted to beat up Father
Roche. He heard the horses clomping out of the yard. He
thought about the Fenians for a while, and Mogue McCabe,
but then Willie Redmond came into his head. He pictured
him on horseback, turning the corner at Clearys', going up
the hill, then down, and on towards the village. He could see
it all clearly in his mind, as if he was there, too. The darkness
of the marl pond, sceachs growing out on to the road. He felt
as if he was on the road with Willie Redmond, but he also
felt that Willie Redmond had taken him over and was inside
his head and his body.

Aunt Mary came over and sat beside him. He was very
fond of her. He had been going with his father to her house
in Enniscorthy for as long as he could remember.

"You'll have to come in often to see me," she said. "Your
father always came to see me when he was in Enniscorthy.
I'm going to miss him terribly."

She started to cry. He didn't know what to say to her.
Willie Redmond was probably at the cross now, turning
towards the village, going down past Bolgers' shop.

After a while Mrs Murphy called him out to the kitchen
for something to eat. She began to cut one of the big cakes
of bread the women had brought the night before. The knife
made a rasping sound against the wood. Two of the Fenians
went outside. The drunken man who had been trying to talk
to Michael earlier was slumped down on the table asleep.

"Will everybody from Kilbride come back? Nearly
everybody is gone," he said to Mrs Murphy.

"They will of course," she said. "They went home to do
the work."

The Fenians outside were arguing loudly. He couldn't make out what they were saying but every now and again he could hear Mogue McCabe's voice raised above the others. He could feel the tension of the argument in his stomach and sometimes he shuddered when a voice spoke angrily. Where was Willie Redmond? Why didn't Willie Redmond come back?

He ate some bread and an egg which Mrs Murphy fried for him. The Fenians at the table were talking about Parnell and the split.

"Tim Healy should be horsewhipped for what he said about Parnell," one of them said angrily.

"Shshsh," Mrs Murphy said. "Mr Redmond and Doctor Guilfoyle are coming back."

The Fenians began to crowd into the house. Willie Redmond made his way through them and stood with his back to the fire. He looked solemn like the priest on the altar.

"I have good news," he said. "We explained to Father Roche that Michael had said an Act of Contrition for his father. Doctor Guilfoyle was sure of that. There was no doubt but that James Carty repented of all his sins before he died. Father Roche said that since God would always welcome the repentant sinner home, he, as God's representative on earth, would do the same. He will receive the remains of James Carty at the door of the church in an hour's time. The funeral Mass and the burial in the cemetery will be tomorrow morning. But, lads, he says no marching, no guard of honour." Redmond shook his head slowly. "It has to be a simple country funeral."

"We'd have to give Jim Carty a guard of honour," one of the Fenians shouted. "That's why we came here. We're not having Roche telling us what to do."

Two or three other voices shouted in agreement but most of the Fenians said nothing.

"I agree with you, lads, and I'd love a guard of honour too, but for Michael's sake, I think we should go along with Father Roche's terms," Redmond said.

"We'll have a guard of honour," Mogue McCabe said, moving into the kitchen, "until we get to the outskirts of the village and then we'll break it up. What Roche doesn't know won't hurt him. We'll fire a volley of shots here at the house."

"All we want to be sure of, lads," Redmond said, "is that there's no trouble. For Michael's sake."

"A guard of honour as far as the village," Mogue McCabe said.

The Fenians began to talk excitedly, all agreeing with McCabe.

"We'll try to avoid trouble," Redmond said, moving towards the wake-room. "The women will want to start saying the prayers now. We'll have to say a rosary before we go."

Mrs Murphy started the rosary. Michael went into the wake-room and knelt beside his Aunt Mary at his father's coffin. He hated being reminded that his father was dead. He had to look down at the corpse, the hands joined and the rosary beads entwined around the fingers. The people were praying together, making a rough sound like the shuffling of feet. This would soon be over and they would all be gone. He would be here on his own.

When the rosary was over people began to move out into the kitchen. Joe Grogan and Dan Murphy, Mrs Murphy's son, put the lid on the coffin and took out nails and a hammer. He wanted to cry out as Joe nailed the lid on to the coffin. He stuck his finger nails into the palms of his hands and he thought of Christ being nailed to the Cross, the men hammering nails into His hands and then hammering a nail through His two feet.

Mrs Murphy took up the candle and Michael helped the

men to carry the coffin out through the kitchen. His father was leaving the house for the last time. He would never see him again in this world. The wind was cold and there was an awful silence among the people standing around the yard. Even the Fenians were quiet. It didn't seem right to speak. Michael remembered running down the lane into the yard shouting loudly, only three or four days before, shouting to tell his father the news that Parnell was dead.

"I'll have to go to the funeral," his father had said. "I'll go into Enniscorthy. There will be people going to the funeral from there."

But he had delayed a while before leaving. He had talked about Parnell. He used to often talk about how hard things were on the land at the end of the Seventies, before the Land League. Falling prices, bad weather, poor yields. Michael didn't remember much of it. He was only three or four at the time. There were evictions, his father said, and eviction notices. Some people were starving. It looked as if the country was going to be destroyed again like it was the time of the Famine.

"Parnell and Davitt started the Land League. That was what saved us," his father had said. "But the people crucified Parnell in the end."

He pushed his father's coffin along the floor of the cart. Huge drops of rain began to fall. The Fenians were putting on black armbands, getting ready to form the guard of honour. He turned to look for Mrs Murphy. He wanted to walk with her and his Aunt Mary. He went over towards Mrs Murphy who was in the middle of the yard talking to Willie Redmond.

"The people all gather in my house at night," she was saying.

"People who gather others together are much to be admired," Willie Redmond said.

Doctor Guilfoyle was standing beside them with his arms folded. They didn't notice Michael although he was close to them. Aunt Mary was back at the door of the house, talking to Mogue McCabe who had his head bent down listening to her. There was no use in going over to them either.

He went and stood on his own behind the cart. They were all too busy to talk to him. His father was gone for good. Jim was in England. He was on his own, and he didn't care if he never loved anybody again, ever in his life, after this day.

Chapter 2

He tried to get used to living on his own. He cried the day he wrote to Jim to tell him that their father had died. Sometimes he thought of leaving Kilbride and going to meet Jim in England, but he didn't think it would be right to leave a farm of land behind, although it was only a few acres and they were in arrears with the rent. He planned each day carefully. He only allowed himself to go to Murphys' once during the day, and again at night. If he went too often they would get fed up of him.

He got up slowly in the morning. There was no use in rushing. It was winter and there was very little work to do. He would milk the cows first and later he would bring the milk to Murphys'. Mrs Murphy had always made their butter along with her own. After the milking he sat at the table and ate his breakfast. Then he read one of his father's books but he found it hard to concentrate. He would go out and bring in fuel although he didn't light the fire until closer to dinner time.

He liked cooking the dinner but he dreaded the hours afterwards. There was nothing to do, and he was on his own. He missed his father. He visited the Grogans' every two or three days and they always seemed glad enough to see him. If the forge was open he went in there. No one ever came to visit him.

He carried the bucket of milk down to Murphys', circling

around a puddle near the gate. Mrs Murphy was out in the yard, scattering meal for the fowl. Strands of her greying hair were blowing in the wind. "Chuck … chuck … chuck …" she was saying, holding her apron up around the basin of meal, as she walked around the yard. "Michael," she said. She sounded surprised to see him although he called to the house every day. "Chuck … chuck …" she said again tilting the basin to scatter the last of the meal. He could see by her that she was in good humour. She was probably looking forward to the day out tomorrow at the fair in Enniscorthy. He was hoping that she would ask him to travel with herself and Dan. He would go on his own if she didn't ask him but it would be nicer to have company for the journey.

The hens pecked the ground and strutted around, cackling.

"Come in," Mrs Murphy said. "I have eggs for you."

He followed her into the kitchen and put the bucket of milk on the kitchen table. She put the basin under the sink and wiped her hands on her apron.

"I'll put fuel on the fire and then I'll get the eggs for you," she said.

She took a big block of wood from the fuel basket and put it at the back of the fire. Old Tom Murphy's chair was empty. He'd had a bad turn a few years before, and she never let him get up until after dinner.

"Will you bring in fuel for me?"

"I will of course," he said, going over to the hearth and taking up the fuel basket.

It was starting to rain. He opened the bolt of the shed. The door had come off one of the hinges and he scraped it carefully along the floor. He didn't know whether she wanted him to go to the fair with herself and Dan or not. He didn't want to ask in case she said no. The first Sunday after his father died he had thought of asking could he go to Mass in

Balyduff with them, and he was very glad that he hadn't. She didn't want to be seen talking to him in the churchyard there. She looked away when he came near, and once she had even turned her back on him. He stayed away from her in the churchyard now. She stood waiting to talk to Father Roche. She was trying to get friendly with him again because she realized that she had made a big mistake by going in to ask him to change his mind about the burial.

He filled the fuel basket with turf and blocks of wood. Some of the hens had followed him into the shed and he shooed them out and bolted the door. He should never have let her come into Father Roche with him that morning. They shouldn't have bothered going. It had been a wasted journey. He carried the fuel back into the kitchen to her. She might ask him to go to the fair with them. The fair was different to Mass in Ballyduff. Father Roche would hardly be at the fair.

She had put the eggs in a bag on the kitchen table.

"We'll go early to the fair tomorrow," she said. "I want to get a good stand in the Market Square, get everything sold and get back here before dark. Will you come up here at first light?"

"I hope I'll wake up in time," he said, pretending he had known all along that he would be going with them.

"I'll send Dan down for you if you don't come up."

He walked back up the lane, delighted that she had asked him. It was only because of Father Roche that she didn't want to be seen with him in Ballyduff. She still liked him. It wasn't until the day of his father's burial that they realized that she had made a mistake by going in to Father Roche. It was old Tom Murphy who said it to her. He wasn't able to go out and he was always bitter when she stayed away from the house for too long and left him on his own.

"I don't know what you had to put your oar in there for," he had said when they came back from the funeral. "It's all over now. It was all solved without you. But it will be a long time before Father Roche calls to this house again."

She stood still in the middle of the kitchen. She looked shocked. "You don't think he'll hold it against me, do you?" Her voice was low and weak.

"He will, of course. He won't have the likes of you challenging him."

"I only went into him because I thought he'd expect me to go in," she said. "He often told me that he thought I was great to be looking after young Michael when his mother died and there was no one else to teach him right from wrong. But you think I made a mistake."

"Michael is after getting you into trouble," Tom Murphy said, laughing jeeringly. Michael knew that Tom Murphy didn't like him.

"We won't talk about the funeral anymore," Mrs Murphy said quickly. "We'll forget all about it." She went over to the dresser and took down the milk jug. "Go out to the dairy and bring in more milk for me, Michael." She stretched the milk jug towards him but kept a grip on it with her two hands even after she must have known that he was holding the handle. "We won't mention your father's funeral again," she said. "We'll settle back down to our ordinary lives." She had seemed weak before but now speaking to him seemed to give her back her strength. He had always loved the unusual deep gravely tone of her voice, but now he could hear a hissing and a rattling in it that sounded awful. "I'll talk to Father Roche after Mass next Sunday," she said. "I'll make sure he knows that I'm on his side."

He had gone out to the dairy. He couldn't believe how tough Mrs Murphy had been. He had never noticed her tough strength before, and he despised it because it was so narrow. In a way he despised all the people of Kilbride. If there was a Rising not one of them except himself would take part in it.

But he was glad to be going to the fair with the Murphys. They were his friends. If he fell out with them he would have nowhere to go at night in Kilbride. He lit the fire, and took potatoes out of the sack in the corner. His brother Jim had never been as close to Mrs Murphy as he had. Michael used to call into her every day on his way home from school. An odd day Jim would go with him.

"You go in first," Jim would say when they came near the door.

"Why?"

"That's the why. She likes you better than me."

It was nice to have Jim following him because Jim was so much bigger. It was great to be sure that Mrs Murphy was going to want to see them when Jim wasn't sure. "Michael," Mrs Murphy woud say. Then she would hesitate, "Oh, and Jim," but her voice would become a bit sharp. Maybe Jim was right to be cautious about Mrs Murphy.

He woke early in the morning and went up to Murphys' in the dark. The horse and cart was in the yard. There were buckets of eggs and boxes of butter on the cart, and he helped Dan to lift up a churn of milk and push it to the back. Mrs Murphy came out and inspected everything. It was beginning to brighten by the time they reached Ballyduff.

"I'm going to call to see Aunt Mary," he said, "I haven't seen her since the funeral."

He was sitting with Mrs Murphy on the floor of the cart. Dan was on the ledge, holding the reins.

"You should keep in touch with your Aunt Mary," Mrs Murphy said. "It would be a pity to loose touch with your relations."

They passed through Killaloe which was deserted in the

early morning. There was a cold wind, and Michael crossed his arms and rubbed them with his hands to stop himself shivering. They came to the outskirts of Enniscorthy, near the side of Vinegar Hill. An old woman walking along the road waved at them. They passed a row of little houses, and turned the bend at the walled cemetery. Donohoes' big shop was at the other side of the road. He loved going to Enniscorthy and looking at everything in the town. He could hear the squealing of pigs from Buttles' Bacon Factory. There were big tall grey shops in Templeshannon. They went over the bridge. The river was wide and rushing noisily along. He saw swans on the island. He thought that it would be great to live in Enniscorthy. There were always people walking around. You'd probably get to know them after a while, and you'd always have someone to talk to. It wasn't like Kilbride. There was no one of his own age in Kilbride. Dan Murphy was ten years older than him.

They got down off the cart and walked up Slaney Street. A man was selling milk from a churn in the middle of the Market Square. Three or four carts were pushed in against the footpaths, and some people were standing around. But it was early still and there was plenty of space for them. Mrs Murphy pointed to a spot outside Jordans' shop and they unloaded the cart. Dan unyoked the horse and left the cart leaning down against the path.

"I'll bring the horse up to the Fair Green," he said. "Will you come with me, Michael?"

They walked up past the Cathedral and up Pig Market Hill to the top of the town. Cows were grazing on the Green, and a few men were standing around. They turned down at Joe Doyle's, and Dan led the horse to drink from a trough near a big sycamore tree. Horses were tethered to trees around the Fair Green.

"I'll go and see Aunt Mary," Michael said. "I'll meet you later in the Market Square."

He crossed the road and turned down into a long street. Aunt Mary's was the last house of the row of little thatched houses. The street was muddy and full of puddles. A wicked dog was barking and snarling and pulling on the rope which tied him to a gate. He knocked a few times on the door of Aunt Mary's house but there was no answer. He expected her to be there. She worked in the kitchen in the Presentation Convent but the nuns usually gave her the Fair Day off.

Mrs Sullivan, Aunt Mary's neighbour, came out from the back of her house. "Mary's gone into the convent," she said. "She had to go in today even though it's the Fair Day. One of the nuns is after dying and they're very busy. It's Michael, isn't it? She should be home after tea."

"Tell her that I'll come back up," he said.

He walked slowly back along the street. He made up his mind that he would stay for the night in Enniscorthy, in Aunt Mary's house, although he knew that Mrs Murphy wouldn't like him doing that. She had always disapproved of his father staying overnight in the town. He stood on the Duffry looking across at the white statue of the Blessed Virgin in an alcove high up in the wall of the Presentation Convent. He didn't want to go back to the Market Square yet and stand for too long in the cold with Mrs Murphy. He didn't want to look as if he was her son. She wasn't friendly with townspeople. She said that you'd never be sure who anybody in the town was. She wasn't like his father who had talked to everyone in Enniscorthy. His father didn't care who people were. The trees were bare on the Fair Green. Vinegar Hill seemed very close to the town. He walked as far as Joe Doyle's and went across the top of Pig Market Hill. A dog was barking at a herd of cattle coming along the far road. A man in a ragged grey coat ran along at the side of the herd, shouting and poking at them with a stick to stop them going down New Street.

Michael wandered along a road out of the town on which he had never walked before. A winding driveway led up to a big house which was in off the road. He turned down a lane of small houses thinking it would lead him back to the Market Square. When he came to the bottom of the lane he saw the courthouse and he knew where he was.

A crowd were cheering and laughing outside Hayes' shop. He moved in among them. There was a monkey dressed in a coloured coat sitting on a narrow chair on an upturned tea chest. A big framed picture of the Sacred Heart was leaning against the front of the tea chest. A man with a gaunt face held out a bun to the animal. Michael had seen pictures of monkeys but he had never seen a real one before.

"The man who owns that monkey is from Hungary," a woman beside him said. "He brings the monkey all over the world. He sells holy pictures too, small ones for a missal and big framed ones for the wall."

The monkey grabbed the bun and stuffed it into his mouth with his paw. The man took pictures out of a leather bag. He put them on the chair beside the tea chest and handed some of them to the people at the front of the crowd. Suddenly the monkey got up and climbed up the back of the chair. He swung out of the side of the chair and waved at the crowd. Everyone cheered and laughed. It was great fun. The monkey made a funny face.

"Sit down," the man said in a foreign accent.

People had gathered up near the monkey around the big picture of the Sacred Heart which was the same as the one in Murphys' kitchen. The man went around the crowd with his cap collecting money for seeing the monkey. Michael put a ha'penny into the cap.

After a while he walked down towards the Market

Square. The fair was getting very busy. Hawkers were selling clothes and ornaments and jewellery along one path. He was definitely staying in the town tonight whether Mrs Murphy liked it or not. There might be other things like the monkey that he would miss if he went home early.

He walked slowly across the Market Square. A woman was standing beside Murphys' cart. Mrs Murphy was putting butter into a brown bag for her.

"I hope the butter is not too salty," the woman said.

"No. It's not," Mrs Murphy said. Her face was very grey. She looked as if she was perishing with the cold. She was trying to sound nice but Michael knew that she might get very cross in a while.

"There's a man with a monkey up in Court Street," Michael said.

Mrs Murphy looked sharply at him. He knew she didn't want him to start a conversation with the woman from the town.

"I saw him," the woman from the town said laughing. She had fair curly hair. "The man is staying in lodgings in Court Street. He'll hardly stay out long today for fear the monkey would get cold."

"He was swinging out of the side of the chair as if the chair was a tree," Michael said laughing.

"You should go up straight away to see the monkey, Missis," the woman from the town said to Mrs Murphy. "The man won't keep him out long in the cold."

Mrs Murphy folded down the top of the brown paper bag and handed it to the woman.

"I don't want to see a monkey," she said. "I came into the fair to do business. I have a farm of land at home."

She took money from the woman and put it in her pocket. The woman made a jeering face at Mrs Murphy and walked away across the square.

"I'm surprised at you talking to foolish people like that, drawing them on us," Mrs Murphy said when the woman was gone out of earshot. "What were you doing up in Court Street? Did you not go up to see your Aunt Mary?"

"She wasn't there," Michael said, "but she had left a message telling me to call back up later. I'm not going to be able to go home with you."

"We can wait for you."

"It's going to be very late. I'm going to have to stay the night in her house. A nun died in the convent and she won't be out until the nuns go to bed at nine o'clock."

He had to tell her lies so that she wouldn't try to make other arrangements for him.

She had everything sold by the time Dan came back to the Market Square. There was a smell of whiskey off him. She hated him drinking. She didn't speak to him but pointed at the churn and buckets as a way of giving him orders.

"Dan will look after everything at home for you Michael," she said. "Don't worry about anything. We'll see you tomorrow."

In a way he was sorry not to be going home with them. It was always good when they were having a disagreement. They wouldn't speak to each other but both of them would be very nice to him.

He wandered around the town on his own. It was cold. He looked for a while at a stall of ornaments at the top of Castle Hill but when he found himself the only person there he moved on. He was disappointed that there was no one to talk to. He missed his father. His father would always know somebody and stop and talk. But his father was dead. He was on his own.

It was beginning to get dark, and a lot of the farmers were going home. He walked up towards the cathedral but it was too early yet to go to Aunt Mary's. The top of the town was

37

covered in dung. He thought he might go down Slaney
Street and along the Island Road to Dempseys' pub where
his father used to drink. The pub would be crowded on the
Fair Day and the Fenians might be there. He wanted to stay
in touch with the Fenians and not become like the people in
Kilbride.

There was a horse and cart full of boxes and crates
halfway down Slaney Street near the lending library. A big
man with a red angry face came out of the lending library
and started to talk to him although he had never seen the
man in his life before.

"Jesus Christ," the man said, pointing at the crates on the
cart. "What am I supposed to do now, son? I can't lift that
big crate on my own. This is shagging awful. There's only
women in that bloody shop, and they couldn't lift a godscow
by the look of them."

Michael was delighted that the man was talking to him.
"I'll help you," he said. He got up on the cart.

The man pointed to a big crate and Michael lifted some
of the boxes out of the way and pushed the crate to the edge.

"The railway sacked my helper," the man said. "They told
me that there was surely a man in every shop in the town
who would help me to lift things. But there's not. They're
telling me they can't get another helper but I know that
they're just trying to save money."

"Why did they sack the helper?" Michael asked.

"He was fighting and giving impudence," the man said.
"Some of these young fellows have no sense. It was a good
kick up in the arse he needed."

Michael laughed. He helped the man to carry the crate
into a shop and out into a shed in the back yard.

"Thank you very much, Mr Brady," a woman with grey
hair said when they came back into the shop.

They went back out on to the street.

"What's your name, son?" Mr Brady asked.

"Michael Carty."

"Would you ever mind staying with me for a while, Michael? I've another few big crates to deliver."

"I'm not going home until tomorrow," Michael said. "I've plenty of time."

"You're not looking for a job, are you? I could bring you over to the railway and tell Kelly that I've found a helper."

"No," Michael said. "I'm not."

Mr Brady led the horse down the street. He stopped outside Shaws' drapery shop. He pointed to a box and Michael got up on the cart and pushed it to the edge for him.

"I can manage this on my own," he said. "Will you wait out here?"

Michael held the reins of the big grey carthorse. He had often thought about how to look for a job if he ever left Kilbride, but it had never occurred to him that he might just be offered one. It was a pity he wasn't looking for a job because working for Mr Brady would have been great.

It was nearly dark, the time of the day he hated most in Kilbride, but the town was still full of life. He saw a man going in to Creanes' pub. There seemed to be a bit of a crowd down in Mary Street. Two women were walking up the path and he had to move out and stand close to the horse to make way for them.

"I got my hair done in Crokes'," one of them said, touching her black hair.

"Who did it for you, Lena or Mary?" the other one asked. She had red hair.

"Lena."

"It's lovely. Look, the young fellow with the horse is looking at you." The red-haired woman caught her friend by the arm. "He thinks you're lovely. He's admiring your hair, and you a married woman twice his age." She screamed laughing.

"Stop it, Katty," the other woman said. "Stop it. Don't be making a show of yourself on the street. Don't mind her," she said to Michael. "Don't take any notice of her."

He laughed but then he became serious. He decided that he was going to stay in the town. He was going to take the job from Mr Brady and stay in Enniscorthy. There was no reason why he had to go home to Kilbride. He didn't own the land, not like the Murphys who had bought theirs under the Ashbourne Land Act. He was in arrears with the rent. He might be looking for a job some other time and he mightn't be able to get one.

"She's too old for you, son," the red-haired woman was saying, pretending to be serious. "She's old enough to be your mother."

"I know," Michael said, laughing again, but he wasn't concentrating on what the woman was saying. He was going to take the job from Mr Brady. Life was much better in the town. Townspeople were great fun. He hated living in Kilbride. He was going to get lodgings and not go back there.

"I'd like the job," he said when Mr Brady came out.

"I thought you said you had to go home."

"I'm on my own. My mother and father are dead. I can do what I like." He was thinking of Mrs Murphy as he spoke. She wouldn't approve of this but he was going to do it anyway.

"I'll bring you over to the railway. With Christmas just around the corner they can't refuse to take you on."

If he didn't like Enniscorthy he could go back to Kilbride in the spring. "I'll have to get lodgings," he said.

"There's a nice lodging house on the Quay."

They led the horse over the bridge. He knew that he had

made the right decision. Mrs Murphy would have no one to ignore now in the churchyard in Ballyduff. She could lick up to Father Roche to her heart's content. He would never have to sit in the house on his own again. There would be company in a lodging house. He would make new friends. The gas lamps had been lit along Templeshannon Quay and he could see the lights reflected in the river. He was delighted. He could hold his head high here among people who didn't know anything about him. But he felt guilty too, guilty about leaving them there in Kilbride without him and without saying a word. They would miss him at night-time in Murphys'. It was wrong of him to be criticizing Mrs Murphy and the people of Kilbride. They were good people. The Irish people would be the best people in the world if only the British were gone. He had to take up the chance of a job in the town. He would take the Fenian oath and help to free Ireland from British rule.

"What will I say to Mr Kelly when we go in to the railway?"

"Say nothing," Mr Brady said. "I'll do the talking."

Chapter 3

July 1892

Margaret Dempsey was ready for Mass. She stood at the bottom of the stairs, in front of the hallstand mirror, pursing her lips as if she had put on lipstick. It was dark and cool behind the heavy oak front door but at the other end of the hallway there was light from the glass kitchen door. She could hear voices in the shop. Maybe there was a funeral. Her father had an undertaking business as well as a pub-cum-grocery shop. Laying her missal on the hallstand, she moved her black mantilla back a little on her head and watched the soft lace fall over her long brown hair.

She turned from the mirror and stood listening to the first faint peals of the twenty-to-eleven bell. As the peals grew stronger, ringing out over the town, she walked up Island Road, underneath the crumbling stone of Roche's maltings, and turned into Old Barracks. Dust rose up from the street as a horse and cart trundled past. She could feel the sun burning into her back. There was a heatwave. It hadn't rained for over a week and the heat seemed to be rising up from the dust and dirt of the road.

Main Street was full of people, dressed in dark Sunday clothes, some coming down from ten Mass, others going to eleven. Margaret stayed on the inside of the path, close to the tall houses. People walked with their heads down, in silence.

Some of the women greeted one another but they all spoke quietly. The streets were quiet on a Sunday. The Protestants were always watching, the nuns told the girls, and they would be delighted to see Catholics letting themselves down.

The granite stones at the front of the cathedral were sparkling in the sunlight and she blessed herself at the holy water font and walked up the centre aisle. She knelt near the pulpit and looked up at the gold tabernacle in the centre of the altar. The light around the huge stained-glass window was radiant. She took out her rosary beads and, feeling the coldness of the silver crucifix against her hands, she began to pray. She prayed for her aunt Julianne. Julianne and Thomas, her mother's sister and brother, still lived in Tomanoole, her mother's homeplace. Margaret's mother was trying to make a match for Julianne with John Bourke. Thomas had been doing a line with a girl for years and they were afraid that he'd get married and then Julianne wouldn't be wanted in the house. When John Bourke's mother died they realized what a great catch John would be for Julianne. He had one hundred acres out in Marshalstown. Margaret remembered her mother getting dressed up to go out to the wake, but it was only afterwards she told them why she had gone. She stayed all night at the wake and spent a long time talking to John. She didn't mention Julianne to him that night but she told him how lonely he would be with his mother gone and she advised him to find a nice girl for himself and get married.

The seats around her in the cathedral were filling up. She knew a lot of the people. Mr Browne, who owned the big drapery shop in Court Street, and Larry Colfer, the postmaster, whose thick wavy grey hair looked like corrugated iron. Mrs Doctor Power and her sister Miss Laetitia O'Connor walked slowly up past the pulpit and knelt in the very top seat.

After a while the shrill presbytery bell rang out and Father Turner followed the altar boys on to the altar. The priest's deep booming voice filled the cathedral. Margaret loved the way he read the Latin prayers, emphasizing some of the words as if they were especially important to him. The altar boys, kneeling at the foot of the altar, were fidgety and inattentive. One of them touched the big altar bell and the high-pitched sound of the beginning of a peal rang out before he quickly silenced the bell.

Margaret tried to pray but her mind kept wandering. She thought John Bourke was too old for Julianne. She didn't like him. She had met him one day in the shop. He was having a drink in the snug and her mother sent her in to invite him up to the parlour for tea. He was small and slight. His hair was grey. Her father was talking to him about a hurling match and John Bourke was nodding. "Aye," he said, "aye." He had his eyes narrowed and he was leaning back with one arm stretched out along the back of the long seat. Margaret didn't think he was listening to her father. She thought he was watching him and sizing him up. But her mother and Julianne were very keen to make the match although Julianne hardly knew John Bourke. He had a big house and land. Julianne would never be poor and she could have children.

"*Gloria in excelsis Deo*," Father Turner sang, his voice exultant, and Margaret listened to the choir singing the Gloria, the song the angels sang to welcome the Christchild on that first Christmas night. The cathedral was crowded and it was very hot. She wished she was out in Tomanoole. When she was younger she spent every summer out there, except for the two summers when her mother fell out with them all. She used to go across the field and wade into the little river. Her grandmother was alive then. Her grandmother would sit on the bank. Even on the hottest of summer days the river water was freezing cold.

She stood for the Gospel. She decided to offer up the Mass for Julianne. After dinner she was going to Tomanoole with her mother and her father. John Bourke had been invited to tea.

*

"Go in again and tell him we're ready to go," her mother said.

They had been sitting in the kitchen waiting for Margaret's father for more than an hour. He had eaten his dinner quickly and had gone back into the shop. Mrs Byrne and Tommy Doyle, local historians from Oulart, were in the snug and he was in there talking to them.

"Why don't we just go without him?" Margaret asked. She didn't want to go into the shop and annoy her father again. They often went out to Tomanoole without him.

"We have to bring him with us, today of all days. He's always the same. I don't know how I put up with him. God grant me patience."

Her mother was getting angry and Margaret moved towards the back door. It was often very hard to get her father out of the shop. Sometimes Home Rulers or local historians came into him, and it could be eight o'clock when he'd come in for his tea.

"Tell him we're leaving now." Her mother stood at the back door shouting after her. "If he doesn't want to come tell him to say so. He promised Julianne, but I don't care what he does. The one day I want him to do something he lets me down like this. God knows I don't ask much of him."

It was dark inside the shop, and cool too, now that the sun had gone away from the front of the house. The men from the Irish Street were still standing in the corner,

45

drinking glasses of black stout and talking quietly. There were dark bottles on the upturned tea chest beside them. Her brother James was behind the counter, his back to the shop, pouring whiskey into a measure. She went into the snug.

"That's the way the Blackwater men came up to Oulart Hill at the start of the Rising," Mrs Byrne was saying, moving a dirty fingernail along the big cream map spread out on the table in front of her. She had a thin, high-pitched voice. "In through the gap there in the ditch, through what would be Farrells' land now."

The men had their heads bent down, poring over the map. Margaret knew that they didn't even know she was there.

"There's a gate in that corner now," Tommy Doyle said, "but there wouldn't have been a gate there in '98."

"I know where you mean," her father said. His voice was dreamy, as if he was talking to himself. "Up the side of the big cornfield."

She coughed and he looked back at her. His two eyes were different. One of them was blue, but part of his other eye was a speckled colour, like a thrush.

"She wants to know will you be ready soon." She spoke in a low voice, half-hoping that Mrs Byrne and Tommy Doyle wouldn't hear her.

"I'll be there in a minute now," he muttered, frowning and turning away from her.

"Are we holding you up Philip?" Mrs Byrne spoke loudly. She was a big woman. Some of her hair was plaited and wound around the front of her head. "Don't let us delay you now."

"No, no, no," he said, leaning back over the map again. Margaret had heard him talking about this map that Mrs Byrne had got in Dublin. She had promised several times to bring it in to show him.

"So they would have ended up fighting beside the men from Ferns then." He moved his finger along the map. He still sounded as if he was talking to himself.

The pony and trap was ready in the yard. Margaret stood at the half-door in the kitchen. Her mother was putting more powder on her face. The grey cat came out from one of the sheds and stood in front of the door, miaowing angrily up at her. He had lost half of his ear in a fight a few years before. She saw the shadow of a crow dart across the ground of the yard and looked up to see the crow disappearing beyond the trees.

Her father came out of the shop.

"Here he is now," she said.

Her mother rushed past her out the door. She dreaded her mother being as angry as this. When she was younger and she did things wrong her mother would get angry like this and beat her.

"Go back into them if you like." Her mother gestured past him back towards the shop. "I don't care what you do. Don't do anything just to please me. Go on back in."

"We're time enough," he muttered. "It's not that late. You're making a terrible fuss about a few minutes."

"A few minutes," she shouted. She could always shout him down but she could never get him to want to be with her. "I'm sitting inside waiting for hours. God grant me patience to continue."

He frowned and breathed heavily down through his nose, making a hissing sound. The trap lurched to one side as he sat down opposite Margaret.

There were children playing on the street and it was hot, but her mother, sitting up straight, with her back to them both, drove the pony hard. He would never drive when she was with him. He said he liked just sitting there. He held his face sideways and very still, as if he was posing for a photograph. His bottom lip was jutting out and there was a harsh expression on his face.

The trees along the road cast shadows of different sizes and shapes. Some were round and jagged at the edges, and there were tall shadows that stretched across the road and then rose up over the long grass at the other side. There were sheep in the field in front of the big Protestant house, some of them lying under the shade of the sycamore tree. At Scarawalsh she looked up the road her father had always pointed out to her when she was a child. It was up past Coolnahorna, the way the rebels travelled in 1798 as they went in to take Enniscorthy. He looked at the road too, and then smiled at her. She thought of asking him to tell her about the map of the Battle of Oulart but she was afraid that her mother might get angry with her if she started talking to him.

Glimmers of light flickered through the tall trees and, here and there, longer shafts of light, brilliant against the shade. Her father raised his eyebrows and gestured with his head towards her mother, his face moving as though he were laughing, but he made no sound. She smiled faintly back at him and nodded too towards her mother's back.

"It didn't make any difference to me if you wanted to stay there with them," her mother said, turning suddenly around, as if she knew that they were making faces behind her back. "I didn't care whether you came or not."

Her father frowned and muttered something. His face was very red.

The pony was moving slowly in the sweltering heat. Margaret looked away, back at the river water, puckered and slow-moving. The Slaney was narrow near Ballycarney, one side of it shadowy and dark, the other side blue. They turned up the bohreen to Tomanoole.

"For someone who is supposed to be so clever – all this

history, 1798 and all that – you find it very hard to make up your mind about simple little things, like who you're going to spend a Sunday evening with." She had her back to them. There was bitterness in her voice.

"I don't know why you're making such a fuss about a few minutes," he growled.

"A few minutes? We were nearly two hours waiting for you. But I'm only an old fool. I wouldn't know the difference between a few minutes and two hours." She sighed angrily. "Jesus, Mary and Joseph, grant me patience to continue."

He muttered and breathing down through his nose made a hissing sound. Margaret was glad they were nearly in Tomanoole. They would never fight too much where other people could hear them.

The gate at the side of the tall stone house was open.

"Lie down Shep, you old fool," her mother said, as the dog came panting out.

The sun was blazing down at the side of the house but there was shade around the back. The apple trees and the damp orchard wall were close to the house and the sun was blocked out too by the tall beech trees at the other side of the house.

"Julianne," Margaret called, opening the half-door and going into the kitchen.

Julianne turned around from the small mirror beside the window. "You're very late," she said. She had clips and a comb in her hand. Margaret was surprised at how cross and flustered she was. "I thought he was going to arrive before you."

"It was Philip. He's always the same." Margaret's mother had come in behind her. She knew her father would delay outside for a while. "We sat in the kitchen for an hour waiting for him."

"Thank God you're here now anyway. I didn't want to be on my own when he arrived."

"We'll get the tea ready," Margaret's mother said, handing Julianne the bottle of whiskey she had brought. "Margaret will wash the china for you."

"I finished the novena yesterday." Julianne looked off in the distance. "I hope he turns up."

"He'll turn up all right. He's lucky to be getting you with the big dowry you have."

They started the work. Margaret washed the delicate cream and blue china. Her mother cut the meat. Julianne spent a long time drying the china sugar bowl. She was very slow at any work but she did things perfectly. Margaret watched her moving the cloth carefully around the handles and in under the rim. She had nearly all the china washed before Julianne had finished drying the sugar bowl. But her composure returned to her and there was the usual stillness about her. Margaret thought that Julianne always seemed still even when she was moving around or working or talking.

"How is Thomas? Where is he?" Margaret's mother asked after a while. Thomas hadn't been too pleased when he heard the amount of the dowry John Bourke was looking for. Margaret's mother had said that Julianne was entitled to a good settlement from the place. She could have made a great match years before but she had stayed at home to look after her mother.

"He's up the haggard, I think. He's not in great form. I don't think he wants to marry Joan Doyle now that he has the chance," Julianne said.

"Don't worry about him. If he doesn't marry her he'll marry someone else."

Margaret dried the rest of the china and put it on the table. Julianne brought the butter in from the safe and

Margaret shaped it into small rounds with the butter bats. She took the cutlery from the drawer and set six places around the table.

"How are the boys?" Julianne asked.

"John is out in Oulart with his cousins," Margaret's mother said, leaning on the table and smiling. "They're picking the strawberries. We left James in charge of the shop."

A fly landed on the butter and Margaret waved it away. There was silence. She saw her father at the door. Julianne saw him too.

"Philip," Julianne said, walking towards the half-door to open it for him. "I'm delighted to see you. Thank you for coming out."

"I hope we're not late, that we didn't delay anything," he said, looking towards Margaret's mother who turned her back on him.

"No, no. You're in plenty of time. I read about the lecture you gave on the Battle of Vinegar Hill. *The Freeman's Journal* was very impressed with it. We're really proud of you." Her voice sounded charming.

Margaret watched her as she stood still in front of him, holding her head back a little, gazing up at him.

"It wasn't too bad, I suppose." He was blushing and smiling.

"It was very good," she said, still gazing at him. Then she laughed. Margaret had noticed that both her mother and Julianne laughed in a special way when they were laughing for men. It was a ringing laugh. There was a certain wildness in it, but it was refined and lady-like, too. It always made men smile. "We're very proud of you."

"Are you?" Her father seemed confused. He looked over at her mother who still had her back to him.

"Of course we're proud of you." She touched his arm.

"Could you do something for me, Philip? Go up the haggard to Thomas and bring him down here."

"I will, Julianne," Margaret's father said.

A bluebottle buzzed loudly near the sink and her mother swiped at it several times with a cloth. It buzzed even more loudly as it disappeared out the door. Margaret put a china plate beside each fork. No one spoke. She knew her mother was waiting to be sure her father was out of earshot. They could hear the birds singing in little short trills outside.

"You're great to talk like that to him," her mother said to Julianne. "I can't anymore. It's different when you're married to them. You get tired. You'll see that yourself soon."

"It's the only way to talk to them," Julianne said quietly. "Are you not very proud of him? He's so clever. It's not everyone who could give a lecture like that and have it reported in the paper."

"I am," Margaret's mother said, "and he's on the committee of the Enniscorthy Home Rule party now, too. But I get tired of it all sometimes. What about me?"

There were flies landing on the meat and her mother told her to put it out in the safe. They put muslin cloths over the bread. She brought the butter dishes out to the safe, too, so that the butter wouldn't run.

"I think I saw John Bourke at the funeral in Marshalstown on Wednesday," Julianne was saying when Margaret came back in. She took a gold compact out of her handbag. "He still has the diamond mourning patches on his coat. I think he was looking at me."

"Was he? What were you wearing?"

"My lavender suit."

"That's lovely on you."

"I got Thomas to bring me past the house, too. It's a fine house but I'd say it will need to be done up." She was standing at the window, holding the open compact in her hand and looking at herself in the small mirror.

"It's a very fine house," her mother was saying. "It's bigger than this one. And the farm is bigger too. You'll have to get him to go to a few auctions with you. The parlour is very shabby. You'd think from the parlour that they hadn't a penny."

Margaret never listened to them when they talked about furniture or auctions. They sat at the end of the table down near the window. She spooned the runny strawberry jam into two dishes. She hated talk of mahogany or oak tables and chairs and sideboards. They often spent hours talking about furniture. She watched them. They seemed so close. She often wondered what caused the row between them that had lasted for two years. It was rarely mentioned, but when it was Julianne always said that she never wanted a thing like that to happen again. It was terrible, she said, but Margaret's mother laughed about it. The only reason she came out to Tomanoole and ended the row, she said, was because she thought her mother was dying. Her mother didn't die then for another three years.

"I'm sure the Boggans are raging about this match," her mother said. "I've heard it said that they had their eye on John Bourke for Lizzie."

"Lizzie Boggan wouldn't be suitable for a big place like Bourkes'," Julianne said. "What have the Boggans? Twenty or thirty acres? Where did they get a notion like that?"

"People get strange notions."

They stopped talking when they saw the men coming in. Thomas took off his hat. His face was weather-beaten but all around his receding hairline the skin was white where it was usually covered by a hat.

"Is he not here yet? What's keeping him?" Thomas asked.

"He'll be here in a minute. We'll go in to the parlour," Margaret's mother said.

"Yes," Julianne said. "I'd like everyone to be sitting down when he arrives."

There was a musty smell in the parlour and the heat was stifling. Margaret sat on the couch inside the door. She saw the calves in the field across the road, flicking their tails loosely to keep away the flies. Julianne went to the window to fix the heavy brocade curtains.

"I had the window open and the curtains hanging out all day yesterday," she said, "but I still can't get rid of the smell."

Margaret's mother put the bottle of whiskey in the mahogany press in the corner. There were glasses and a jug on a silver tray on top of the press. The men sat in the armchairs on either side of the tall dark marble fireplace. Thomas lay back in the chair and closed his eyes. His face was glistening with sweat.

"It's great that Philip is here. We can always depend on Philip to keep a conversation going. You couldn't get better than Philip for an occasion like this," Margaret's mother said, looking across the room at Julianne. Her voice was sad but Margaret was glad that she was trying to get friendly with him again.

"Yes," Julianne said. "We're delighted you're here, Philip."

"That's why I wanted you to come, Philip." Her mother's voice sounded flat and sad like it had been when she told Margaret that her grandmother had died. "You're great at talking. You can always be depended on to say the right thing."

"I'm not that good," he said. He was smiling.

"Is the room all right?" Julianne asked.

"It's lovely," her mother said. "I know he'll be very impressed. I always think that china cabinet is a beautiful piece of furniture. And it's the very same mahogany as the mahogany in the firescreen."

Julianne sat down on the couch. "We'll say a decade of the rosary," she said, blessing herself. "We'll pray for God's blessing." She covered her face with her hands to give out the rosary. There was a severity and a gloom in her voice. She gave out the Our Father and then the Hail Marys, not particularly slowly but bringing out the meaning of each familiar phrase. Margaret thought her own voice, merging with the other voices in response, sounded careless in comparison with Julianne's intensity. Her voice while praying sounded different to her usual voice. There was no calm or charm in it but instead Margaret heard a desperation, and maybe a roughness too, or a determination to force God to give her what she wanted. As they finished the "Glory be to the Father" they heard a cart coming into the yard.

"Here he is," Margaret's mother said, blessing herself. "Thanks be to the good God who answers all our prayers."

Julianne went over to the big mirror above the fireplace. She pursed her lips and then stroked her cheeks gently with the tips of her fingers. Thomas took a handkerchief out of his pocket and wiped the sweat off his face. They all watched in silence as a slight figure in a dark coat passed by the window. Julianne went to open the big front door to him.

"Good evening, John," Margaret heard her say. Her voice sounded refined and charming. "Come on in. We're in the parlour. We've been looking forward to your visit."

Chapter 4

May 1900

As she walked down the Railway Hill Margaret watched the men who were gathered around the stile leading down to the bank of the river. One of them must have remarked on her because they all turned to look. Fingering the hard embroidered pattern on the neckline of her dress she looked away and pretended not to have noticed them. They came mostly from the small houses in the side streets of the town.

She was going to a dance in the Athenaeum. It was nearly ten o'clock and it was getting dark. As she turned up Slaney Street she glanced over at the group of men. One of them was still looking at her. She recognized him. It was Michael Carty who worked for the railway and brought deliveries to the shop. He had been in the yard the day before.

Three men, dressed for the dance, were walking ahead of her. There were others at the top of the hill going towards the Athenaeum. She stopped halfway up the street and knocked at the halldoor of the hardware shop where Kitty Furlong lived. Margaret's mother could never understand why there wasn't a greater take on Kitty. She was an only child and the man who married her would fall in for the shop and some land out the country too. But Kitty had eyes for no one except Walter Mernagh. His family owned a farm out in Davidstown. Even though he would let weeks pass without coming in to see her, Kitty believed that he would marry her in the end.

"I hope he's here tonight," she said as they walked in through the big doorway of the Athenaeum.

They walked up the stairs. Long discordant notes were coming from the ballroom as the musicians tuned their instruments. They paid at the door and the first person Margaret saw when she went inside was her brother John. She hadn't seen him for more than a week. He spent a lot of time out in Tomanoole. Thomas had never married, and they were hoping that he would leave John the land. Julianne who had married John Bourke often said how foolish Thomas was not to find a nice girl for himself.

She waved at John who was over in the corner of the ballroom with some of the committee of the Island Hunt. She noticed a stranger at the edge of the group. He had brown hair and he was taller than John. He was rubbing his knuckles with his fingers.

The viola player came on to the stage. The cellist was slowly turning the pages of a music book. Margaret and Kitty stood under the second window down from the stage. The ballroom was filling up. The girls were standing on one side, the men on the other. There were rows of velvet-covered chairs pushed in against the wall. In the winter sometimes those chairs would be in the middle of the ballroom for concerts and plays.

Margaret had been coming to dances in the Athenaeum for about five years and she mostly danced with the same men. She had walked out with some of them for a while and had been invited to most of the big balls that took place over the winter. But she knew that there was no question of marrying any of the men who regularly asked her to dance. Some of them wouldn't be in a position to get married for years until farms or businesses were handed over to them.

She didn't like some of them but she often reminded herself not to be too critical. She would have to settle for one of them soon because it was time for her to get married. Her brother James had been courting Nancy Doyle for years and they couldn't get married until Margaret did. Her mother said that you couldn't have three women in the one house.

The master of ceremonies announced the first dance and the quartet began to play. Margaret danced two or three waltzes and then stood with Kitty, talking quietly. It was dark outside. The top of the blind on the window opposite was torn and Margaret could see the blackness. Men were crossing the floor to find partners for the next dance. She saw Walter Mernagh down at the end of the ballroom but she didn't say anything to Kitty. Walter Mernagh would take his time before asking Kitty to dance.

The stranger she had noticed earlier was walking along in front of the rows of girls. He had his head turned towards the dance floor, away from the girls, but every now and then he would glance at them, blinking. He had his mouth open. His shoulders were bent. He stopped in front of her and held out his hand.

"Will you dance?" he asked and turned away immediately, sure that she was going to follow him.

"What's your name?" she asked after a while.

He bent his head down to answer her. He had his arm on her waist and he was holding her although there was a pause in the music between dances. "Patrick Stone," he said. His face was near hers and she knew that he wanted to kiss her.

It took her a while to remember where she had heard his name before. He was a hurler and he was on the Wexford County hurling team. He had come to live with his uncle in Cherryorchard and he had also started to play with the Rapparees, the local Enniscorthy team. She had heard her father and her brothers talking about him. He was a great hurler.

"See you later," he said when the dance ended.

She saw him again when she went downstairs with Kitty to the reading-room for supper. Two of the men from the Island Hunt were leaning against the fireplace and he was standing in front of them nodding in agreement with everything they said. He didn't look like his uncle, Tommy Rafter. Margaret knew Tommy Rafter because for a while he drank a lot in her father's pub and he was often brought into the kitchen for his dinner. When his wife died suddenly he had taken to the drink out of loneliness after her. People said that she was a lovely woman, full of charm and talk, and that he couldn't bear to be in the house on his own without her. He had neglected the farm and even sold some of the stock to pay for drink. She hadn't seen him for months. He probably wasn't drinking as much since Patrick Stone had come to live with him, or maybe he was drinking in another pub.

Her brother John came in for supper and Kitty and herself stood in the corner close to the fireplace talking and laughing with him. Patrick Stone was watching them. He held the saucer close to his chest and kept a grip all the time on the handle of the teacup. After a while John turned around to talk to the men who were with Patrick Stone.

"Do you think Walter Mernagh saw me? We should have gone in to the billiard room for supper," Kitty said. "That's where he is."

"I think he's still upstairs," Margaret said. "I saw him when we were walking out."

"We're standing in the wrong place upstairs," Kitty said. "We should be down nearer the door. We're wasting our time up there at the top."

Patrick Stone was smiling and nodding as John spoke. He

had got to know the important men in Enniscorthy very quickly. Margaret could see that he was determined to become well-known. He wasn't just going to be one of the farmers who came into town for the fair or to buy groceries on a Saturday night. They kept their heads down and spoke quietly and looked embarrassed sometimes when their wives were with them. A lot of people weren't sure what their names were or where they came from. Shopkeepers had to be nice to them if they were making money from them but nobody really cared whether they came or went. Other farmers were different. They strutted around the street, talking loudly, and behaving as if they owned the town as well as their land out the country. Townspeople wanted to talk to them and tell other people what they had said. Patrick Stone was going to be one of those although she didn't think he would ever talk loudly. He had a soft sort of a voice.

"Is that your sister?" she heard him asking John as she moved off.

He knew now who she was, that John and James who played hurling and rode with the Island Hunt were her brothers, and that her father had a good-sized business in the town. He looked shrewd, the sort of man who would marry well. He needed money to restock the farm. It would be obvious to him that she would have a big dowry. She was certain that he would ask her to dance again before the end of the night.

They were playing the Treasure Waltz when she went back upstairs. It still reminded her of the man she had been in love with. They had been playing that music the first time she saw him dancing with someone else.

"Here he is," Kitty whispered.

The music stopped and she saw Walter Mernagh, walking along, scanning all the faces looking for Kitty.

"Hello Kitty," he said.

After a while she saw Patrick Stone walking up the ballroom. His arms were hanging loosely out from his body and they looked too long. He held out one hand as he asked her to dance and with the other he moved his fringe back so that she could see the white skin at the top of his forehead. He was blinking as he smiled at her but under the surface of the smile there was a distant expression on his face.

"You're Margaret Dempsey," he said.

She nodded. She had her arm on his shoulder and she thought that she could probably get used to him if he liked her.

"Will I walk you home?"

"If you like," she said.

*

He was standing at the corner of the Abbey Square, on the bottom step of the Bank of Ireland building. Two RIC men were walking down Castle Hill. She had been nervous all day at the thought of meeting him. He jerked his head when he saw her and walked out on to the square. He was rubbing his knuckles with his fingers.

"Am I late?"

"No. No," he said.

They walked past the co-op and the Presbyterian church. There were grey clouds swirling around in the grey sky. She waited for him to talk but he said nothing. The seagulls were squawking down by the river.

"There's the train," she said as a shrill whistle sounded out from behind them. "If we walk a bit faster we'll see it coming out of the tunnel."

"Where?"

He didn't know that the train went right under the town. If you stood on the Railway Bridge, she told him, you could see it going into the tunnel. In the shops in the Market

Square you could hear it rumbling down under the ground. They crossed the road and stood at the wall looking towards the tunnel. She laughed as the train came chugging and hissing out. They crossed the road again and stood at the ditch watching it disappearing among the trees.

"It sounds like thunder when you hear it in the shops in the Market Square," she said.

He didn't answer her and she decided not to say anything else for a while. She thought she sounded too excited. It would be better if she could get him to talk. They walked slowly along, high above the river. The ditch was lush and overgrown with grass and nettles and sceachs. There were some early blackberries, still small and white, not yet ripe. She knew that the men sitting on the low wall at Arnold's Cross were watching them.

"Do you like living out in Cherryorchard?" she asked after a while.

"It's all right," he said, jerking his head and stopping at a stile in the ditch. "I get a bit lonely sometimes. I was always used to a house full of people. The uncle doesn't talk much."

They were standing above a bend in the river and the tide was coming in. Margaret's father often talked about how important the tidal waters of the Slaney were in the history of Enniscorthy. The Normans came from Wexford on that tide. Later, the Butlers came up the river to raid the town. Her father had been sick on and off over the last few years. He wasn't able to write history anymore. The river looked deep and dark. Among the trees on the other bank there was the huge red-brick mental asylum.

Patrick Stone walked slowly on and she followed him.

"I think it's going to rain. The sky is full of clouds," she said.

"No. No," he said, looking up. "I wouldn't say so."

"Maybe not."

There were sheep grazing in the mill field. The ditch was low, and huge fields, yellow and green, were sloping upwards on the other side of the river. They walked over the bridge and up past Davis's mills.

"You were born near Wexford, weren't you?"

"Yes. In Killurin. We lived near the Randles, the people who make the hurls. I suppose that's why I started to play hurling. We always had hurls at home. Like all the young lads I used to hurl the sliotar along the road to school. But if you're ever going to be any good you have to practise on your own. I practised on my own as well." He had his head tilted upwards, sideways, away from her. She was delighted he was talking but it was as if he was talking to himself.

"That's why you're good at it," she said.

He looked startled when she spoke as if he had forgotten she was there. "Yes. For as long as I can remember the only thing I ever wanted was to get on the Wexford team."

"You must be delighted to be on it now."

"I am when I'm playing well. But I hate playing badly. I was playing well last Sunday, in the game against Offaly. I scored a goal and three points. They had their best player marking me but I won all the tackles." He was smiling and blinking. But even though he was smiling she thought that there was anger hidden in his face. He had a cruel look, too, but then she told herself that it wasn't anger or cruelty that were in his face, but just the determination that any man would need to win a tackle and score a goal. "That goal on Sunday," he said, "was the best goal I ever scored. A lot of players would have gone for a point from that angle near the middle of the field. A point was a safe bet but a point would have been no good. We needed a goal to win. A good hurler has to take risks. I took a risk and I won."

She was surprised at the way he was boasting. People

didn't usually say good things about themselves. They waited for other people to say them.

The chestnut trees were growing in over the narrow road, and little white spiked chestnuts had fallen early on to the ground. He had gone a few steps ahead of her and she rushed to catch up with him.

"We're playing the Duffry Rovers on Sunday. I hope I'll be in good form for that," he said frowning. "The shoulder is giving me trouble. It was paining me last Sunday, too." He moved his hand lightly over his right shoulder and down over his arm. "The mother is coming up during the week and she's bringing up the rub I used to put on it. Maybe it will be all right."

"I hope so," she said. "Is it very painful?"

"Sometimes, but don't tell anyone about it. I shouldn't have told you that at all." He looked worried and his voice had become high-pitched. "I never talk about it. The mother advised me not to. If word leaked out and the selectors heard, they mightn't pick me. And if the other team found out that I had a weak shoulder they'd hop off it. You won't tell anyone?"

"Of course not," she said. "But even with the pain you played very well last Sunday. They said you were very good."

"Who? Who was talking about me?" He stopped walking and turned to face her.

"My brother and the men who work in our shop were at the match."

"They were talking about me. What exactly did they say about me?"

"They said you scored a goal and two points and that you played very well." She tried to sound light-hearted. He looked so alarmed.

"Did they say anything else? Did they mention the free I got?"

"No. They just said that you were a very good hurler."

"Did they say that?" He looked away from her with a little smile on his face. "Patrick Stone is a very good hurler." He smiled as he rubbed his knuckles with his fingers, first the knuckles of one hand, then of the other.

They walked under the light green ash trees and then they passed the huge gnarled oak at the entrance to St John's Manor and turned up the road towards Red Pat's Cross. He stopped and looked back along the road and when he saw that there was nobody around he kissed her. He put his hands on her breasts and after a while he began to fumble with the buttons of her blouse trying to open it. She moved away from him and then took his hands in hers and entwined her fingers in his and held her face up so that he could kiss her again. She wanted him to think that she liked being close to him but she didn't want him to get the impression that she was fast.

She started walking again along the middle of the road and she held his hand for a while. It was getting late and the light was beginning to change. The mountains in the distance were a deep blue. He asked to meet her again. His mother, he said, was coming up to Cherryorchard for a few days to see him playing in the match against the Duffry Rovers on Sunday. He thought that she would probably go home on Tuesday or Wednesday.

"I could meet you on Thursday night," he said, blinking. He was stooped down over her.

She went for a walk with him every Tuesday and Thursday night that Summer. The first thing they always talked about was the last match he had played. With his head tilted sideways away from her, he would describe the play of the game, glancing down at her every now and again as if to check that she was listening. He always asked her what James and the men had said about the match.

"They said you played very well," she would say. She listened carefully when hurling was discussed. The men would talk all through dinner time about a hurler or a team or the match they had been at the previous Sunday. They were delighted that she was going out with Patrick Stone. They looked at her when they mentioned his name. She had got up from the table to get the teapot from the range and James had turned right around in the chair to meet her eye as he said what a great hurler Patrick Stone was.

"I never saw anything like that solo run he did up the field last Sunday. None of them could catch up with him. He's the best hurler I ever saw."

The men who sat on the wall at Arnold's Cross recognized him and one old man leaned forward on his stick and called over to him about a goal he had scored in the match against Ballyhogue. He went over to the wall every night after that. He stood in front of them and they all looked at him. Even when someone else was talking they all watched him. He discussed the match with them and praised other players and listened carefully to them. She noticed that he never bragged or boasted to them. He ran himself down and then he would smile a little as they praised him.

"I'm only in Enniscorthy a few months and I'm well-known already," he would say to her as they walked past the mill and up towards Lucas Park. "Everybody is talking about me. What did James and the men in the shop say about me after Sunday's game?" He often looked a bit aggressive when he asked that question, as though he might go after them and beat them up if he didn't like what they had said.

He would look over both shoulders and when he was sure that there was nobody around he would kiss her. He would open her blouse and she would wait for him to put his hand up her skirt and between her legs. One night they climbed over a stile and stood at the side of a huge field of wheat. He kissed her.

"We'll lie in the ditch," he said.

"No, Patrick," she said.

"It's the same thing," he said. "Standing up or lying down. There's no difference."

She shook her head. It was hard to know what to do. She couldn't refuse him without being too severe. Yet she had to be careful not to give him the impression that she had courted a lot of men.

"We'll lie in the ditch for a minute," he said.

They walked along the side of the field until they came to a grassy part of the ditch where there was no nettles or sceachs. He kissed her and touched her breast. He took her hand and put it on his penis. She could feel his erection. She was glad that he had taken her hand because she had been wondering for a while should she touch his penis. If she did he might think that she had been with a lot of men. No man would marry a woman who had a reputation for being loose with other men. He unbuttoned his trousers. She put her hand on his penis and fondled it. She lay there wanting him to hurry and move his hand between her legs but when he did and she began moaning a bit with pleasure she stopped herself. It must always appear as if he was having more pleasure than she was. When he slid his hand down her back and began to try to remove her underwear she stopped him. They had done too much already. If he did something once he would do it every night from then on, and where would it all end?

"I don't want to find myself expecting a child, Patrick," she said.

"I know that," he said, looking anxiously around the field. "I don't think anyone saw us. Do you think there was anyone looking?"

Some nights he talked about his four brothers and two sisters and she preferred stories about them to all the talk about hurling. One of his brothers, Joseph, was in St Peter's College in Wexford, studying for the priesthood. His brother Peter had gone to America and was married out there. Dan and Nick were at home on the farm. He had two sisters, Sara and Mai. Sara was married down in Tacumshane and Mai was a Poor Clare nun up in Carlow. He had told her about how Mai entered the convent. It was the year his father died. None of them had known that she was thinking of joining the nuns. She had been doing a strong line with a man called Tom Murphy, a butcher from Wexford town, and they all thought that she would marry him. She stayed out courting Tom Murphy until five o'clock in the morning the night before she entered the convent.

"How often is your mother allowed to visit Mai?" she asked him one night as they walked home up Munster Hill.

"Once every three years," he said, "but she has to talk to her through a grille. She will never again be able to touch her. Unless Mai died. If Mai died they'd let the mother into the wake."

They had gone for a shorter walk than usual because it was the Thursday night before the Leinster Final against Kilkenny and Patrick Stone didn't want to overdo things before the match. They stopped and waited near the top of the hill for Cosgraves' cows to go into the field. The boy ran around the cows to open the gate. The dog was yelping and the cows rushed doggedly along.

"Your mother is going to the match," she said, "and your uncle, and Joseph and Peter. What about Nick? Is he going?"

"He is, I suppose, if he can get away from the Kavanagh one," he said with a smile on his face. "This one from Castlebridge. She's mad after him for years." He laughed derisively. "Anna Mai Kavanagh. She has a big mouthful of teeth," he said, cupping his hands around his mouth, "and a pair of knockers on her, and by jaypers, they'd meet you halfway down the lane." He moved his hands out expansively from his chest. "She's mad to marry Nick. He wouldn't go next, nigh or near her only for the big farm of land she has."

Margaret thought he was being very rude about Anna Mai Kavanagh but she was very interested in what he was saying. She had often wondered why Dan and Nick were both at home on the farm. Dan was the eldest so he was going to inherit it. She thought they had about eighty acres which was big enough for one family, but not big enough to divide.

"Anna Mai Kavanagh is keen on Nick then but he's not keen on her," she said.

"I don't know. He might marry her in the end. The mother thinks he should. She had a brother but he died young. So she stands to fall in for the farm. She's mad after Nick and he says she's a right one. She's mad for it." He chuckled and rubbed his hands together. "She'd spread her legs anytime."

Margaret was shocked at the way he was talking. The cows had gone into the field and she walked on ahead of Patrick Stone. She had never heard a man speak like that before. She was very sorry she had ever lain in the ditch with him. She hoped he wasn't saying things like that about her.

"I don't think that's a nice way to talk," she said when he caught up with her. "It's not right to talk about a girl like that."

He blushed. "She's a common sort of a girl. She's not a lady like you. Well you're a lady most of the time." He was looking down at her and there was a big sneering grin on his face.

"What do you mean?" she asked, although she knew what he meant.

"You know what I mean," he said. "You talk like a real lady but you're as good as any of them in a ditch."

"That's a lovely way to talk," she said. She felt like punching his face. "I can tell you I'll never be near a ditch with you ever again."

"You will," he said.

She walked on ahead of him.

"You're taking this too seriously. It's only a bit of fun." He caught up with her. There was still a smile on his face but he was blushing and his eyes were half-closed. His eyelids looked like little hoods down over his eyes.

They were walking along under the workhouse wall. She was very angry but she told herself not to say anything hasty. She needed time to think about this. She didn't want to make any mistakes.

"Maybe we should change the subject, Patrick," she said. She was glad that her voice sounded haughty.

It was getting dark as they walked into the Market Square. Two men sitting on the windowsill of the butcher's shop were watching them.

"That sort of talk is only a bit of fun," he said. "You're taking things too seriously." He looked earnestly at her trying to get friendly with her again. "I'll see you on Tuesday night and you'll be after forgetting it all by then."

As she worked in the house during the week his jeering laugh kept coming into her mind, and she began to think how much she disliked him. She got angry every time she remembered him saying that she was as good as any one else in a ditch. She didn't think she could bear to listen to any more of that foolish talk about hurling and what people were saying about him. She was slowly drying a plate and thinking with revulsion of the contrast between the brown-tanned skin of his lower arm and the white skin of his upper arm.

"You're lucky," her mother said, putting another plate on

the draining board. "If you play your cards right with Patrick Stone you're going to get out of here. You've some chance of making a life for yourself but I'll still be stuck here in this little street. If I had my life to live again I'd do things differently. It's well for you."

"I don't know. It mightn't work out," Margaret said. She dried the last of the big dinner plates and carried them over to the dresser. She didn't think she could possibly marry Patrick Stone but if she said that to her mother there would be a terrible row.

"Play your cards right now and he'll marry you." Her mother dropped some cutlery noisily down on the draining board. "But I wouldn't have him playing hurling at all. I never liked James and John playing hurling either. Get him to give up the hurling and take up cricket. You get a much better class of person playing cricket."

"I don't care what game he plays," Margaret said, picking out the knives from the wet cutlery.

"You'd want to have a bit of sense." Her mother was clattering more cutlery around in the basin. "Get to know the right people. You have a chance to have a good life, out the country away from all the riff-raff in the town. All my life I've had to put up with your father bringing every Tom, Dick and Harry into the kitchen and expecting me to talk to them. It's even worse since he got sick. I'm worn out minding him. There's not another woman in Enniscorthy who would put up with what I have to put up with."

There was cabbage on one of the knives. Margaret threw it back into the basin.

"God grant me patience to continue," her mother said, throwing the knife out on to the draining board again with the cabbage still on it. "That pain in my arm is worse than it ever was. The tablets that Doctor Power gave me are not agreeing with me at all. Your father gets all the attention but I'm not well either."

"Go up and lie down for a while," Margaret said. For the last few years her mother hadn't been able to do much work in the house. Mrs Foley from the Irish Street came in to help but Sunday was her day off. "I'll finish the washing-up."

"I don't know what I'm going to do when you're gone. James is bringing a woman in on top of me now and only God knows what will be the end of me."

"But you get on well with Nancy," Margaret said. "Nancy is lovely."

"How lovely will she be when I'm living with her? I've had a hard life, and the end of it is not going to be easy either."

Margaret grimaced as her mother banged the glass door. She didn't know how she would listen to her shouting or maybe crying when she heard that it was all over with Patrick Stone. The daughters of the women she played cards with had made great matches for themselves. She had had a very hard life, she would say. Why did nothing ever work out for her? Her father would get upset when her mother started to shout. Maybe she could make an effort and learn to put up with Patrick Stone.

It was late on Sunday night when James came home from Dublin. Wexford had lost the match. The score was Kilkenny eleven points and Wexford one goal and six points.

"Patrick Stone wasn't playing as well as usual," James said. "He went for goals twice and he missed. He could have easily scored a point both times but he made the wrong choice."

On Tuesday night she walked slowly towards Patrick Stone who was standing on the bottom step of the Bank of Ireland in the Abbey Square, kicking at the mud scraper. There were crows pecking grain from the road. She didn't want to see him or listen to him talking about the match.

"I can't believe that we lost," he said. "Can you imagine what they're all saying about me now?"

"I'm sure they're all just as disappointed as you are, Patrick," she said. "You did your best. That's all anyone can do."

"I know they're blaming me."

"You did your best. How could anyone blame you?" She didn't know how she was going to keep repeating the same thing over and over for two or three hours.

"I should have scored two goals," he said. "I made two terrible mistakes. I know everybody is giving out about me."

"People have no reason to give out about you," she said. "You scored the only goal of the match. You have every reason to be proud of yourself. I know I'm very proud of you."

She didn't know why she said that to him. She wasn't thinking, and suddenly she found herself saying what Mother Superior used to say at prize-giving in the Loreto Convent years before. Mother Superior would sit behind the big table at the top of the study-hall and Mother Gonzaga, the Mistress of Studies, would stand beside her and call out the names of the prize-winners, one by one. Margaret had often won prizes. Mother Superior would take her hand and tap it lightly.

"You have every reason to be proud of yourself, dear," she used to say. "I know I'm very proud of you." There were some strange brown splotches on Mother Superior's face. She was old and frail. Gonzag used to have to hold her arm and help her walk up through the study-hall.

"Are you really proud of me?" Patrick Stone had stopped outside the mill and he was beaming at her.

"I am."

"And you think I should be proud of myself?"

"Yes. Of course."

"I suppose you're right," he said, looking off in the distance. "I scored the only goal of the match."

He looked down at her and she knew that he was waiting for her to say more.

"Put that behind you and look forward to next year," she said. "You might win it next year."

"I'd love to win an All-Ireland medal," he said, "because then everybody would know about me. I thought of standing in the next elections for the new county councils. I'd love everyone voting for me."

"That would be great," she said.

"But you're proud of me even though I didn't win." He bent his head down on to her shoulder and moved his hand gently over her hair. "I love you, Margaret," he said.

This was terrible. She didn't know what she was going to do. He was slowly kissing the side of her face. She knew that she was wrong to have said something that she didn't mean. Mother Superior used to say it over and over again to everyone who was getting a prize.

"You have every reason to be proud of yourself, dear. I know I'm very proud of you."

Gonzag would smile, and move the white starched front of her veil which always dug into her forehead making it look red and sore.

"Will you marry me, Margaret?" Patrick Stone asked.

She hesitated for an instant and listened to the harsh tearing sound of cows pulling grass from the earth in the field beside them.

"Yes." She couldn't say no without thinking more about it. This was what she had always wanted, to make a good match.

"We'll keep it a secret for a while," he said. "Until after the county championship. Too much excitement is not good before a match."

She tried to persuade herself that she wanted to marry him, live in the same house as him, be with him, day after day, night after night. She lay in the ditch with him but she began to hate courting him. Sometimes she couldn't make herself react when he touched her.

"What's wrong?" he asked.

"Nothing," she said.

She would have to tell him sooner or later that she wanted to stop going out with him. But not now with her father sick.

"You're not in the mood," he would say bitterly after a while, and shrug and lie back in the grass. He had jeered her for being too interested in courting but he didn't like it when she wasn't interested either. They walked in silence along the road.

Two weeks later her father took another bad turn and she was able to cancel arrangements to meet Patrick Stone. He expressed concern about her father in a stilted sort of a way as if he thought of himself as a person who expressed concern about sick people. He was nice about the arrangements being cancelled. She thought that he had grown tired of her and was glad not to be meeting her. Her mother and Julianne told her that she was foolish not to keep going out with him. Life had to go on, they said. You wouldn't want to let a good catch like him slip through your fingers. But she liked to sit with her father in the evenings. When her father got a bit better she would tell Patrick Stone that she didn't want to marry him.

Chapter 5

The knocking on the front door woke her. She heard someone running across the landing and down the stairs. She thought immediately of her father. Maybe he had taken another bad turn. She lay very still, listening. He had been bad for the past few weeks and Julianne had come in from Marshalstown to help nurse him. She sat up and leaned over on her elbow. She thought she heard Father Bolger's voice but it was hard to be sure. She held her breath and listened carefully to the footsteps on the stairs and the timber creaking. Her father's bedroom door clicked closed. James must have gone up for Father Bolger. He had gone for him another night, too.

She was shivering. She lay down and pulled the bedclothes over her arms and shoulders. She wondered should she get dressed and go down to them but it was very early. There was a dull brightness in the room but no sound yet out on the street. The doctor said not to have more than one or two people in the room with him because too many people would over-excite him. He tried to talk to everyone, and to smile and laugh, but his mouth was crooked and it was hard to know what he was saying. He had been very quiet yesterday. Her uncle Peter, his brother, had come in to see him and he had made no effort to talk after Peter left. Her mother said that Peter had upset him.

She heard someone rushing across the landing and up the

top stairs to her bedroom. She got out of bed. He must be very bad. Please God, make him all right, she prayed as she opened the door. Julianne was at the top of the stairs.

"He's dead, Margaret. He died a few minutes ago. Lord, have mercy on him," Julianne said in a low voice. "Your mother knew he was low and she sent James for the priest but he was dead before Father Bolger arrived. He went off very peacefully." She was dressed even though it was so early, in the new beige outfit Mrs Whelan had made for her.

"I'll go down to see him," Margaret said.

She got dressed quickly and as she went down the stairs she could hear her mother and Father Bolger saying the rosary. Her mother was mumbling the prayers in a low monotone but the priest's voice was loud and clear. The bedroom door was open. Margaret hesitated on the landing. They were kneeling at the far side of his bed. Her mother was wearing the black satin dressing gown with the coloured lanterns on it.

"Jesus, forgive us our sins, save us from the fires of Hell, lead all souls to Heaven, especially those in most need of Thy mercy," Father Bolger said, and then he paused. "The fifth Sorrowful Mystery. The Crucifixion," he said, and looked at Margaret's mother expecting her to give out the prayers, but she sighed loudly and slumped down on the bed. She moaned. She wouldn't make any effort to behave normally. She had become closed in on herself over the last few years. She focussed more and more on her dissatisfaction with her life.

"You're not able to say the prayers, Mai," Father Bolger said gently. He stood up and walked towards the door. "The good Lord will understand that. Margaret is here. Margaret will go down and get Julianne to hurry up with the tea."

"It takes them hours to do even the simplest of a thing," her mother said. "I don't ask for much."

Margaret gripped the banisters and her hand stuck to the timber as she went slowly down the dark stairs. How could God take her father from her? Her eyes were full of tears. If it was her mother who had died she wouldn't have cared, but how could God take her father from her? The grey light in the hall startled her and made her remember that it was just an ordinary winter's morning. It was a day the same as all other days. People would open up their shops and stop and pray for a minute when they heard that he was dead, but then they would work, and talk and laugh as usual, as if it didn't matter.

James and Julianne were standing at the range in the kitchen.

"I'm waiting for Tom Kirwan to come in to help me to lay him out," James said.

Julianne was stirring porridge, and every now and again the spoon scraped off the bottom of the saucepan. Nobody spoke for a while and Margaret gripped the edge of the table. Everything outside would continue as usual. She pictured swans rising up, flapping their wings and flying above the river.

Tom Kirwan came across the yard and James went to the door to let him in.

"I'll miss him," he said after he sympathized with her. "I was always terrible fond of him."

"We'll go upstairs, Tom," James said.

"I'll go up and try to get your mother to come down for the tea," Julianne said. "It's not good for her to stay up there for too long."

The glass door rattled as it closed. The kettle began to make a rough, rumbling noise coming to the boil. She felt weak and hardly able to lift the kettle to scald the teapot. Patrick Stone would probably come to the cathedral for the funeral Mass. She pictured him craning his head above a crowd of men making sure that he saw everybody and that they all saw him. She was crying as she took the crockery from the dresser and began to set the table. As she went to the drawer to get cutlery she saw James opening the front door to let Father Bolger out. The bare branches of the sycamore tree in the back lane were moving stiffly in the wind. The day he died was a cold, windy winter's day, she said to herself, as if his death was a story she was telling.

"She won't come down," James said, rattling the knob of the glass door. "She's gone into the parlour with Julianne. You may bring up the tea to her."

She got the tea-tray ready and carried it upstairs to the parlour. Her mother was sitting in the big armchair near the hearth, and Julianne had pulled one of the low chairs up beside her.

"I'm sure Peter didn't mean to upset Philip," Julianne said. "He probably thought that Philip couldn't hear what he was saying."

Margaret put the tray on the table between the two windows.

"Very well, Julianne," her mother said loudly. "You know what happened even though you weren't there. I was in the room with them, but I wouldn't know what was going on. I'm only an old fool."

Margaret moved the small table close to their chairs but she kept her head down and didn't look at either of them. Sometimes now her mother's mind seemed to get stuck on someone who had slighted or annoyed her. She would rant about them for days, unable or unwilling to get her mind to move on to the next day's happenings. Uncle Peter had annoyed her yesterday.

"You're taking things too much to heart," Julianne said gently. "You're tired and you're upset but I don't think you should start a row with Peter. He's Philip's brother and he's the only one of the family left now."

"I'll do exactly what I like. I'll start a row with him if I want to. Philip wouldn't have died so soon if Peter hadn't come in and upset him. Imagine coming in here and standing over poor Philip and saying, 'He won't last much longer. He looks very low. Two or three more days, that's as long as he'll last.'" There was venom in her mother's voice as she imitated Peter.

Margaret winced as she brought the cups of tea over to them.

"Poor Philip was lying there," her mother continued, "and I was after trying so hard not to let him know he was dying and then Peter came in and ruined everything. I'm after putting up with too much from Peter over the years and I'm going to tell him now what I think of him. That's enough, that's plenty," she said irritably as Margaret poured milk into the tea for her. "He didn't want Philip to marry me," she continued, looking off in the distance. "I'll never forget the first time I went out to Oulart after I got engaged to be married. Peter didn't speak a word but he tapped with his fingers on the table every time there was silence. It was very hurtful. I could never forgive him for that."

Margaret stood still beside them for a while. Her mother was gazing at Julianne who nodded sympathetically. Even when they were arguing they always appeared to be so close.

Margaret moved quietly towards the hearth and knelt down to clean out the fire. There was a spark here and there among the hot ashes and she moved the poker along the grate, trying not to make too much noise.

"I know you're after putting up with a lot from him over the years," Julianne said after a while, "but I wouldn't say a word if I were you. There'll be a big crowd in here for the wake and you wouldn't want them all talking about you."

"I don't care about any of them. They're all the same, every one of them who ever came in to the house to see Philip. None of them ever had any consideration for me. I'm after going through too much. I'm not letting Peter away with any more."

"I know," Julianne said coaxingly. "It was terrible but I wouldn't say a word to him. Not in front of everybody. They'll all be talking about us."

Julianne was so gentle and charming. It had been great to have her in the house, talking cheerfully about frivolous things like clothes, while he was sick. The shovel scraped against the stone of the hearth as Margaret cleared the ashes out.

"I suppose I should just mind my own business. It's nothing to do with me," Julianne said after a while. "Maybe I should go home and not interfere."

"No. No. I'd never have got through the last few weeks without you," Margaret's mother said, putting her cup and saucer on the table.

"You couldn't have been better," Julianne said. "You were great and you stayed so cheerful all the time."

"I didn't want him to know he was dying. Often I could have broken down in front of him and cried but I never did. I'm going to miss him," her mother said sobbing.

Julianne reached over and gripped her arm.

Margaret put paper into the grate and pieces of kindling and cinders. Her mother sighed and sobbed. A dog barked somewhere up the town and the wind was rustling in the chimney. She set a match to the fire. There was a knock on the front door.

"I'll go down," Julianne said. "You wouldn't know who that would be."

Margaret put small pieces of coal on the fire and tried to think of something to say to her mother who had her head bent and was hunched in over the fire. Her hair was matted against the back of her head.

"Bring up a damp cloth and clean the hearth," she said, standing up and gripping the front of her dressing gown. "I'll have to go and get dressed before there's a whole deluge of people in on top of us."

It was great to get downstairs away from her, and there was a lot of work to do. Josie Flood and Mrs Kirwan, Tom's wife, came to help in the kitchen for the day. All the china and the good cutlery had to be taken down and washed. James brought a big ham from the shop and it was put on to boil. They talked about how they would cater for all the people. James said to be careful not to insult anyone or leave anyone out. It was at a time like this that a shop could lose custom. People would take offence if they thought that they weren't treated as well as their neighbours. People who had dealt in a shop for years could easily move to another shop if they felt that they had been slighted. Kitty Furlong arrived after a while and said she would stay all day and help with the work.

"I don't know what we're going to do when Peter comes in," Julianne said.

People began to come to the wake. After a while Margaret went upstairs with Julianne to see him laid out. Two of the neighbours were standing on the landing and they sympathized with her. There were women in the parlour with her mother and neighbours sitting around the wake-room talking quietly. They all watched Julianne who was dressed glamorously. She smiled graciously at them.

"I hope they're not going to sit there all day," Julianne said quietly. "It's ridiculous to give the likes of them the run of the place. They look awful."

"They're our neighbours," Margaret said. "My father loved talking to them."

She knelt at the bed. All the colour was gone from her father's face. He was in a brown shroud and one of the white starched sheets was covering him. She started to cry and she stood up and went out.

She didn't know what time it was when she saw Patrick Stone in the parlour because she had a feeling all that day that it was no time, not any time of day, nor any particular day. The parlour was crowded and he was standing in the corner with a group of men. He had a glass of whiskey in his hand. He was blinking and smiling that distant smile of his. He reddened when he saw her and she knew that he didn't like the idea of men watching him talking to a woman. He frowned as he shuffled quickly out of the corner towards her.

"I'm sorry for your trouble," he said in a low voice. "It's hard on you all but particularly on your mother." He had his head bowed and his voice was very low. What he was saying was commonplace but he was very anxious that no one would hear him. It was as if there was something illicit in a conversation with her. "It's always hard on the wife."

"Yes," she said.

"I know he was sick but I'm sure his death was a shock to you," he said in a whisper. He began to awkwardly rub his knuckles and the whiskey splashed from side to side of the glass. "Tell me," he said suddenly, his face becoming animated. "Is he going to be buried in Oulart or in Enniscorthy?"

"In Enniscorthy," she said.

"Had he bought a grave?" He seemed excited now and his voice was louder.

"No," she said. "James went out to the cemetery earlier."

"He was an undertaker and he hadn't bought a grave? Wouldn't you think he'd have bought himself a grave? It's not as if there was any shortage of money." He looked around the parlour and his eyes focused for a while on the big mahogany sideboard. "I can't believe that an undertaker hadn't that arranged for himself," he said excitedly. He turned away from her and looked back at the men he had been standing with. "Enniscorthy," he said loudly. "Lads, it's Enniscorthy he's going to be buried in, not Oulart, but he hadn't bought a grave."

How could he speak like that about her father? She was certainly never going to have anything to do with him again but she couldn't tell him now in the middle of her father's wake. She walked away from him.

"I saw you talking to Patrick Stone," Julianne whispered excitedly. "James pointed him out to me. He's a very fine-looking man."

Margaret went downstairs and out into the yard. She was angry with Patrick Stone, and angry with herself for having spent time with him. But Patrick Stone didn't matter. Her father was dead upstairs. She went across the yard and leaned against the crates of bottles underneath the bar window. There were banks of dark cloud moving quickly across the sky. She was shivering with the cold but she stood there for a long time, glad to be alone.

When she went back into the kitchen her mother and Julianne were sitting at the table drinking tea.

"I'm worn out," her mother said. "I wish all those people would go home and I could get a bit of a rest. They're all staying too long. I thought Joan Delargy would never go. I had a pain in my face looking at her and trying to smile."

"When you look back on all this, Mai," Julianne said, standing up and taking her gold compact from the dresser, "you'll be very pleased about some of the people who came to the wake. Doctor Power and Mr Sinnott were here for hours. And Mrs Grattan-Flood. But I thought Mrs Bennett from the Castle was such a lovely refined woman. It was so good of her to come down the minute she heard the news.

Henry Bennett is away in London." She stood beside the oil-lamp, dabbing at her face with the powder puff and gazing at herself in the mirror.

"Philip used to waste a lot of time talking history to Henry Bennett. Doctor Power is all right, and Mrs Grattan-Flood, but I'm not bothered with that Sinnott man. He's a terrible old bore."

"Did you see those men from the Home Rule party? I made a very good impression on them," Julianne said. She seemed to be enjoying the wake. She often said that she hated living out in the heart of the country, not seeing anyone apart from her own family from one Sunday to the next. "I talked to them for a long time. I'm glad I told John Bourke not to come in until tomorrow. I don't want him hanging out of me with all those people around. That man with the dark beard looked very distinguished. Who's he?"

"He's from the Gaelic League," Margaret said.

The saucers rattled against one another as she put them on the draining board. She turned around and looked at her mother and Julianne. Her mother was crouched over the table, frowning determinedly. Her eyes were almost closed. She seemed intent on spreading her gloom and her despair as far as she could. Julianne was putting on bright red lipstick and rubbing her lips slowly together, smiling at herself as she gazed into the mirror, desperately clinging to glamour. It occurred to Margaret that her mother and Julianne were both, in different ways, extraordinary, and she thought that it would be better to live in a more ordinary way, without extremes of gloom or glamour.

She held her breath when she saw her uncle Peter coming into the kitchen. He had lovely soft grey hair and dark grey eyes. He was older than her father and much more serious. There was a nervous feeling in her stomach at the thought of a row between her mother and Peter.

He stood at the table looking down at her mother. "How are you, Mai?" His voice was low and grave. He was sad and he seemed humble and gentle because of his sadness. There was a gravity and a dignity about him that pervaded the room and Margaret thought for an instant that Peter's mood was strong enough to keep her mother quiet.

But her mother looked up. "I didn't think you were going to come in here today, Peter," she began in a monotone which sounded calm but Margaret knew that it would turn vicious very soon. "You certainly took your time about coming into your brother's wake."

Peter's eyes moved a little. He made a low whistling sound under his breath but he said nothing.

"The wake is upstairs, Peter," Julianne said in her most charming voice. "In the bedroom. Didn't poor Philip go off quickly in the end?"

"That's no surprise to Peter," Margaret's mother said. Her voice was loud and angry now. "Didn't Peter know he wasn't going to last? Peter is so smart that he was able to tell us last night that Philip wouldn't last. You should never have said that in front of a dying man. You upset Philip last night, and you upset me too. I don't know why you didn't stay out the country instead of coming in here to annoy us all."

There was silence. Margaret began to dry the dishes. Her stomach felt queasy as if her mother's bile was seeping into her.

"I'll go upstairs to the wake, Julianne," Peter said after a while. His voice sounded weak.

Margaret finished drying the dishes and put them on the dresser. There was a thudding behind her forehead as she listened to her mother gloating about how pleased she was that she had finally told Peter what she thought about him. She hadn't finished with him yet, she said, she'd talk to him again later.

It was good to get away from her to go up to the wake-room again. It was night-time and the house was filling up with men who had finished work. Patrick Stone had gone home. She sat close to the top of the bed in the wake-room watching her father. He would be gone forever from her soon.

The men who drank in the bar came into the room and prayed and sympathized with her and shook her hand. They stayed in the house for a while, drinking. After a while, she heard the clinking of bottles in a crate. Drinks were being brought upstairs from the bar. Then there were shouts for quiet outside and when the talk gradually stopped 'The Croppy Boy' started on the mouth organ. The music sounded shaky and uncertain, the way mouth-organ music always sounded. She was glad that it was the music of 'The Croppy Boy' and not the words. The words were too sad and she didn't want to cry. The music was raw and loud and she thought it was coming from the hallway, somewhere close to the front door. She pictured the mouth-organ player with his head to one side and his hands taut, covering his mouth, gripping the mouth organ. The words of the song began to come into her head.

> As I was walking up Wexford Hill,
> Who could blame me to cry my fill?
> I looked behind and I looked before,
> But my tender mother I shall see no more.
>
> As I was mounted on the platform high,
> My aged father was standing by;
> My aged father did me deny,
> And the name he gave me was the Croppy Boy.

The song was too sad and, in a way, she had always hated

the 1798 Rising. It was heroic, and everybody in Wexford was very proud of it, but sometimes she thought that it had been a mistake. It had ended so badly with the leaders being hanged and their heads displayed on Wexford bridge. All the odds were stacked against them. The whole might of the British Empire was used to put them down. It was wiser to stay at home and do nothing. She forced the sad lines of the song out of her head and made herself concentrate on the music until the men on the landing began to sing the last verse of the song.

> *It was in Duncannon this young man died,*
> *And in Duncannon his body lies;*
> *And you good Christians that do pass by,*
> *Shed a tear, say a prayer, for the Croppy Boy.*

She wanted to join in the singing but she stopped herself. Her father was lying dead. How could she want to sing at her father's wake?

The music ended and there was loud talk outside. She sat watching her father, and John came and sat beside her for a while. There was a lot of noise in the house but inside her head was completely still. She was startled suddenly when she heard calls for quiet for a singer.

"Come on, Mylie," a man shouted.

She was delighted that Myles Reilly was going to sing. She stood up and went to the door of the wake-room. She didn't know where Mylie was, in the hall, or maybe the kitchen, and she wanted to hear the song properly. Of all the singers who sang in the bar, Mylie was the best. He had won prizes for singing songs in Irish at the Oireachtas in Dublin but before he ever won prizes she had known that he was a great singer.

"Stay quiet, lads," someone said.

She crossed the landing, past groups of men, and stood at the top of the stairs, leaning on the banisters. She could hear Mylie coughing and clearing his throat as he got ready to sing. She went quickly down a few steps of the stairs and she could see him in the hallway. He was a small man with a moustache. He worked in Bolger's drapery. He coughed and straightening himself up he began the song. It was a song she had never heard before and she tried not to make the slightest sound as she moved further down the stairs to hear it better. It was a sad air and it was in Irish. She didn't understand the words, but as she closed her eyes and listened to the long slow notes, she knew that it was the most beautiful song she had ever heard and that it was a love song.

Chapter 6

A sudden heavy shower of rain began to beat against the kitchen window and she looked at the pitch dark outside. She finished the washing-up after the tea. It was six weeks since her father died. Her mother was taking his death very badly. She had the sciatica again, and she couldn't sleep properly or work much with the pain. She hated to be left alone, and Joan Delargy came to the house to sit in the parlour with her.

The rain eased off, and there was a buzz of talk from the bar. It was Martyrs' Night, and the town was crowded. She had decided to go out to see the procession. It was the custom that people went out as little as possible after there was a death in the family, and for a while after her father died she hadn't wanted to go out. It was as if everything had stopped for her, and she didn't want to know about anybody else. Her grief seemed to make her self-contained, to take her over completely, to make her feel so painfully alive within herself that she didn't need anyone or anything else.

But she was tired now of spending so much time in the house. She had slipped out last night and had gone up to Kitty Furlong's. Kitty came often to see her. Patrick Stone hadn't come to the house since her father's wake. She was sure that he had changed his mind about her, just as she had changed her mind about him. She couldn't convince her mother and Julianne that it was all over with Patrick Stone.

They said that he hadn't come to visit her because he knew that she was in mourning.

"It shows how highly he thinks of you, the great respect he has for you, that he wouldn't expect you to break any customs for him," Julianne had said.

She swept the floor and got ready to go out. The rain had stopped. As she crossed the dark street she could hear the river roaring along, and the bands in the distance. The Irish National Foresters organized the annual procession to honour the memory of Allen, Larkin and O'Brien, the three Fenian martyrs who had been hanged in Manchester by the British. Her father had always taken part in the procession and she used to stand on the street watching out for him among the men. She came to the top of the hill and saw the lights on the bridge. The music stopped for a while and then it started up again. The strains of 'God Save Ireland' came from the other side of the bridge, and she realized that she had missed the first half of the procession which began in the Abbey Square.

There was a crowd lining the paths on both sides of the bridge. She walked slowly along behind the people looking for a spot from where she would have a good view.

"Hello, Margaret." It was Mr O'Callaghan, a retired teacher who had been a friend of her father's. He moved back to make a space for her.

Four men with lighted torches led the procession on to the bridge. The Irish National Foresters came next carrying a big banner with their name on it. They marched four-deep across the bridge. A man carrying a torch led the first band which began to play 'Deep in Canadian Woods'. The music was loud and rousing. She thought of Irish men in Canada, and all over the world, who would tonight commemorate the Manchester Martyrs, and pledge themselves to win freedom for Ireland. There were more torch-bearers next, and then the Enniscorthy branch of the Home Rule party. She looked down when she saw the banner, not wanting to see a gap, or a gap filled, in their ranks where once her father had been. The front of the procession went along Slaney Place and more groups came on to the bridge. The spectators began to leave the bridge and some of them went up Slaney Street to the Market Square for the final gathering of speeches and music. She watched the Gaelic League men marching into Slaney Place, and she headed up Slaney Street.

People were standing on the footpaths waiting for the procession. There was a gang of young fellows fooling around on the corner'. She could hear the music of 'The Croppy Boy' in the distance. She walked along past Cronins'. Steam was rising up through the grille outside Jordans'. The wet footpath was gleaming under the light of the street lamp. She thought that Kitty Furlong might be somewhere in the Market Square. And then out of the blue she saw Patrick Stone leaning back against the wall of Jordans', rubbing his knuckles with his fingers.

"Hello," he said. He pushed back his fringe as he moved out from the wall.

"Hello, Patrick," she said.

There was silence. She didn't know what to say, how to start talking to him. She didn't know how she had ever spent time with him.

"I was going to write you a letter," he said in a low voice, "but I thought I'd wait until a while after your father died. I think we'll leave it so, now." He was blinking. "We'll leave it so," he repeated in a half-whisper. He had his shoulders bent over and his head bowed so that he was very close to her.

"Yes," she said.

"I hope you don't think it's callous of me when your father is just after dying, but we'll leave it for a year or so now." There was a slight smile on his face.

"Yes," she said. He had got tired of her. She was tired of him, too.

"I think the procession is coming." He pointed towards George's Street, and straightened himself up and craned his neck, as if she wasn't there. Then he moved away from her, almost running down the path towards Floods'. He had a loose swinging swaggering way of moving the bottom of his body, but his shoulders were always taut. He couldn't wait to get away from her. Drops of rain were beginning to fall and she stood in Jordans' doorway as the procession came into view.

It had been awful talking to him but she was glad that it was over with now. She would wait until Julianne came to visit on Sunday and then she would announce that Patrick Stone had broken it off with her. There could be no more talk of him then.

She brought breakfast upstairs to her mother the next morning. "I won't be able to eat anything," her mother said, lifting her head a little off the pillow. "The sciatica is gone worse. I didn't sleep a wink all night. The pain is darting right down my arm. I'll try to drink the tea but bring the rest of it back downstairs. Don't open the shutters. I couldn't bear any light in the room."

"Maybe you should get Doctor Power again?"

"No, no. There's no use. He told me it would get worse before it got better. Would you send the messenger boy up to ask Joan Delargy to come down and sit with me for a while? I know sometimes she talks too much, and she stays too long. She talks about her daddy. She'll wear me out, but I'd like to see her all the same."

Willie Comerford was behind the counter in the shop. James had gone off early to do Matty Kavanagh's funeral out in Davidstown. He came back from the funeral just after midday. She went upstairs to tell her mother and Joan Delargy that the dinner was ready.

"It was a huge funeral," James said, stretching forward and tilting the dish of potatoes towards Joan. He was a great talker. He could keep a pleasant conversation going with anyone.

"Is that right, James?" Joan said and smiled at him. She had a very squeaky voice. She had never married and she lived with her elderly father above their shop in Main Street.

"Tom Kirwan said he never saw as big a crowd in Davidstown church," Willie Comerford said.

"They all go out to funerals," her mother said scornfully. "They're like vultures. They love a spectacle. But there's very few of them would care about you at the back of it all. One or two are loyal, and don't think I don't appreciate that." She paused and looked first at Willlie Comerford and then at Joan Delargy to show that it was the two of them she was referring to. "Don't talk to me about big funerals," she continued. "I was bad enough without having that big crowd at Philip's funeral. I think a small funeral is more dignified. That's the kind I am. I'm different to other people. I like a bit of dignity."

James looked at her and moved his head slightly. He wasn't disagreeing with her, he would never openly disagree with anyone, but, being an undertaker, he was hardly agreeing with her either.

"I'd say you're right, Mrs Dempsey," Willie Comerford said. "It's good to be dignified."

"I like a bit of dignity," she repeated.

No one spoke for a while.

"How is your father, Joan?" James asked.

He talked about Joan's father and about the people he had met at the funeral. He made such an effort to be charming and well-mannered. An undertaker had to be able to do that. If you were in charge of a wake or a funeral you couldn't be too silent or bad-tempered. It didn't matter how sad other people were; James had to be able to keep things on an even keel.

"I was talking to Walter Mernagh," he said, "and do you remember Nora Mernagh, Margaret? She was at the funeral too. She came down from Dublin when she heard that Matty had died."

"Nora Mernagh was in my class in the Loreto Convent," Margaret said.

Her mother was looking at them with a puzzled bitter look on her face. She was annoyed with them for talking about younger people whom she didn't know.

"Matty Kavanagh supplied all the horses to the railway and to Donohoes'," James said, pouring more water into Joan's glass. "I suppose his son will keep that up. I remember my father buying a horse from Matty, one time. A lovely grey mare. A beautiful horse."

"I always thought that Matty Kavanagh used to make a cod of your father," her mother said. "Your father was lovely in many ways, but he was a fool, too. The likes of Matty Kavanagh would always get the better of him. I used to advise your father but he didn't always take my advice."

James moved his head slightly as if acknowledging that he had heard what she said. "I don't know will the son be as good at running the place as Matty was," he continued, without making any comment on what she had said. "The son asked for the inscription on the headstone to be written in Irish. I told him it would cost more but he said he didn't care. Matty was after getting interested in Irish before he died."

"Is that right, James," Joan said.

"I think that's lovely," Margaret said. "Irish. Our own language."

95

"I think it's stupid. Pure foolishness. A waste of money," her mother said. "Has he no sense? What sort of a fool of a son did Matty rear? He'll ruin the place wasting money like that."

"I think he's right. Irish is our own language," Margaret said. "It's the language we should be speaking only the British stopped us."

"They were right to stop us from speaking it," her mother said. "Irish is a backward language. English is being spoken all over the world. Even in darkest Africa the blacks are trying to learn English. Even the black people know that they should give up speaking their own language and learn English."

Willie Comerford nodded. He was wearing a brown shop coat. James never wore a shop coat.

"I suppose," James said.

"Kitty is learning Irish. You know Kitty Furlong from Slaney Street, Joan? She's going to Gaelic League classes to learn Irish," Margaret said.

Joan didn't answer.

"It's hard to know," James said.

"It's not a bit hard to know," her mother said. "People all over the world know. English is the language you'll make money in. All other languages should be got rid of, and Irish should be the first to go. God doesn't want all those languages at all. He only wants Latin for the Mass, and English. Just English."

"I'm going to go to learn Irish after Christmas," Margaret said.

"Very well," her mother said. "Don't listen to me. I'm only an old fool. Do what you like."

"I met Kitty's father out at the funeral," James said. "He was in great form." He was so good at changing the subject to make sure that things didn't get too unpleasant.

He seemed so calm and content after dinner as he went back out to the shop. There was the same intense stillness about him sometimes as there used to be about Julianne.

"You shouldn't have let all those people into the house to your father's wake," her mother shouted after him. His calmness annoyed her a lot sometimes. "You should have shown some consideration for me, and sent half of them home."

But James had gone into the shop.

Julianne came to visit on Sunday and Margaret brought tea up to the parlour. Julianne's two youngest children, Thomas and Anna, were playing quietly in the corner.

"You seem in better form today," Julianne was saying. "You look much better than you did last Sunday."

"I don't think I'll ever be the same again," her mother said. "I'm not like other people. I don't think I'll ever get over his death."

Margaret handed them the cups of tea, and stood in front of them with the milk jug and the sugar bowl.

"Did you go back to Doctor Power?" Julianne asked.

"I haven't the heart to go out of the house," her mother said, sighing.

"Send for him to come over here. That's what I'd do. I'd send for him. That's what he's for. I'd make him come over here." Julianne moved her head up and down determinedly. She didn't seem still like she used to. As she grew older sometimes she would become very intense and excitable as if she realized that there wouldn't be many more chances to grab all the things she wanted.

Margaret poured milk into Julianne's cup.

"I was thinking about Patrick Stone the other day when I went to view the auction out in Fairfield," Julianne said to her. "Did he call? I saw a beautiful mahogany hallstand at the auction."

"He didn't call," Margaret said, "but I met him up in the Market Square on Martyrs' Night and he told me he didn't want to see me anymore." She spoke slowly to make sure they couldn't pretend they hadn't heard.

"You're not serious," Julianne said. "You're not joking with us about a thing like that, are you?"

"I am serious," Margaret said. "He said that he didn't want to see me anymore."

No one spoke then for a while. The fire was spitting and crackling.

"Wouldn't you think I was after going through enough," her mother said, "without this on top of everything else?"

"This is after upsetting your poor mother," Julianne said.

"God grant me patience to continue. You'd think your family would provide a bit of consolation to you in your old age but all they do is give you trouble."

"James and John are good to you," Julianne said.

"They're only all right," her mother said, looking into the fire.

They talked on and on. Margaret sat on the couch beside the door, fingering the lace on the antimacassar. It was getting dark. They were going round and round in circles, repeating the same things again and again, and Margaret realized then that they had forgotten all about her. She was only important to them when she was doing something that they liked. They noticed her standing up and they stopped talking and watched her. It seemed as if she had wounded them. She felt desolate as she slipped out of the room although she told herself not to take any notice of them. She couldn't keep trying to be like them.

*

After Christmas she went with Kitty to the Gaelic League classes. Her mother wasn't talking to her since she told her that the line with Patrick Stone had ended. It was great to get out away from her. The classes were held in a room above Senan Doyle's bakery in New Street and Kitty had been going to them since September. The teacher's name was Muiris, Kitty said, and he was a native speaker from the Corca Dhuibhne Gaeltacht in Kerry. He lived in New Ross and travelled on a bicycle to all the towns around to teach Irish. They walked up the narrow stairs of Senan Doyle's house and into a long room off the landing. Five or six men were standing around the fire, and other people were sitting at a big table in the middle of the room. The young boy who worked as a gofer in the post office was gripping the table and tilting his chair dangerously backwards. Old Mrs Doran of Doran Grocery Stores was beside him.

Margaret sat with Kitty near the top of the room at the window. There was an easel and a blackboard propped up against the wall in front of them. She guessed that the man with the beard standing in front of the fire was Muiris, the teacher. He looked about fifty. He seemed serious and intense. After a while two of the men lifted out the easel and blackboard and set it up beside the fire. The other men moved down to the back of the room. Kitty pulled across the shutters on the windows and Muiris closed the door. It seemed as if the class was about to start but then Muiris noticed her. He came over.

"*Cé hí seo?*"

He reminded Margaret of a bird, because of the way he moved his head all the time and seemed to be so intensely alive.

"*Seo* Margaret," Kitty said.

"*Mairéad is ainm di. Mairéad is ainm duit,*" he said.

She understood what he was saying because she knew that Mairéad was the Irish for Margaret, but she understood very little else during the class. Muiris walked around at the top of the room, talking. He banged his fist on the table a few times, and once he banged it against the blackboard, and she thought that the blackboard would fall. He asked questions, and pointed at different people who answered him hesitantly. One woman spoke for a few minutes, and she seemed to be good at Irish, but all the other voices sounded flat and expressionless in comparison with Muiris's voice. Muiris, Kitty had said, spoke with a great blas, and Margaret was amazed at how proud and contemptuous his Irish sounded. She had expected it to be gentle and melodious, this beautiful language which the British had tried to destroy. But Muiris was making a 'ch' sound deep in his throat, and some nasal sounds, which were very unpleasant, and he seemed to enjoy throwing out these sounds, and muttering, and moving his shoulders, as if he was very proud of himself for being so good at Irish. He narrowed his eyes and he seemed to be giving out about something, probably the British. Maybe he was talking about Home Rule, or '98, or the treatment of Irish prisoners in British jails, or the Famine.

A man at the back of the class said something. Margaret thought he was asking a question. Muiris nodded and, taking a piece of chalk from the easel, began to write on the blackboard. He said the English meanings of the words as he wrote them down. "*Fearthainn*" was rain. "Gaoth" was wind. It was easier to follow when he wrote on the blackboard. But suddenly he was talking about seanfhocail or old sayings. "Is olc an ghaoth nach séideann do dhuine éigin." It's an ill wind that blows no good. "Mair, a chapaill, agus gheobhair féar." Live, horse, and you'll get grass. He moved quickly from one subject to another. "Capall" was horse, "bó" was cow. She wrote it all down. Kitty had shown her beforehand how to write in the Gaelic script, and she had practised it at home.

She loved making the strange-looking letters, the waves at the bottom of the A, the twirl at the top of the D.

The verb came first in the sentence in Irish. There were strange things called *forainmneacha réamhfhoclacha*, prepositonal pronouns, which Muiris wrote on the blackboard. Orm, ort, air, uirthi, orainn, oraibh, orthu. "Tá brón orm" meant I'm sad. When she went home she learned everything that she had written down, and went over and over it again until she knew it perfectly. It was great to have something special to do, something that she had to make time for every day. Vocabulary was easy to learn. She used to write out a list of words and have them with her in the kitchen all day. She often thought about her father who used to sit in the kitchen with her when he didn't feel well enough to work in the shop. Peann. Leabhar. Litir. Scríbhneoir. File. Dán. After a while, she could pick out words here and there when Muiris was speaking, and sometimes she could understand a whole sentence.

There was a man in the Irish class. Michael was his name. Michael Carty. He lit the fire every night and made all the arrangements with Muiris. She knew that he worked in the railway because he made deliveries to the shop. He was standing at the door one night when the class was over, waiting to put out the lamps. She had crossed the room thinking that Kitty was following her, but when she looked back Kitty was talking to Mrs O'Connor.

"It's hard to get them all to go home," he said. "I'm tired. I was out late last night. One of the lads from the railway got married and we didn't get home until morning. I nearly fell asleep several times during the class. Do I look tired?" He was talking to her as if he knew her well although this was the first conversation they had ever had.

"No, no," she said. "You don't look tired."

He was watching her carefully, as if he was trying to learn about her. He seemed to like her.

"I'll go to bed as soon as I go home," he said.

"I'll call Kitty," she said, "and the others might leave, too."

"No," he said. "They'll leave when they're ready."

Kitty and Mrs O'Connor came over, and Michael Carty was very friendly with them, too. He was friendly with everybody. He had dark hair. He was a bit taller than her, but he wasn't too tall. He stood sometimes with his arms loosely folded. Maybe he was married. But there was no use in thinking about him because he wasn't good enough for her. He followed a horse for the railway.

"Is Michael Carty married?" she asked Kitty one night as they walked down Slaney Street.

"No," Kitty said. "He lives in lodgings up in Court Street. You're not interested in him, are you?"

"No," she said.

But when she was on her own at home she often pictured his face. He talked and laughed and seemed to enjoy himself, but several times she had seen him look off in the distance as if there was something different on his mind. He had blue eyes and a big wide forehead. His face looked angular.

She was walking across the Market Square one day, going up to Bolgers' to buy wool. It was Thursday, Market Day, and the square was busy. A man lifted a sack of potatoes from a cart on to his shoulders and carried it into Byrnes' grocery shop. There was a carthorse coming along. She stopped and waited. She was looking up New Street, at the green dome above the Loreto Convent, and she wasn't taking any notice of the horse and cart. Then someone leaned off the cart, sideways towards her, and smiled at her, and she recognized him. It was Michael Carty. He touched his cap, and she waved, but he was gone then, up New Street. The horse thudded loudly away from her, and she stood for a few seconds looking after him. She found herself thinking how wonderful he was. He stopped the horse outside Carrolls' public house, and she forced herself to walk quickly up George's Street. He might see her looking after him. He wasn't good enough for her. Why was she thinking about him? She would have to forget about him but she could see his face in front of her eyes. It was lucky for Mrs Carroll. He had gone in to Carrolls' pub, and Mrs Carroll who was an old woman was talking to him.

Some nights at the classes he would talk to her, but other nights he didn't even look at her. He would be sitting down at the back when she came in, and she wouldn't look because she didn't want him to know how often she thought about him. She would make herself listen to Muiris and pretend that Michael wasn't there. But every now and then she let herself bask for a while in the feeling of his presence behind her, and she would conjure up his face before her eyes, although sometimes his face appeared before her without any prompting.

Muiris was writing a verse of a poem on the blackboard. It was a verse out of "*Cabhair ní ghairfead*" by Aodhagán Ó Rathaile. The blackboard was dry and shiny and every so often Muiris licked the chalk before starting a new word. Margaret wrote down the verse, and Muiris's translation of it.

Do thonnchrith m'inchinn, d'imigh mo
    phríomhdhóchas,
poll im ionathar, biora nimh' trím dhrólainn,
ár bhfonn, ár bhfothain, ár monga 's ár mínchóngair
i ngeall le pingin ag foirinn ó chrích Dhóver.

My mind quaked, there was no hope left in me,

a hole in my guts, poisonous arrows through my heart,
our land, our homes, our woods, our own countryside,
all gone for a penny to a crew from the land of Dover.

She loved the poem, which Ó Rathaile wrote after his patrons, the MacCarthys, lost their land to the planters. Muiris said that it was his favourite of all the poems he had ever read.

The class was over. Michael stood at the top of the room with the men and he didn't look around as she passed. She stood close to him waiting for Kitty, but he folded his arms and talked to the men. He went over to the corner and got the fireguard and put it in front of the fire. She thought that he didn't like her. She was a fool to be spending her time thinking about him.

The *modh foshuiteach*, the subjunctive mood, the tense for prayers and wishes. She sat at her dressing table and wrote the heading in her notebook. She put the pen down on the blotting paper. Sometimes it wasn't that the thought of Michael Carty came into her head, but that a desire for him rose up in her body. She wanted to court him, to feel him close to her. She wanted him to kiss her, and she sat there at the dressing table for a while, and let herself imagine courting Michael Carty. He watched her while he was talking to her as if he was trying to understand something about her. She forced herself to pick up the pen. Michael Carty followed a horse for the railway. Did she want to go hungry, owe money in every shop in the town? He didn't earn enough money to keep her. As if trying to wake herself from a dream she forced herself to write down a sentence in the *modh foshuiteach*. *Go dté tú slán.* She wondered where was Michael Carty now? What was he doing? Was he on his own or was he with other people? Who was he with?

Chapter 7

It was beginning to get dark, and the rain was lighter than the darkness, pouring down, hitting the cathedral yard and splashing back up. Benediction was over and some people stood in for a while in the porch of the cathedral, waiting for the rain to ease off.

"I've an umbrella," Kitty said. "I think we'll go."

They walked close together under the shelter of the umbrella, looking down, trying to avoid puddles. The rain was rolling in streams down Main Street, and they could hear it glugging into shores and beating off corrugated iron rooves. It dripped heavily off the edge of the umbrella and wet Margaret's shoulders and her arm. She pulled up the collar of her coat and felt a trickle of cold water on her neck. They turned up into Hogans' lane and when they came out into New Street the rain had eased off a little. Kitty let down the umbrella and they went inside. Suddenly they heard the rain pouring down again, even heavier this time than before.

"Listen to that," Kitty said, putting the umbrella into the hallstand.

There was an umbrella already there and Margaret knew that Michael Carty was upstairs.

He was kneeling down in front of the grate. He was trying to light the fire but the coal was too wet. There was no flame, and there wasn't even much smoke.

"That's a terrible night," he said, turning and looking up at them. "Are ye drenched?"

"We had an umbrella. We're not too bad," Kitty said, moving into the room.

Margaret stood just inside the door. Often when she saw him she felt confused, and she didn't know what to do or say.

"Take off your coats," he said, standing up. "They'll dry out in no time when the fire lights up."

He moved sideways towards the door, towards Margaret. He held his hands out awkwardly in front of him because they were dirty from the fire.

"You'd want to get a damp cloth, Michael," Kitty said, pointing towards the fireplace, "and clean the grate and the hearth. Did you ever do that?"

"No," he said.

"The hearth and the fireplace are very dirty and dusty," Kitty said, shaking her head. "They need to be washed, don't they Margaret?"

"I suppose," Margaret said. She felt uneasy about the casual way Kitty spoke to Michael, and said his name. Margaret had never been able to say his name to his face. She looked at him. He seemed fragile to her. He might be very hurt by criticism.

"I must do that," he said. "I'll get a cloth from Senan, the next time I'm down in the kitchen."

"And bring up a brush from the kitchen," Kitty said. "The floor needs to be swept."

"I'll do that next week," he said. "I hope the fire will light up. The coal is very wet. I'm just after bringing it up from the yard."

"I'd say it will light in a minute," Margaret said. "You have paper and sticks in there too. It will light."

A puff of smoke came from the front of the fire, and then a small flame came from nowhere and danced in a zig-zag movement over the top of the coals. It didn't touch the coals, but it buzzed for a while, and they watched it until it disappeared.

Kitty went down to the back of the room to close the shutters.

"It's hard on a miserable night like this," he said, "to imagine the heat of the summer, when you'd look forward all day to a swim down the banks in the evening."

Kitty closed the shutters on the bottom window with a bang. She came up to the top of the room and stood for a while with her back to them looking out the window. A long flame burst through the damp shiny coals at the back of the fire and it blazed, red and orange, up the chimney.

"Will you come for a walk with me on Sunday, Margaret?" It was the first time he had said her name.

"Yes," she said.

He smiled at her. As Kitty closed the shutters they heard voices outside on the street. The rain seemed to have eased off. The timber on the stairs creaked. Other people were arriving.

"I'll meet you on the bridge on Sunday," he said.

"About two o'clock," she said.

*

He was standing near the cotton tree as she came down the railway bridge. There was a sprinkling of light green leaves on the trees above the Turret Rocks. Those trees had been bare, like skeletons, all through the winter. As soon as he saw her he walked towards her. She was nervous, afraid that he wouldn't like her.

"Will we go across the bridge," he said, "and up the Hurstbourne Road? There's a great view of the town from the Hurstbourne Road."

They walked past the stile leading down to the bank of the river, and turned on to the bridge.

"It's a great day for a walk," he said. "It's great to get a fine Sunday when we have the day off."

He walked faster than her, and sometimes went ahead, but he stopped to look at her each time he spoke. They crossed the bridge and turned down the quay. Jagged rocks jutted out at the bottom of the high Mission House wall.

"I was out this road yesterday," he said. "We often have to do deliveries out here, myself and Billy. We have to walk most of the way. The horse is not able for the pull. Do you know Billy Dagg?"

"No," she said. "I don't think so."

"He came to the Irish classes a few times, but then he gave up. He said it was too hard. He's great company on the cart, and he knows everyone. He tells stories about all the people out in the Mile House where he lives."

They walked under the high rocks of the Hurstbourne Road, and he talked to her about Billy and the other people he worked with. He talked to her as if he knew her well, and as if he thought she knew everything about him. She hadn't expected him to be like he was. She thought he would be quieter and more serious. But he seemed excitable, and he talked about people, not about serious things. She didn't know the men he was talking about, Billy and Nick and Martin who worked on the railway with him. But he looked down at her and she loved the slight movement in his face as he spoke. It occurred to her how much her mother and Julianne would have despised them all, men with badly paid jobs who would never own anything. But Michael liked them. He seemed to like most people. They turned the corner on the Hurstbourne Road. She wondered when would he kiss her.

"I've been out this road as far as Screen," he said as they

went up towards Drumgoold. "You pass through Ballymurn first. There are always peacocks out on the street in Ballymurn. We stop the horse to look at them."

"The peacocks from the manse often come down to our yard," she said. "Father Rossiter owned them and since he died they wander around the town. Our cats are afraid of them. They run into the sheds as soon as the peacocks come strutting into the yard."

They walked along the road, past a row of small mud-cabins. She had always known about the squalor of Drumgoold but she had never been here before. The poorest people in Enniscorthy lived here. The men drank too much, and late at night there were fights here, and women and children were thrown out on the side of the road. Some of the hovels weren't much higher than the ditches in front of them. There were holes in the thatch. Ragged clothes were drying on the bushes. How could people live decent lives in hovels like that? The British should improve things for the Irish people. She thought Drumgoold was a terrible place but she didn't say anything to Michael in case he would be insulted. Maybe he knew people who lived here. A mangy dog tied to a post at the side of the road began to bark at them. She was glad when they turned on to the tree-lined road towards Ballycourcy.

"Isn't that oak tree extraordinary," she said, pointing at the gnarled bark of the tree. "It's probably hundreds of years old. There are so many beautiful trees, and there should be even more but Sir Henry Wallop cut down the forests and sold the timber."

"They came here and they destroyed our countryside, and they've nearly taken our language from us." He stood still on the road but he didn't look at her as he spoke. "It's time for the Irish people to stand up to them. They left us to starve during the Famine while shiploads of grain were exported to keep landlords living in luxury over in London. The Irish people are too quiet. They've got used to being treated badly. But somebody has to stand up and strike a blow. The British will have to be got rid of sooner or later."

She looked up at him but he was looking away. He looked serious and he seemed distant from her for the first time that day.

They turned a corner and he stopped and kissed her. They walked along the road again and he was quiet for a while. She caught his hand. She thought that he liked her.

"I think this is the road that they escaped along in '98, after the Battle of Vinegar Hill," he said.

"Yes," she said. "The ones who escaped through Needham's Gap."

She wanted them to keep walking along this road. She didn't ever want to go home. But after a while he said that maybe they had gone far enough. They should turn back. He told her that he was going to play cards that night in the Workingman's Club. It was a while since he played because he was busy with the Irish class. He kissed her again before they came too close to the cabins in Drumgoold.

They turned the corner and stood at the wall on the Hurstbourne Road, looking at the town and the river. The tide was coming in and the river was full. Seagulls circled above the water and every now and again one of them swooped down on to the river. She could see the roof and the top windows of her own house on the Island Road.

"From up here, the houses look crowded together," she said. "You can't see the streets between them."

He put his arms around her and he kissed her, pushing his tongue far into her mouth. She loved how strong he seemed, and how firmly he was standing on the ground. She was standing in front of him, and after a while she put her face down on his chest. He put his hands on her hips. She didn't ever want to leave him.

*

They walked back along the Wexford Road and on to the quay. There had been a drought, and several patches of the stony river bed had dried out completely. He went down the steps to the bank of the river and walked along the narrow ledge above the water. She followed him. He jumped out on to one of the stony patches on the river bed.

"Are you all right?"

"Yes," she said, although she felt weak and dazed. She had been courting him for too long in a field out the road.

He bent down to look for stones to skim along the top of the water. She stood on the narrow ledge beside the river watching him. The chestnut trees on the far bank were round green shimmering reflections in the dark water. The castle and the cathedral rose high above the houses.

"Come on out here," he said.

She jumped over the narrow water on to the dry stones. The white and grey gravel crunched under her feet. He was inspecting the stones that he had picked up. He threw some of them back down, and put the others into his pocket. He went over close to the water, took out a stone, and gripped it between his thumb and his forefinger. Stooping slightly he bent his hand backwards towards him, and eyeing the water he flicked his wrist and skimmed the stone across the river. The stone touched the water in three or four spots, causing little splashes, and then it sank. He took another stone out of his pocket.

She picked up a few stones but threw some of them back again because one side was round or jagged. She handed him some flat smooth stones. He narrowed his eyes and, bending forward, skimmed one of the stones across the river. She watched him, thinking that he had got the angle wrong and that the stone would sink as soon as it hit the surface of the water, but it skimmed along, three, four times, and it kept going. It hit the water six times before sinking.

"I think that's the best I ever saw," she said. "It kept on going."

"It was good all right," he said.

They had decided to get married. She was going to have to tell her mother tonight before they went up to the manse to ask the priest to call out the banns.

*

Smoke gushed out when she opened the oven, and the rich smell of the stuffed steak filled the kitchen. The bubbling fat spit and hissed as she lifted the heavy roasting-dish and put it down on the range. The house and the bar had been extraordinarily quiet all the morning. There had been a terrible row in the bar last night, and Martin Quigley had been barred. It was over by the time she got home. She had gone out past the mill with Michael, and when she came back it was dark but there were people out on the street, talking about the row and looking at the big front window of the bar which had been broken and was boarded up. Martin Quigley had thrown a stool through the window and had smashed bottles and glasses on the floor. He was on a terrible batter and had been drinking whiskey in different pubs around the town all day. He was very drunk when he came into James' bar. James gave him one drink but told him that he'd have to go home after that. All hell broke loose then. Her mother was very upset. James hadn't wanted a row with Martin Quigley. His relations were very respectable people, but Martin was the black sheep of the family. When he was on a batter sooner or later he caused a row wherever he went.

She lifted the meat on to a plate, and got a knife from the dresser to cut it. She hadn't told her mother or James last night that she was getting married. There had been too much else going on. She was surprised at how calm she felt now. She would tell them after dinner.

James came into the kitchen. She put the dish of parsnips and the dish of new potatoes on the table, and James's plate in front of him. The stairs creaked. Her mother was coming downstairs. "I'm not the better of that row last night," she said when she came in to the kitchen. "Where's Willie Comerford?"

"I sent him home," James said. "It's quiet out there today and I can manage on my own. He was very good last night. He came down the minute I sent up for him."

"There's no one like Willie," her mother said.

The row seemed to have calmed her down. It had taken her out of herself. She had included Margaret in the conversation last night, and had looked at her as she spoke.

"I didn't sleep a wink last night," she said. "I can't stop thinking of Martin Quigley's poor mother. She's in the house on her own with Martin coming in drunk. I think I'll go up and see her some day. I used to be very great with her years ago. I'll get Joan Delargy to come with me, and we'll visit her."

"It's hard on Martin Quigley's mother," James said, "but it's hard on us, too. He did a lot of damage out in the bar. I'll be getting a bill from Ned Sullivan for a new window. I've a bruise the size of a football on my leg from the kick he gave me. It wasn't easy to get him out."

"You'll be all right," her mother said. "You're young. Young people always recover. It's his poor mother I feel sorry for." She had talked a lot about Martin Quigley's mother last night, too. She often got stuck like that, talking all the time about one person or thing. "No one understands the way mothers suffer," she said. "It's hardest of all on Martin Quigley's mother."

"I suppose," James said. "There's another meeting of the 1798 Rising Commemoration Committee tonight," he said to change the subject. "I think we're going to make the final decision that we'll get Oliver Sheppard to make a statue. The money is pouring in, even from America and Australia. Oliver Sheppard is the best sculptor in the country and he's doing a statue for the Wexford Committee, too. He has proposed having two figures in our statue – Father Murphy and the Croppy Boy. He's doing a single figure for the Wexford Committee, a pikeman."

"Where will you put the statue?" Margaret asked.

She would have to tell them soon about Michael. She could see that her mother was annoyed about the change in the topic of conversation, and was eyeing them suspiciously, waiting for a chance to get back to talking about the row and Martin Quigley's mother.

"We're not sure where we're going to put it," James said, taking a pinch of salt from the salt cellar. "Maybe up on Vinegar Hill."

"Men are great for getting statues made," her mother said. "Anyone could make a statue. But there's no one to help a poor widow woman like Martin Quigley's mother. Men long ago had a bit of authority. They'd have gone in after a fellow like him and frightened him so that he wouldn't upset his mother. But the men nowadays are no good."

James moved his head slightly. He was about to speak but her mother continued.

"What use are statues? You're all full of talk about statues," she said, "but there's not one of you any good at the back of it all."

Her mother was stuck on Martin Quigley's mother and wasn't going to move on to anything new. There was a good side to her mother even if it was hard to listen to her. She was often really good to someone who was in trouble. She would do anything she could to help Martin Quigley's mother. If she stayed stuck on her maybe she wouldn't be able to react too strongly when she heard about Michael Carty.

They ate in silence for a while. She would have to tell them now before James started on something else or her mother got back to Martin Quigley's mother.

"I'm getting married in the autumn," she said. "I'm getting married to Michael Carty."

"What?" her mother said.

James moved his head towards her and then looked down.

"You know Michael Carty, James," she said. "He often comes into the shop. He works for the railway."

James kept his head down and slowly cut the meat. James knew about herself and Michael. He had seen them walking around the town together but he had never mentioned it.

She faced her mother. "I'm sure you've often seen him in the yard. He does deliveries to the shop."

Her mother's eyes sparked. "He follows a horse for the railway, and you're telling us that you're getting married to him." She put her knife and fork down on the plate.

"We're going up to the manse to see the priest tonight," Margaret said. "September. We're getting married in September." She tried to speak loudly and to stay cheerful, to maintain a different tone to her mother's. Her mother's moods were so strong that they spread out over people who weren't making a huge effort to hold their own.

"You're joking," her mother said.

"No. I'm not joking. I'm getting married in September."

"I knew there was something going on," her mother said angrily. "You think I'm an old fool but I'm not. I knew you weren't up in Kitty's all the time, or at your Irish class, but of course you wouldn't tell me that you were making a show of yourself courting some trick of the loop working for the railway. What did you say his name was?"

"Michael Carty."

"You can't marry him," her mother said. "You can't let us all down by doing a thing like that. We'll be the laughing stock of the town."

"Michael is very highly regarded in the town. He knows nearly everyone. Everyone stops to talk to him," Margaret said.

Her mother sat up straight. "What do those sort of people matter, the sort of people who would stop to talk to the likes of him? I won't be able to hold my head up high among my friends. You were never any good. I never wanted much, but I always wanted to be able to say that my daughter married well, but I should have known that there wouldn't even be one bit of good news after all I'm after going through. I don't know what Julianne will say. We'll be the laughing stock of the women when we go out to play cards."

"Michael Carty comes into the bar an odd time," James said. "He seems a nice enough fellow."

"A nice enough fellow," her mother said. "Don't be talking nonsense. Ye have no sense. He has no money and he has no prospects. It's not much use being nice."

There was silence for a while.

"We're going to see about renting a house on Bohreen Hill," Margaret continued brightly. "One of the houses there is vacant."

"God grant me patience to continue," her mother said. "Life is after dealing me many a bitter blow. No one knows all I'm after going through."

She seemed to have completely forgotten about Martin Quigley's mother. There was silence. Margaret took a potato

117

from the dish and began to peel it. James poured more water. Her mother sighed loudly.

"God grant me patience to continue," she said again. "You always thought you knew everything but one thing you never knew was how to treat your mother. You wouldn't tell me things that the whole town probably knows. Everyone must have seen you walking out with this fellow, you must be walking out with him for a while, but I'm the last to know."

"I am seeing him for a while. But I didn't tell you because you don't talk to me."

"You never told me. You think I'm against you." She started to cry. "I never could … You think I'm against you but I'm your mother. I always only wanted what was best for you. I never wanted things to be wrong for you."

"I know," Margaret said.

"You know nothing," her mother said, wiping her eyes with her fists and getting angry again. "But you'll find out soon enough. I don't know where I went wrong rearing you. I reared you too soft. You don't know what hardship is like, but you'll find out if you marry that fellow."

"Michael works," Margaret said. "I'll live on his wages."

"What sort of wages would a fellow like that be earning? And that's all very fine but what will you do if anything happens to him? Will you come back here looking for us to support you, and a houseful of children? Go on. Go off. If that's the sort of life you want for yourself go and lead it. But leave me out of it. I've had a hard enough life, and I'd like to get through the end of it with a bit of comfort. I don't want to hear about all the hardship you'll have to go through, about the money you'll owe. People sneering at you and looking down on you."

Margaret could feel her mother's gloom and anger spreading through her. She sat up straight and made herself think about Michael. She wished she could walk out of the house at that moment and never have to come back to it. Never to have to listen to any more of this.

"Look. Here's Joan," James said, gesturing towards the window. "Isn't that great now." He stood up and opened the back door.

"I came as soon as I heard about the row, James," Joan said. "Martin Quigley is a terrible man when he's drinking. Are you all right? How is your mother?"

"She's bearing up well enough, Joan," James said.

Her mother had started to cry again.

"What's wrong, Mai? What happened? You're very upset," Joan said.

"I'm all right," her mother said. "But I'm after hearing very bad news." She stood up.

"Bring her upstairs to the parlour, Joan, and we'll send you up tea," James said.

Joan came over and put her arms around Margaret's mother. They went out into the hall. Her mother's shoulders were hunched and rounded, and the bones down the middle of her back were sticking out through her fine summer cardigan.

James peeled another potato. Margaret sat and watched him.

"It's terrible hard to listen to her sometimes," James said, putting butter on the potato. "I don't think she means a lot of what she says. She gets all caught up in things. But we have to try to move on. The past is the past."

Chapter 8

July–August, 1914

Michael Carty wheeled a handcart to the edge of the railway platform and stood waiting for the Dublin train. Two swans rose up above the river and flew towards the town. He looked across the island at the row of houses among the trees on Bohreen Hill. Margaret was at home there with the baby, and the boys were probably home from school. There was a dead heat. The sky was dark, and angry clouds threatened rain. A cart rattled into the Railway Square, and he walked down the platform to look out. It was usually quiet on Thursdays, a half-day in the town, but it wasn't going to be quiet today. Fennelly, a school teacher and one of the new leaders of the IRB in the town, was getting a crowd together in the Railway Square to boo and jeer at a detachment of soldiers who were due to arrive on the mail- train from Waterford. There would be ructions in a while. He was looking forward to it.

The shrill whistle of the Dublin train sounded in the distance, and he walked back up to the handcart. Mr Kelly, the stationmaster, had come out on the platform and was walking down towards the signal box. The signal went up.

"Martin." He called in to Martin Webster, his helper on the cart, who was in the storeroom reading the paper and having a smoke. Martin was in the IRB and the Irish

Volunteers along with Michael. "Kelly is down at the signal box," he said.

Martin came out and stamped on his cigarette butt. The train was coming in to view. Martin did a mock practice march across the platform. The Irish Volunteers held regular marches through the town, and people lined the streets to see them marching in their uniforms. There were thousands of Volunteers all over the country, and five hundred in Enniscorthy, although the movement had only started before Christmas.

The Dublin train came slowly to a halt in front of them, and a few people got out of one of the carriages. The guard opened the door of the baggage carriage and they lifted the boxes and crates for Enniscorthy on to the handcart. The faint sound of cheering was drifting across the town from the polo match in the Showgrounds. As they wheeled the handcart towards the storeroom the guard was banging the carriage doors closed. The whistle blew and the train pulled out of the station.

Martin rubbed his hands together gleefully. "The trouble will start soon," he said. Fennelly had told the people to come down to the Railway Square ten minutes after the Dublin train left. The detachment of British soldiers was en route to Blackwater to replace the regular coastguard which had been recalled to England because of the threat of a European war. Fennelly said it was a great opportunity to get the people together to demonstrate their hostility to the British.

"Look at Kelly," Martin said as they wheeled the handcart over to the storeroom. Kelly was inspecting something at the bottom of the signal box steps. He had been fussing around the station all day anxious to have everything right for the arrival of the British soldiers. "He's all spruced up, delighted with himself, going to meet British soldiers," Martin said. "He'll get some fright when the crowd gathers."

They laughed. Kelly was a terrible West Brit.

"It's great that it's a half-day," Michael said. "There will be a big crowd off work. The Mackens will get a great crowd together from the Shannon."

They wheeled the handcart into the storeroom and were lifting one of the crates when there was a light knocking on the open door.

A small squat man was bending forward through the doorway. "What time is the mail-train from Waterford due in at?" There was a smile on his face as if he was trying to become friendly with them. Michael had seen the man before. He was the driver of a jarvey-car, from somewhere out the country.

"It should be here in about five or ten minutes," Martin said, pushing a crate into the corner. "There's a waiting room. You can sit in there if you like."

"Ah no. I'll be alright here," the driver said. He took two or three steps into the storeroom. "You haven't a cigarette, have you? I'm dying for a smoke."

Martin gave the driver a cigarette and, lighting one up for himself, sat on the window sill of the storeroom. The driver sat beside him.

"I'm here to collect baggage," he said, pulling on his cigarette, "for a detachment of the Shropshire regiment. They're going to march from here to Blackwater but I'm going ahead with their bags."

"The Shropshire regiment? The British Army?" Martin said slowly, shaking his head as if he didn't know. Fennelly had told them to do exactly what they did every single day, and not to pretend that they knew anything.

"There's one thing you can be sure of with the British Army, lads," the driver said. He was leaning forward with one elbow resting on his knee, holding the cigarette a few inches away from his mouth. "You can be sure that they'll pay you."

He genuinely didn't seem to see anything wrong with working for the British Army. Even if he was to starve, Michael was saying to himself, he wouldn't do it. You couldn't call yourself an Irishman and work for the British Army.

"I've a grocery shop and I wouldn't like to tell you how much money I'm owed," the man said. He was smiling and looking up at Martin who had given him the cigarette. "Some people wouldn't care if they never paid you," he said, leaning back against the window.

"You should go down and talk to Mr Kelly. He's the stationmaster, and he's a great admirer of the British Army, too." Martin stood up. "I'll show you where he is," He went out on to the platform. The man followed him.

Michael finished unloading the handcart and wheeled it out. There was a brilliant glare among the clouds where the sun was trying to break through. The driver was standing talking to Kelly down near the signal box. Martin had gone up to look out the door of the station into the Railway Square. Michael stood on the platform as if it was just an ordinary day and he was waiting as usual for the Waterford mail-train.

Martin came back. "There's a crowd gathering," he said quietly. "There are women and children with the men."

The whistle sounded and the Waterford train came around the corner through the trees, clacking against the iron of the railway track. Kelly walked briskly down the platform. He rubbed the dust off the shoulders of his stationmaster's uniform. The engine chugged along the tracks. The long front carriage was full of British soldiers. Some of them were sitting down, others standing up, reaching into the baggage rails, lifting down rucksacks and bags. Enniscorthy wasn't a garrison town, and Michael didn't have to see British soldiers too often. The sight of them reminded him of Cromwell's soldiers tramping through the land, sending Irish Catholics to Hell or to Connaught, of British armies with guns and cannon advancing on Vinegar Hill in '98, eager to slaughter innocent Irish men, women and children.

As the train slowed down, the soldiers, holding rifles and rucksacks, pressed forward towards the door. He closed his eyes and when he opened them all he could see was the dusty black of the goods' carriage slowing down in front of him. The carriage full of soldiers had passed on.

He heard booing behind him and he turned around. A group of men had come on to the platform. Some of them were standing back against the wall while the others were just inside the station door. He recognized some of his comrades in the IRB. They were booing and stamping their feet.

"It's starting," Martin said, rubbing his hands together. "This is going to be great."

The stationmaster was so anxious to greet the soldiers that he was running slowly along the platform holding the door of the carriage. He stopped when the train stopped but then he almost fell forward as the train chugged on again. The men on the platform shouted and roared laughing.

"You're an eejit, Kelly," one of them said.

Kelly looked around. Then he turned back, as if he hadn't seen the men, and opened the door of the train.

More men were coming on to the platform. They began to shout at the soldiers who were getting off the train. Kelly and the driver were shaking hands with the soldiers. Kelly was bowing and he seemed to be making a little speech to each soldier. The men who had come into the station booed loudly and moved slowly up the platform towards them.

The guard came up from the back of the train. He was an officer in the IRB in Waterford, and it was he who had sent word to Fennelly that the soldiers would be passing through Enniscorthy.

"This is great," he said. "Ye're doing a great job. That will show them what the Irish people think of them." He opened the goods' carriage.

"Isn't it terrible to watch Kelly fawning over them," Michael said.

"And the driver," Martin said. "Just look at the driver. You'd think he was play-acting on a stage."

The driver was imitating Kelly, and bowing at the soldiers.

They got into the goods' carriage and began to pull out the Enniscorthy baggage.

"At least the soldiers didn't put their luggage in here," the Waterford guard said, dragging out sacks of mail. "I stayed away from them, down at the end of the train. I couldn't bear to go near them."

Michael threw a small sack on to the handcart. Near the station-door the platform was crowded with men, booing and stamping their feet. Further down the platform the soldiers were eyeing the crowd and standing around as if they were guarding trunks and rucksacks which they had put on the platform. Kelly was talking to a soldier who was older than the others and who seemed to be in charge.

Martin jumped out on to the platform. "It's even better than I thought," he said. He pointed to a large crate near the door. Michael and himself lifted it out.

"That's everything now," the guard said, closing the door of the goods' carriage. "I'm sorry to have to go. I'd say ye'll have a great time here. There's a good spirit in Enniscorthy. It would be very hard to organize a thing like this in Waterford."

"We'll tell you all about it tomorrow," Michael said.

"We'll go slowly, up past Kelly," Martin said. "I'd love to hear what he's saying. They must be getting frightened."

They wheeled the handcart slowly towards the storeroom, delighted with the loud booing chant.

"Go home to England," a voice shouted above the chanting. "Get back on the train. Get out of here."

The chanting continued and there was shouting coming too from the Railway Square.

Martin stopped the handcart beside Kelly and the soldiers and they stood listening.

"You have a long march ahead of you, Sergeant," Kelly said to the oldest of the soldiers.

"The regular coastguard, Mr Kelly, has been recalled to Devonport because of the threat of war," the Sergeant said loudly in a posh English accent. "The Shropshire regiment has been asked to take over."

"Isn't that nice Sergeant?" Kenny said.

"We're honoured to serve His Majesty's government," the Sergeant said.

Michael knew that Martin would roar laughing as he repeated this conversation again and again in the months to come. He pushed the handcart over towards the storeroom. But Martin stopped because the driver of the jarvey-car had started to shout.

"Could we load up the car now? Could you hurry up? Come on." His voice was high-pitched and screeching. His face was very red. He was looking in horror at the crowd of men on the platform.

One of the men in the crowd began to imitate the driver in a screeching woman's voice. "Could we load up the car now? Could we load up the car now?"

The rest of the crowd roared laughing and surged forward.

The driver seemed to lose control of himself altogether. He stamped his feet and waved his arms. "I'm in a hurry," he screeched. "Could we load up the car now? I'll go off with the baggage, and youse can march whenever youse like."

"Yes. Yes," the Sergeant said. "Calm down, man. We're moving as fast as we can."

The crowd was laughing and shouting and jeering.

"Could we load up the car now?" someone screeched in a high-pitched voice.

"I want to be heading off before the rain comes," the driver screeched. "Could we load up the car now, Sergeant?"

A door banged, the whistle sounded and the mail-train began to move slowly out of the station. Kelly gestured towards the side door and led the way towards the verandah to avoid passing the group beside the main door. The Sergeant pointed at the soldiers who took up the baggage and followed Kelly.

"We won't unload the handcart," Martin said. "We'll leave it in the storeroom, and close the door. I don't want to miss anything."

The men who had been on the platform were going back out through the main door of the station on to the Railway Square to continue to harass the soldiers. Michael and Martin followed them. Michael couldn't believe the huge crowd that had gathered in the Square. Fennelly was a great organizer. There were a lot of men standing in the middle of the Square. Most of the women and children were over at the wall of Donohoes' mineral-water factory. Twenty or thirty men were standing at the side door around the jarvey-car. Jimmy Macken was there. Some more men were coming around the corner by the timber yard. The news seemed to have spread like wildfire through the town. He saw Larry Prendergast and a group from the *Echo* newspaper coming in to the Square. Prendergast was one of the leaders of the IRB, and Michael thought he might come up near the soldiers. But then he lost sight of him as more and more people pushed into the square. He didn't know where Martin had gone. He had lost him in the crowd. He moved up towards the jarvey-car. The soldiers were beginning to load up the rucksacks, and as they did, the men shouted at them. Jimmy Macken was arguing with the driver.

"You're the traitor of an Irishman who's driving them," he said. "You're worse than them if there could be anything worse than them."

"I'm only trying to make a few bob, lads," the driver said frantically. "That's all I'm doing. If I didn't drive them someone else would."

The men began to jeer and boo, and suddenly it seemed as if everyone in the square was booing and shouting different kinds of abuse at the soldiers, but also at the driver. A large group of men had joined with Jimmy Macken to tackle the driver. Kelly had covered his face with his hands and was shaking his head. The Sergeant and the soldiers watched as the men argued with the driver.

"The British army is bad enough, but whoever is driving them is worse. No decent Irishman would have anything to do with them," a man shouted.

"Do you see that crowd? How do you think you're going to get through that crowd?" Jimmy Macken asked, pointing towards the square. "They'll kill you if they get their hands on you."

"All right. All right," the driver screeched, turning around to the Sergeant. "Take off the baggage. Get them to take off the baggage, Sergeant. You can carry it yourselves." He gestured wildly at the Sergeant and Kenny.

The Sergeant looked so angry that for an instant Michael thought that he was ordering the soldiers to shoot at the crowd. Kelly and the Sergeant talked for a few seconds. Kelly kept nodding his head. The Sergeant shrugged and pointed at the soldiers and at the baggage on the jarvey-car. There was loud cheering and clapping as the soldiers began to take the rucksacks down from the jarvey-car. Kelly had his hands joined as if in prayer and he spoke earnestly to the Sergeant. They led the soldiers back into the station, and the crowd roared and cheered as they went. Some boys had climbed up on to the wall in front of the railway field. More and more people were coming into the square. Michael wondered were his sons, Philip and Aidan, somewhere among the crowd. Cormac was still a bit young to be allowed wander too far away from home.

"The polo match up in the Showgrounds must be over," a man said to him. "The crowd from the polo match are arriving now. This is great, and it's getting better."

Jimmy Macken was laughing and shouting as the driver, his face red with anger, got into the car. The crowd cheered and clapped as they made way to let him through. They were delighted that they had got the better of him. But as soon as he was gone there was a silence in the square, as if nobody was sure what should be done. They had about twenty British soldiers as their prisoners in the station. Michael wasn't sure was this what Fennelly had intended, or what he would want them to do now. The train was gone. There was no way out of the station for the soldiers except through the Railway Square, and the Railway Square was blocked. If the people decided to storm the station ... but they couldn't storm the station because the soldiers had guns.

The crowd was quiet as if they were waiting for someone to tell them what to do.

"Look who's coming now," Jimmy Macken said.

Michael saw the horses and the blue uniforms of the RIC coming around the corner, and the crowd pushing in towards the walls to let them through. Jones and Manning were leading the way on horseback and there were five or six other RIC men carrying batons marching behind them. There was a deadly quiet as they moved towards the station. Michael watched Manning who was hunched forward on the horse. His face was twisted and his eyes looked lit up with madness. People said that he was the most brutal policeman who had ever been stationed in Enniscorthy. The crowd moved aside as the RIC men approached the side door of the station. Kelly and the Sergeant came out to meet them.

"Look. Father Cummins is at the back of the crowd." Martin came up behind him.

Father Cummins was tall and it was easy to pick him out among the crowd. He was wearing a black soutane and he stopped to talk to some of the women. He was friendly with everyone. He often came to inspect the Volunteer parades and to bless the men before they went off on manoeuvres. He was friendly with the RIC, too. It was hard to know what he believed in.

"Father Cummins is sending Moll Reilly home," Jimmy Macken said. "She has the twin babies with her. She should never have brought them down here. I'd say he's giving out to her for bringing them out."

Some of the women at the back of the crowd turned and went home with Moll Reilly. "He'll send everyone home," Jimmy Macken said.

"We won't argue with Father Cummins." It was Fennelly's Kerry accent. Fennelly was standing beside Jimmy Macken. He seemed to have appeared out of nowhere. He was very excited. "We'll let Father Cummins send everyone home, and no one will ever know who brought them all down here."

"Do we have to go?" Jimmy Macken asked.

"Yes," Fennelly said. "We've done what we wanted to do. We've let people demonstrate their support for Irish freedom. We've given the British army and the RIC a bit of a fright. It's over now. I'm going back to school. I have some more copybooks to correct."

"And we have deliveries to make," Martin said. "Baggage to sort and deliveries to make, haven't we Michael? None of this had anything to do with us."

*

He sat at the kitchen table listening to Margaret moving around upstairs, and saying goodnight to the boys. It was hard to settle them down. They were noisy and excited after seeing the British soldiers in the Railway Square earlier. It was nearly dark, and as the cathedral bell began to ring out ten o'clock he looked around to watch her coming slowly down the stairs, carrying the baby.

"It was amazing," she said, sitting in the low chair beside the range, "for a big crowd like that to gather in the Railway Square."

"It was a great day," he said, turning his chair around to face her. "A sign of things to come."

"I'm glad I didn't know what was going on." She opened her blouse and settled the baby at her breast. "I'd have been worried about the boys if I had known."

"There was no danger," he said, "although, I suppose, you could never depend on the British Army. Father Cummins persuaded some of the people to go home, and the others agreed to march as far as Clonhaston with the soldiers to make sure they got out of the town. Nobody would go against Father Cummins."

"Did Mr Kelly say anything about it afterwards?"

"No. He never mentioned it to us. He went out to Clonhaston with the RIC. We stayed in the station, and when he came back he was very anxious to be friendly with us. You know what he's like. He's afraid of his shadow in a way."

"It's just as well that there was no trouble," she said. "There's no use in a fight unless it's going to lead somewhere. The whole country will have to join in. Look at what happened to Wexford people in '98 when we went it alone."

He didn't say anything. She knew more about '98 than he did. He often said that if she was a man she could deliver a lecture to the Uí Chinseallaigh society. She was better than any of the men whose lectures were reported in the paper. She knew all the usual things, about the battles and the leaders, but also strange stories about people hiding out for months after it was all over, and a story that always made her shudder, about a woman, married to one of the Colcloughs, whose hair turned white overnight after her husband was hanged on Wexford bridge.

"Kitty was here with me," she said. "We heard cheering and shouting but we thought that it was a hurling match or a drill practice."

"How is Kitty?" He stood up to light the lamp. He could never understand why Kitty hadn't got married. He thought she was a lovely woman, but Margaret said that Kitty had never got over Walter Mernagh marrying the Englishwoman.

"Kitty is in good form." She paused. "When you get your wages on Saturday I'm going to send Philip up to pay off the money we owe in Furlongs'. Kitty didn't mention it, and I know she won't ever say a word about it, but I'm going to pay it all off even if that leaves us short during the week."

He nodded.

She had lost so much when she married him – money, property and the esteem that went with owning those things. They never had enough money. He often wondered was she sorry that she married him. In the beginning she used to talk about how differently some people treated her, in shops and on the street, once they realized that she wasn't well-off any more although she was still the same person. It was strange and sometimes hurtful, she said, and it had made her more distant with people than she used to be. Some people only wanted to talk to her so that they could get pleasure out of making some remark which would remind her of her changed status.

"Will you come up with me to the Market Square on Monday night to hear Seán Mac Diarmada speak?" He sat down at the table again. "He's a great orator. Anyone who heard him speak would be converted forever to the Republican cause."

"Ah, no," she said. "I'll stay here and you can tell me what he says."

"You have to hear it yourself. I want you to come with me. I can describe him to you and tell you all the things he says, but it's not the same as seeing and hearing him yourself. I can't get across the spirit of the man."

"I have three children and a baby. There's a lot of work to do in the house. I have sewing to do, books to read. I don't want to be standing around on street corners as if I had no home of my own to go to," she said. Sometimes she sounded very proud. He liked it when she talked like that, so sure of herself and of her own importance, although she hadn't been like that when he knew her first, before he married her. It was as if, having left the money and the status of her family and class behind her, she took on their attitudes, maybe to protect herself.

"You might change your mind," he said.

She stood up and walked up and down, between the window and the chair, gently rocking the baby. It was always hard to get him asleep.

"I'd like to walk up the Irish Street with you," he said after a while.

She laughed. "Who will mind the baby?" She turned at the sink and walked towards the door.

"Philip will mind the house for us," he said. Philip was eleven years of age, old enough to be left in charge for a while.

*

"We'll stand near the monument," he said as they walked up Irish Street, "near Father Murphy and the Croppy Boy."

She moved towards him, out to the middle of the path to avoid the steps in front of the doorways. Most of the doors were still open although it was getting dark.

"Did Mac Diarmada say when he arrived in the railway station what his oration was going to be about?" she asked.

"No," Michael said. "But he has to be careful. The RIC will be there and they take down every word he says. If he goes too far he could be charged with sedition. I suppose he'll talk about Britain having declared war on Germany. Maybe he'll mention bringing in the guns at Howth."

Mac Diarmada had arrived at the station on the four o'clock Dublin train. Larry Prendergast had been there to meet him. Michael and Martin stood with Prendergast on the platform waiting for the train. Prendergast was a reporter on the *Echo* newspaper. Most of the people working in the *Echo* were involved in all the different nationalist movements. As well as being an officer in the IRB, Prendergast was heavily involved in the Gaelic League, the Irish Volunteers and Sinn Féin.

"I have to bring Mac Diarmada to the *Echo* first. He's great company. The men would go mad if I didn't bring him into the office," Prendergast said.

"He was in Stafford's public house only once," Martin said, "but Mrs Stafford is always asking for him. He made a great impression on her."

"He's full of humour and fun," Prendergast said, "but there's no more committed Fenian than him in the whole country. It was himself and Tom Clarke who brought new life to the IRB, and put an end to all the old squabbling about rules and constitutions."

Mac Diarmada had looked thin and pale as he got off the train. He had a limp in his right leg. He had worked so hard for the IRB, travelling around the country without stopping, that he had got rundown and contracted polio. He used to travel on a bicycle but since he got sick he had to go by train. His eyes were sunken in his face and he seemed tired, but as soon as he saw Prendergast he smiled and held out his hand to greet him.

"How are you? And all the men in the *Echo*?" He laughed. "The Echo newspaper – just around the corner from the RIC barracks in Abbey Square, isn't that right? Our friends in the RIC won't have to travel too far if they want to arrest you."

"I'd say they might be more interested in arresting you," Prendergast said.

"Why would anyone want to arrest me?" Mac Diarmada had a lovely voice. He was from Leitrim, and his accent was very different to the Wexford one, harsher in a way.

"I hope I'll have more time to talk to you later," he said, shaking hands with Martin and Michael before he left the station.

"What age is Mac Diarmada?" Margaret asked as they turned into the Market Square.

"I'd say he's about thirty. He worked in Scotland and England for a few years, and he spent some time in America. If I'm talking to him again I'm going to ask him did he ever come across Jim – you know, my brother Jim – in England. It's years since I've heard from Jim."

The Market Square was filling up with people. It had

been a beautiful warm summer's day but it was getting cold as darkness fell. They walked slowly across the square towards the statue.

"Do you remember the great day we had when the statue was unveiled?" She linked his arm and led him around to look up at the statue, the two figures, the pike and the flag. "Do you remember how we stood outside Jordans' with the children while Father Kavanagh delivered the oration?"

"Yes," he said.

"Cormac was a baby," she said. "I remember thinking to myself that it was one of the good days in our life, one of the days we'd look back on."

They walked around to the back of the statue, and stood among the crowd facing a makeshift wooden platform which had been erected in front of the Technical Institute and from which Mac Diarmada would speak. A Sinn Féin banner was nailed to the wall behind the platform.

"Mac Diarmada is staying in Prendergast's house in New Street," Michael said. "I think they're leaving to come down now."

Eight men walked down the street, two abreast, carrying torches. The crowd became quiet as the men rounded the corner into the Square, the torches blazing above them. Mac Diarmada followed them slowly, alone, limping. He looked small and weak, and Michael felt he was with Mac Diarmada as he came around the corner, aware of the pain in Mac Diarmada's foot as he dragged it up the steps to the platform.

The men held the torches aloft, around him, and his face looked pale and wan, but his voice was strong and firm. He began by speaking about '98, saying how humble he felt walking along streets where the great men of '98 had walked – Father Murphy, John Kelly from Killanne, Bagenal Harvey.

"Wexfordmen are well-schooled in rebellion, and when

Roisín Dubh calls again I know that they will not be found wanting," he said.

The crowd cheered, and Michael was smiling because Mac Diarmada was smiling too, but even before the cheering stopped Mac Diarmada was speaking again, determined and fanatical now, talking about the war and condemning as slavish all those who would encourage Irish people to join in the British war effort.

"Let them wave their flags and blow their bugles, but as they march into battle we must watch and wait, wait for our chance ..." He paused, and then gestured dramatically towards the RIC men on the corner of George's Street. "I'm speaking too quickly. I must slow down to let the note-takers catch up with me." The crowd laughed and cheered. "I'll make it easy for them," he continued to loud laughter. "I'll speak in their native tongue." He was so funny, so fearless and brave, and he was standing there laughing with the crowd, enjoying himself. He loved the crowd, and they loved him.

Mac Diarmada was speaking in Irish but Michael found it hard to understand the Northern dialect, and when he changed back to English again his Leitrim accent was even more pronounced. Each sound seemed to have been twisted around somewhere in his throat or nose so that it sounded as if it had been first of all blown up and then flattened. But Michael stopped listening to the words and he watched the man, his face pale against the glare of the torches. Suddenly he was reminded of a martyr being burned at the stake, and he shook his head to get that idea out of it, not to feel the pain of it.

Mac Diarmada was talking about freedom. "It is our duty to fight for freedom, to free ourselves from oppression and injustice, to fight for a country where we can live as free men and women and not as slaves."

Michael was aware of a stillness in the square. It was as if everyone was enthralled by this man who seemed to be the very embodiment of the struggle for freedom. The sanctity and the suffering of the Irish cause were in Mac Diarmada's body, in his voice, in his face. No one could witness him without steeling himself to leave everything and follow him to fight and, if necessary, die for Ireland.

"While they call their troops to the flag and march in procession, let us not forget the great dead who died for Ireland: Wolfe Tone, Robert Emmet, Allen, Larkin and O'Brien. Let us prepare to continue the fight. The time is coming soon when a blow must be struck. This generation must act now, a blood sacrifice must be made soon, to keep the soul of patriotism and the spirit of freedom alive."

There was silence for a few seconds after he finished, as if no one wanted to break the spell he had cast. But when the applause came it filled the square, and people began to move closer to the platform.

Michael remembered that Margaret was beside him. "What did you think?"

"He's like a saint," she said, "so good and true and beautiful. He's inspiring but I'm afraid for him. I know to look at him that he's too good. The British would love to get him into one of their jails and destroy him."

"No. No," Michael said. "Don't say that. No one could destroy Mac Diarmada."

Chapter 9

October 1914

The cool early morning mist had burned off, and there was good heat from the midday sun. Michael stood on the platform waiting for the train. A man wearing a British Army uniform came into the station, and five or six people hesitantly followed him. The man walked out to the edge of the platform, and the group waited for him near the station door. Since the war broke out the railway had been the worst place in the world for an Irish republican to be working. During the first weeks of August hundreds of the reserve had left Enniscorthy station to go to war, and most of them had been members of the Volunteers. They had pledged themselves to fight for Ireland, but as soon as war broke out they went off to join the British Army. The station had been crowded day after day as their families came to say goodbye to them.

The man in the uniform looked up towards Ferns to see was the train coming, and Micheal got a terrible shock when he realized that it was Jimmy Macken. He couldn't believe that Macken would join the British Army. A big crowd of men had gone to Wexford to enlist after the Split in the Volunteers, but no one said that Macken was among them. How could he of all people wear the uniform of the British Army? He had led the crowd against the Shropshires that day in July, and it looked as if he was committed to fighting for

Irish independence, but now he, too, was betraying the cause. It had seemed that the worst of this war was over. There had been a lull for a few weeks after the reserve left, but then Redmond told the Volunteers to go and fight for Britain, and now, day after day, men were heading off to Flanders.

The best thing to do was to ignore the people who joined the British Army. He moved down the platform away from the Mackens. They were all following Redmond and the local gentry. Macken would have got a nod of approval from Colonel Henry Bond when he declared his intention to enlist, and there would be a chance of a job in Bonds' mills, or the foundry, for one of the Mackens. But Michael didn't think he would ever be able to talk to him again. The only thing he would want to say to him was that he was a traitor, and there were things that were best left unsaid.

The war had changed his life in Enniscorthy. He had always spoken to everyone who came to the railway station. It was how he had got to know people when he came to the town first. In those early days it had been on his mind that he knew very few people, and he forced himself to talk to people and to remember their names. He wanted to feel part of things. But since the war broke out he had no choice but to pretend not to see people. If he spoke to them he knew he would sound angry and bitter.

The whistle blew and he could hear the train in the distance. Martin Webster came out from the storeroom and stared at the Mackens.

"Will you look who's down there? Jimmy Macken," he said. "I heard he was going. The wife is crying, but I'd say she'll cheer up when she gets the dependants' allowance. I'd rather have money any day than Jimmy Macken."

Martin had laughed and jeered about the war from the beginning, but Michael couldn't laugh at it. The train stopped in front of him. He got into the baggage carriage and helped Martin to lift out some crates. He didn't ever want to see Macken again. But as he went towards the storeroom he noticed, out of the corner of his eye, the wife clinging to Macken, and Macken loosening her hands one by one, tearing himself away from her. The guard was banging the doors of the train closed and Michael stood at the back of the storeroom waiting for the train to pull out. Macken would go to Waterford first and probably on to Fermoy from there. Fermoy was a garrison town.

"I'd say Macken's wife will take to the drink when she gets the dependant's allowance," Martin said. "She's one of the Powers. Her mother was a terrible woman to drink."

"I always liked Macken," Michael said. "I think it's a pity he didn't stay with us."

"The one good thing is that we've kept the name 'Irish Volunteers'," Martin said, scraping a crate noisily across the floor. "The crowd going off to France are only 'National Volunteers'. There might be more of them, but we have the right name."

"I wonder what news will Prendergast get from the IRB when he goes to Dublin," Michael said. "He'll be meeting Mac Diarmada and Clarke."

They heard the gates of Donohoes' mineral-water factory closing and they knew that it was dinner time. After dinner they would do deliveries. They walked together through the Railway Square, and Martin went up the Shannon. Michael could hear the pigs squealing as he turned into Templeshannon. It was Wednesday, the day for slaughtering in Buttles' Bacon Factory, and the river near the slaughterhouse was full of blood.

He saw Philip and Aidan, his two eldest sons, turning the corner at the bottom of Bohreen Hill. Aidan was playing with a hurl and sliotar, throwing the sliotar up and tapping

141

it with the hurl as he walked along. He was a great hurler. Men often stopped Michael to tell him about some great save Aidan had made.

"Where's Cormac?" he asked.

"He went back early to play in the yard," Philip said. "It was on the *Echo* about the Gaelic League concert in the Athenaeum. It named all the songs and all the singers."

"Did they put in about us being there?"

"No." Philip laughed.

"What's for the dinner, Aidan?" Michael called after Aidan who had passed him by, still playing with the sliotar. Aidan didn't usually bother to join in conversations, but seemed always in good humour, laughing and smiling, playing with something.

"Bacon and cabbage," Aidan said, raising the sliotar skilfully from the ground up on to the hurl.

"Bacon and cabbage," Michael repeated. He often found himself repeating the few words Aidan said.

"There's a letter for you," Philip said. "I nearly forgot to tell you."

They had been expecting a letter from Jim. Fennelly had heard from the IRB in Dublin that two leading members living in England were coming home to Enniscorthy. Jim Carty was one of the names mentioned.

Margaret took the letter from the dresser and gave it to him as soon as he went in.

"I'd say it's from Jim," she said. "He might have decided when he's coming home." He opened the envelope and took out the single sheet of paper. Then he sat at the table, and read:

Dear Michael,
I'm sorry I didn't write to you before now to tell you of my plans to return to Ireland, but I wanted to have

all the details arranged before I got in touch with you. I expect to arrive at the station in Enniscorthy, along with a friend of mine, Stephen Bolger, on the last Friday in October. I believe that employment and lodgings are being organized for us by good friends. We will be working in Hogans' Leatherworks, and our lodging house is on Nunnery Road.

So many years have passed, and I look forward to seeing you again, and to meeting your wife and children.

> With kind regards,
> Your brother,
> Jim.

He folded the letter and put it down on the table. He had hoped that this talk about Jim returning to Ireland was just a rumour. He wasn't looking forward to seeing him although he wouldn't admit that to anyone. He knew he should want to see his brother, but Jim couldn't have picked a worst time to come home. There were too many changes, and the split in the Volunteers was bad enough, but when Jim arrived there would have to be talk about their father's death, about Father Roche and about how Michael had left Kilbride. He didn't want to remember. He had never gone back to Kilbride. He should have gone back to see them. They were good Irish people. When he didn't come home after the fair that time Mrs Murphy had sent Dan in to Enniscorthy to find him. Dan tried to persuade him to come back to the land but he had refused. He had been so glad to escape in spite of all they had done for him. It wasn't their fault about Father Roche.

The dinner was on the table, and Margaret was taking the potatoes out of the range.

"It is from Jim," he said, taking up the letter and handing it to her. "Do you want to read it?"

She stood with one hand on the back of her chair, reading the letter. Sunlight was flickering through the bushes in the field above the yard.

"He sounds nice," she said when she had finished reading. "I'd say we'll all like him. It's good he's coming back now," she said, sitting down at the table beside him. "He'll come here to visit us, won't he?"

"I'd say so. He'll be very important with the IRB men because he has spent time in jail."

"He might just call in to visit us," she said, "but we'll invite him down on Sundays for his tea."

"I suppose Dan Hogan is giving them the two jobs that the Butler brothers from Carley's Bridge had. They enlisted last week."

"I'd say Hogans' is a nice place to work," she said. "There's a lot of talk there. Everybody always seems in great form."

He peeled a potato. He wasn't going to tell Jim too much about how he had left Kilbride. Most people presumed he had been evicted and he never contradicted them. A few times he had told Margaret parts of the true story but he couldn't bear to go over all the details of it. The whole thing was somewhere tied in a knot at the back of his head and he wasn't going to let Jim open it up. He had treated the people of Kilbride badly by leaving without saying a word. A few months after he left Joe Grogan had called to the railway with a box of books from the house and money from the sale of the cow. He felt guilty ever since and he always avoided people from Kilbride at matches or on fair days. The Kavanaghs, Joe told him, had taken over the few acres of ground. He had nothing against the Kavanaghs but he hated them getting the land.

"Any news over in the railway?"

She startled him when she spoke and it took him a few seconds to think what to say. The yard outside darkened as the sun went behind a cloud.

"Jimmy Macken went off this morning," he said. "The whole family came down to say goodbye to him. I was disappointed. He was in the same company of the Volunteers as me, and I marched beside him at parades. But I suppose none of that means anything now. Most of the men have let us down and joined with Colonel Henry James Bond in the National Volunteers."

"Maybe you expected too much of them all," she said. "You know how I often talk about Palm Sunday. Do you remember? When Jesus was coming into Jerusalem the crowd loved him so much that they covered the road with palms to ease his way, but one short week later the same crowd shouted 'Crucify Him. Crucify Him'. You can't expect too much from a crowd."

"I don't think I expected too much from them," he said. "I expected them not to join the other side. I thought they might believe in something, and stay loyal to a cause. But now it seems that they were only dressing up in the uniform of the Volunteers, and pretending to believe in Irish freedom. But we'll win in the end, even if we have to wait a long time. That's the only thing that keeps me going."

*

"How long is it since you've seen your brother?" Tom Byrne asked. He had come to the railway from his wife's lodging house to meet the men from England.

"Twenty-seven years," Michael said. He knew the answer because everybody was asking him that question. The whole town knew that Jim was coming home. "I suppose he'll have changed a lot."

"I can't understand why Michael's not a bit more excited," Martin said to Dan Hogan who had brought a horse and cart for the luggage. "He's going to see his only brother again after twenty-seven years and he doesn't care."

"Everybody else is excited enough to make up for me," Michael said. "Maybe I won't even recognize him."

But he recognized Jim immediately. He had a look of their father although his colouring was darker. The others hesitated, looking at one another, unsure whether to approach the two men who were getting out of a carriage at the front of the train. But Michael nodded at them, and Dan led the way towards the men who were lifting suitcases down on to the platform. Then for one instant he wasn't sure if it was Jim. The small thin man definitely wasn't, and maybe the heavier man with the tan coat wasn't either.

"Hello" the man said, smiling as he put out his hand to shake hands with Dan. "This is Stephen Bolger," he said, gesturing towards his companion, "and I'm Jim Carty."

It was Jim, but Michael would have known him anyway, once he spoke, because of the enthusiastic, affectionate way he greeted Dan. Like when their father used to meet people in the village after he'd had a few drinks. You always knew he was delighted to see them.

Jim started to laugh when he saw Michael. "There's no need to ask who you are. I'd know you anywhere," he said, shaking Michael's hand and gripping the top of his shoulder. "Isn't this great?" He laughed again and everybody else laughed, too. He was moving around, yet each time before he moved his feet looked firmly rooted to the ground. He seemed delighted with himself. "You haven't changed a bit. Well you haven't changed much anyway." Everybody laughed with him again.

"Your voice is still the same," Michael said. He was

pleased that Jim didn't even have the slightest trace of an English accent.

"Your suitcases, Jim. Come on, Jim. Your suitcases," Stephen Bolger said, picking up one of the cases. He was breathless and wheezy. "I'm not carrying the heavy one with the books."

"This man is getting on to me the whole way home from England. I'm after having an awful time with him," Jim said.

He was smiling as he went back to pick up one of the suitcases.

"I'll carry the heavy one, the one with the strap around it," he said. "I won't have people giving out about me. They might all decide they didn't like me."

It was hard to imagine anyone not liking him. He was funny and pleasant and he made a big effort to talk a lot.

"We'll see ye later, lads," Martin said, heading towards the goods' carriage, "at the meeting in Antwerp. Prendergast will be home from Dublin and he'll have all the news."

"You'll both come out to that, to the IRB meeting in the Gaelic rooms in Antwerp, won't you?" Dan said in a low voice, turning to Stephen Bolger and Jim, who nodded. They moved towards the station door, carrying the cases, but Jim turned back to Michael.

"I'll see you at the meeting tonight," he said. "I often wondered over the years was I remembering Enniscorthy right, but I'll know now. My father always loved coming in here. I remember rows of houses on hills. And there's a cathedral."

Michael nodded. "There's a castle too," he said.

The others were gone out into the Railway Square.

"I don't remember a castle," Jim said. "But I remember being in Hayes' pub with my father. That's the earliest memory I have of Enniscorthy. There were two old women who used to give me bottle-lids to play with."

147

"I remember being in Hayes' with him too," Michael said. "They're all dead now. They were lovely old women, very soft-spoken."

"It was always dark in the pub, wasn't it? Most of the window was covered in a board, I think. I remember my father sitting on a stool, laughing. It was hard on him, left on his own, out the country, with two children."

"He missed you when you left," Michael said. "He was always talking about you, wondering how you were getting on."

"Was he?" Jim hesitated, as if unsure whether or not to continue. "I didn't get over his death for years," he said. "I'd have loved, more than anything else, to have talked to him one more time before he died."

"We're all waiting for you, Jim." Stephen Bolger came to the door of the station. "Hurry up."

"I had better go," Jim said. "I don't want them to go off on me."

"I'll see you at the meeting tonight," Michael said.

He stood watching Jim leaving, not wanting him to go.

*

Margaret lifted her hand from the baby's shoulder, and moved on tip-toe towards the bedroom door. She thought he was asleep at last, but when she turned to check he was stirring. He had his eyes open by the time she got back to the cot. She began to rock the cot again and to hum a lullaby for him, but he was smiling at her and trying to get up. She held him firmly down and turned her face away from him. When he didn't have a sleep after dinner he was cross for the rest of the day. She looked out at the long wet grass in the field behind the window as she rocked the cot.

Jim would be arriving at the station in a while. It was hard to imagine what it would be like for Michael to meet him again after all the years. She hoped he wouldn't have changed too much. Michael said that he used to be friendly and funny, but a British jail might have changed him. They said that Tom Clarke sat sideways for hours in the confined space behind the counter of his shop in exactly the way he had sat in his narrow prison cell. She turned back to look at the baby and thought from his breathing that he was asleep. She stopped rocking the cot. When he didn't stir she lifted her hand slowly from him and began to move quietly across the room.

She was halfway down the stairs when there were three loud knocks on the front door. She stopped to listen in case the noise had wakened the baby. It was her mother's knock, although she wasn't expecting her mother and Julianne to call. They had visited the day before, and they wouldn't usually call again for a week or two. Her mother was very busy. She had settled down over the years to being a widow, and had a great life for herself, playing cards and visiting. There was another knock on the door. They could easily waken the baby banging on the door like that. She was on her way out to them when she saw *Irish Freedom*, one of Michael's newspapers, on the table and she went back and put it in the press of the dresser. She took off her apron and put that into the dresser, too.

Her mother had her hand on the knocker, about to start knocking a third time, when Margaret opened the door. She always noticed how glamorous they both were, and how thin they had got. The glamour was extraordinary at their age. They were wearing the beautiful new winter coats that Miss O'Rourke had made for them, and Julianne had red lipstick on, and a lot of powder and rouge. It was as if neither of them realized that they had grown old. They went around from house to house like young girls.

"Hello," Margaret said.

149

Her mother turned away and waved at the driver of the pony and trap to tell him he could go.

She was surprised that neither of them said anything. For several years after she got married her mother had had nothing to do with her, but since they got friendly again, at John Bourke's wake, they were normally very polite to one another.

"I was upstairs putting the baby to sleep," she said.

Her mother shook her head and narrowed her eyes, but said nothing. She looked cross and angry as she stepped into the hallway. Margaret stood back, holding the door for them. Julianne closed her eyes and turned her head away as she came inside.

"Has she the fire lighting in the parlour?" Julianne asked, shivering. "If she hasn't the fire lighting we'll have to go into the kitchen."

"She has it cleaned out but she hasn't got it set," her mother said, looking into the parlour.

They were talking about her as if she wasn't there.

"The kitchen is very draughty," Julianne said. "I hate sitting here, but we couldn't sit in the cold in the parlour."

Margaret followed them into the kitchen. She didn't want a row with her mother. Michael had been very pleased when they got friendly again. He always liked to hear that her mother had called, and it would be hard to explain to the children if their grandmother suddenly stopped visiting. The children were very fond of her, and she was kind to them, bringing them presents and telling them stories about out the country long ago. Sometimes it occurred to Margaret that her mother was acting like one of the gentry visiting a local cabin, but she let it pass. Her mother talked about her friends and their houses and furniture, and card-games. She visited only at times when she knew Michael would be at work. If Margaret mentioned him a blank puzzled expression would come on her mother's face as if she wasn't sure who he was, and couldn't understand why anybody would talk about him. She would interrupt to ask Julianne about clothes or furniture, or to talk about some of the important women they visited.

"Should we take off out coats? I don't think we should take off our coats," Julianne said, shivering again. "We're not staying long. We were supposed to be visiting Mrs Jeffrey Bond out in Kilcarbery, the Bonds of the Maltings, but your mother said we'd have to come in to you first."

They sat down in the two easy chairs in front of the range without taking off their coats. Margaret sat at the table.

"I came for a particular reason. You needn't worry. We're not going to start visiting you every day," her mother said. "But I have something to say to you. I was playing cards in Flaherty's last night. I've had a hard enough life, but I try to keep going, and Mrs Flaherty has been very good to me. There's many another would have lain down under all the blows that I've been struck but I've kept going."

It was years since her mother had spoken like this, in a pained dull monotone. She had been in great form for a few years, and this sudden reversion was terrible.

"I think you're great the way you've kept going, Mai," Julianne said, "and you're after being such a help to me since John Bourke died. I'd never have managed without you."

"Some people appreciate me," her mother said. "I always do my best, but I've got nothing only knocks." Her voice was beginning to rise in anger and she was looking at Margaret. "I was in Mrs Flaherty's last night," she repeated, "when the new maid came in with the tea, and stood in front of me and said 'You're Michael Carty's mother-in-law, isn't that who you are?'" Her mother imitated a squeaky country accent.

"The cheek of the maid to speak to you. I can't believe it," Julianne said.

"She spoke to me in front of all the women as if she knew me although I never laid eyes on the girl before," her mother said. "She stood in the middle of the parlour floor. 'Isn't it great about his brother coming home? Michael Carty's brother Jim is coming home from England. He's in the Fenians. He's after being in jail over there. He was in jail for Ireland. Michael is delighted with his brother coming home.'" She imitated the maid's accent, but then her voice became angry. "I was in here visiting you yesterday and you never said a word to me about it. You wouldn't tell your own mother. You left it to a stranger to tell your mother. And why are you letting him come home here on top of you? What about the children? Wouldn't you think you'd be after getting a bit of sense? Haven't you a hard enough life here?"

"I blame Mrs Flaherty for letting the maid talk to visitors," Julianne said. "I'm surprised that a woman living in a big house in the town, a solicitor's wife, wouldn't know more about how to handle a maid. It makes me wonder about Mrs Flaherty. Who was she before she married him? I always told the maid to speak only when spoken to."

"The maid in Flaherty's told the whole card school about Jim Carty who has spent time in jail. I never heard of him before, but he's a convict related by marriage to me apparently, and he's coming home now to live here," her mother said. "I couldn't believe that you didn't tell me. If I had known I could have stopped her as soon as she started. I'd have thought of something cutting to say that would have stopped her. But you didn't tell your own mother. Of course, I'm only an old fool. That's the way you always treated me. You never had any time for me. I don't know why I waste my time coming here to visit you, but I'm a foolish old woman and I'm after growing fond of your children. I don't know what's going to become of me. You wouldn't talk to your own mother. You'd leave it to strangers to tell me."

"You should have told your mother," Julianne said. Julianne had become very dependent on Margaret's mother since John Bourke died. She used to be able to disagree with her at times and follow an independent line. She had given Margaret all the old baby things from Marshalstown. Her mother hadn't even visited her when Philip and Aidan were born. But John Bourke's death had weakened Julianne.

"We didn't want to talk about him too much until he actually arrived," Margaret said. She hadn't told them because she didn't want to have to listen to them giving out about him.

"The whole town was talking about him. James told me this morning that they were talking about him in the bar last week. But nobody said a word to me. I'm only a foolish old woman. My own family think nothing of me. I never thought I'd end my days with my own family making little of me. They're old that know their end." She sounded sad and bitter.

"We were afraid it was only a rumour and we didn't want to talk too much about it," Margaret said. She knew that she should have told her. "I'm sorry."

"You didn't tell me because you look down on me," her mother said quietly. "You only let me in here because of the children. You wouldn't care if you never saw me. Whatever sort of a person you are, you wouldn't care if you never saw your own mother."

"That's not true," Margaret said. It wasn't true. She liked to see her mother an odd time, mainly because the children liked her. She used to feel very guilty when she got married first because then she had wished never to have to see her again.

"I'm just an old fool," her mother said, "and maybe you're right to look down on me. You're so good and perfect. You take after your father and your father's family. I see Nancy with James's children and she's no good with them. They're troublesome and wild. I can't talk to them. You're much better with the children than she is. The boys here are lovely, and I'm glad because they're my grandchildren. But you look down on me. You despise your own mother."

"I don't," Margaret said, shaking her head. "No. I don't."

"You do. I see you looking at me sometimes and I know. I didn't want you to marry him because I didn't want you to be poor. I love your boys and I hate to think of them being poor."

"I know you love the children," Margaret said, "and they love you. I don't look down on you. It's terrible if you think that."

"There's no use in talking about it," her mother said. She was crying. "But you shouldn't look down on me. I'm not all bad."

"Of course you're not bad. I think you're great. I was delighted when you started to visit me again," Margaret said.

Her mother was crying and wiping her eyes with a handkerchief. Margaret knew she should stand up and hold her mother's shoulders or her arm, and tell her not to cry, but she hesitated. She couldn't imagine touching her mother. She didn't ever remember touching her.

"You're after upsetting your mother," Julianne said. "You should have written to that fellow to tell him not to come home. What right has that fellow to come here and upset us all?"

"I couldn't have done that," Margaret said. "He has a right to come back to his own country if he wants to."

"I'm an old woman and you may not have me for much longer," her mother said, wiping her eyes. Her fingers were twisted and gnarled with arthritis. "I'm only asking you to do one thing for me. I want you to go over to the railway station and tell him you've changed your mind. Tell him he can't bring his brother to live here with you."

"But …" Margaret trailed off. Her mother thought Jim was going to come and live in Bohreen Hill but she was wrong.

"We'll stay here and mind the baby," her mother continued. "Tell him that you've changed your mind. Tell him when you got a chance to think about it you changed your mind. If you let that fellow sleep here for even one night you'll be stuck with him for good."

"But Jim is not coming to live here," Margaret said quietly. She knew she should have said it sooner and not let her continue being mistaken, but she wasn't used to contradicting her. "Is that what you heard? He's coming home, but he's going to stay in Mrs Byrne's lodging house on the Nunnery Road."

"Oh," her mother said, and then there was silence. Her mother didn't usually admit to being wrong. Even when Julianne had brought the row with Margaret to an end, at John Bourke's wake, her mother had just begun to speak again, but the five years of silence had never been mentioned.

"Even if he is going to stay up in the Nunnery Road he'll still draw trouble on you," her mother said. Her voice sounded distant and distressed. She moved forward in the chair as if she was dragging herself back from some distant place where she had been alone. "He's after being in jail over in England, and the RIC will be watching you. You should have written to him to tell him not to come, that you didn't want him. I hate my grandchildren having anything to do with him."

"I'm sure it will work out all right," Margaret said. "He wrote us a letter and he seemed a very nice person."

"Nice. What use is nice? I don't know did I ever tell you," her mother said, "how much I hate my grandchildren having the surname 'Carty'. I hate that name." She shuddered. "I hate to think of them being poor for the whole of their lifetime. They'll never make anything of themselves around here with a name like that. Everyone knows that they're poor and that their father came from nothing."

"There's nothing wrong with the name Carty," Margaret said. "The children can be proud of their father. There's not a better man than Michael in the town."

"They'll be twice as clever as the men they'll be working for," her mother said, "but they'll be made little of all their lives. The best they can ever be in this town is clerks. They'll be doing all the work for some of the big noises in the town, they'll know twice as much as them, but they'll have to bow their heads with respect every time they see them. Maybe we should get them to leave – go to England or America. They might do better over there."

"I worry about their future, too," Margaret said. "But there's no use in worrying about it. I can't change the world and make it perfect for them. We have to believe in God's will and God's goodness. I pray for them every day. The only other thing I can do for them is teach them to be good."

Her mother didn't answer, but sighed loudly. Julianne was slumped back in the chair and didn't seem to have been listening. They heard a tapping on the front door, and a dog barking.

"Is that Cormac home from school? That's the dog that always follows him," her mother said. "He'll get a surprise when he sees us here."

"He will," Margaret said. "He'll be delighted." She stood up and went towards the hall to open the door. "You won't say anything against Jim in front of Cormac," she said turning back into the kitchen.

"What do you think I am? Do you think I'm a fool? Do you think I know nothing?" Her mother sat up straight in the chair, in fighting form again. "I'm such a foolish old woman that I wouldn't know what I should and shouldn't say in front of a child. I don't know how you put up with me. Weren't you very unfortunate to have such a stupid mother? I'm very lucky I have you to advise me because I know nothing. I'd never know what to do or say. I'm only an old fool."

"You're not an old fool," Margaret said.

"Go out and answer the door. Don't keep the child waiting," her mother said. "I saw him going into the town with Aidan the other day. I stood at my parlour window and watched the two of them walking up the Island Road. They reminded me of my own two boys, of James and John."

*

Michael introduced Jim and Stephen Bolger to a few of the IRB men. They were sitting facing the window in the Gaelic room in Antwerp. Fennelly went behind the table to get the meeting started. Martin Webster nodded at him and pointed towards the stairs, signalling that he would stand guard at the front door to watch out for the RIC. Bill Kavanagh stayed at the window looking out on Mary Street and the bridge. Prendergast sat at the table beside Fennelly and told them about his visit to Dublin, to Tom Clarke's tobacconist shop on Parnell Square. Prendergast had a wad of small blank sheets of paper on the table in front of him. *Echo* reporters always had paper and pencils in their pockets.

"I met Clarke and Mac Diarmada," Prendergast said.

"Mac Diarmada sends you all his greetings." He lowered his voice. "The Supreme Council has decided that there will be a Rising before this war is over. No details of it will be forthcoming until the last minute for obvious reasons. IRB members are to do as they have always done – continue to work within the Gaelic League and the GAA to spread nationalist ideas, but particularly all IRB members are to work with the Irish Volunteers. The Irish Volunteer Convention last week is deemed by the Supreme Council to have been highly successful. We are to forget about the National Volunteers and the war. Let them go off to die for England. But if we are to regenerate the spirit of the Irish people we must be ready for a blood sacrifice."

There was a buzz of excited talk as soon as he finished speaking. At last there were men in charge of the movement who were going to lead a Rising and try to awaken the spirit of the Irish people once more. Fennelly called the meeting to order and asked were there any questions.

"Did you ask Tom Clarke what he thought about pikes?" Pat Lambert asked. "Should we be manufacturing pikes to use in a Rising?"

"No," Prendergast said. "I didn't get a chance to mention that. Clark and Mac Diarmada and Pearse have to deal with the general picture. They've to take the overall view. It's hard to expect them to know about local issues."

"Pikes were good enough in '98," a man said. "We should have them this time too."

"We make all the military decisions ourselves," Séamus Walsh said. "What buildings we'll take over, how we'll man them. We should be trying to arm ourselves as best we can. Pikes and rifles and shotguns. Revolvers. Anything we can lay our hands on. And explosives. We should all learn whatever we can about making explosives."

"What about recruiting posters for the British army? There are recruiting posters all over the town," someone said.

"Tear them down," Fennelly said.

Chapter 10

The Gaelic room in Antwerp was crowded. It was the Saturday night before Feis Charman and the last minute arrangements for the Feis were being made. Michael was standing in front of the table where Séamus Ó Dubhghaill, the secretary of the Feis committee, was assigning duties for the following day. More than ten thousand visitors were expected in the town for the Feis, and most of them would come by train. Michael had to work in the railway in the morning, and again at night, but he would be free to help the Feis committee during the middle of the day.

"*Beidh tusa san Athenaeum ag a leathuair tar éis a haon, mar sin, a Mhichíl,*" Séamus said.

"*Beidh,*" he said, and he watched Séamus turning the pages of the hardbacked copybook and writing "Mícheál Ó Cárrthaigh" halfway down a page headed "Athenaeum".

Michael moved back from the table and stood with a group of men who were talking about the Feis. He had his arms folded, and with his right hand he could feel the revolver in the inside pocket of his coat. He had brought the revolver to the Bridge Inn where Walshe was looking over the guns held by members of the IRB. After a while he made his way through the crowded room, and went downstairs and out into the Hollow. It was getting dark. There were groups of men standing around under the trees. Michael looked for Jim, and saw him sitting on a window-ledge talking to some men from Hogans'. They were laughing, and he guessed that they were talking about the sedition trial and Prendergast. Everybody was laughing at the RIC since they arrested Prendergast's two lodgers, Hegarty and Bolger, but let Prendergast slip away, although he was in the house when they went there. Guns and explosives had been found under Prendergast's bed, and the Casement pamphlets which had been printed in the *Echo*, were in the dining-room. The RIC had been the laughing stock of the town ever since because Prendergast would have been a much better catch for them than either of the other two. Hegarty, an IRB man from Cork, and Bolger, an Echo journalist, had been in custody since February and were on trial in Dublin charged with sedition. Prendergast was on the run, and a rumour had spread around the town that a German submarine had picked him up near Ballyconnigar, and that he was gone to Germany.

"Wherever he is I'm sure he's having a great laugh at the RIC," Jim was saying when Michael went over.

"If he's caught he'll be in for a long sentence. Tim Healy is laying all the blame on him at the trial to get the other two freed. Healy has the whole country laughing at the RIC," Dan Hogan said, and pulled on his cigarette. He was sitting on the window-ledge beside Jim.

"I hope Tim Healy's wit works to some benefit this time. He wasn't so funny when he was destroying poor Parnell," Stephen Bolger said.

They heard the windows on the first floor of Horgans' shop rattling and looked over to see Tony and Joan Horgan hanging out a banner for the Feis. Some of the men went over to the bottom of Slaney Street to talk to the Horgans.

"You'll be down for your tea tomorrow." Michael moved over to lean against the wall beside Jim. "I'll have to go to the railway at about six, but Margaret and the boys will be there."

They stopped talking because Stephen Bolger had started to cough. Jim stood up to go to the lodgings with him. Stephen hadn't been well since he got a bad flu in the spring.

Michael was about to go home when Martin Webster jumped down from the road into the Hollow.

"The RIC have put up those recruiting posters again," he said, gesturing at Michael, but looking at the other men who were standing around. "On the Railway Bridge. On the side of Roches' Maltings."

The IRB men kept pulling down the recruiting posters all over the town but the RIC always put them up again. The two high walls of Roches' Maltings, which were looking down the hill, were the worst places of all to let them have posters. Nobody could go up the hill without seeing them.

"We'll tear them down," Michael said. "They surely don't think we're going to leave those up on the day of the Feis with all the visitors coming to the town."

He walked up out of the Hollow with Martin, and some of the men followed them. It was dark, and it wasn't until he got to the top of the hill that he could see the posters. The first one was singing the praises of an Irish soldier called Michael O'Leary. The second one was even worse. "Will you answer the call? Now is the time, and the place is the nearest recruiting office," it said, and there was a picture of a harp and Caitlín Ní hUallacháin on it. It was terrible to see Irish symbols being used to try to fool Irishmen into joining the British Army.

He had gone on ahead of the others and he went over the bridge to the far poster. He looked around to check that there was no one watching who might inform on him, and then he climbed the wall, holding on to the big stones at the top, and fitting his boots into the gaps between the smaller stones further down. Martin started to climb beside him. The men whistled, and shouted encouragement. Michael stood up on the wall of the bridge and leaned in against the high wall of the Maltings. He could feel the revolver pressing against his ribs. He pulled the poster away from the wall. It tore above the centre, and he pulled the bottom half down, and let it fall into the grounds of the Maltings.

"Good man, Carty," one of the men shouted.

He looked back at Martin and saw his poster falling to the ground. The men were shouting and laughing as Michael stretched in as far as he could and gripped the rest of the poster. He pulled it firmly, and most of it came away from the wall except the very far corner which was blank. As he turned to clamber back down the wall he noticed two men crossing the road, coming towards the town. He couldn't understand where they had suddenly appeared from. They were gesturing to one another and they seemed to be going to join the crowd behind him. He got his feet into gaps between the stones and, gripping the top of the wall, let himself fall on to the road. The two men were coming towards him. He rubbed his hands together to get the dust off them. The men seemed to know him, but he wasn't able to make out who they were in the dark. They were probably on their way up to Antwerp.

"Goodnight, men," he said, sure that he would recognize them when they came closer.

They began to run towards him, and he couldn't believe it when he recognized one of them. It was Fleming, Constable Fleming.

The RIC had been hiding, hoping to catch someone pulling down the posters.

He saw Martin disappearing into the crowd, and he ran, but he knew that the RIC men were too close. They were going to catch him, and he had the revolver in his pocket.

They grabbed his arms, and he tried to keep running but they ran into him, and as he staggered they knocked him down. His forehead banged against the ground. He felt their weight on top of him. They were holding down his arms, their knees digging into his back. He tried to struggle but they had him pinned down and he could hardly breathe. His forehead and his nose were throbbing with pain.

"The other fellow got away," he heard Fleming saying.

"Who did we catch? Who is it? Do you know him?"

Michael thought that it was Rogers, the new Constable from Kilkenny, who was with Fleming. He felt Fleming's cold hands on his face, lifting his head. He gasped as his neck was twisted.

"It's Carty. He follows a horse for the railway," Fleming said.

He managed to stop his head from banging against the road as Fleming let it go. There were lights in front of his eyes. He could hear the men booing at the RIC. "Sit up. Come on. Get up." The RIC men dug their knees into his back as they stood up. "Get up, Carty."

"All right." He tried to get up but all the strength was gone out of one of his hands, the hand he had fallen on, and he knew he couldn't lean on it. He raised himself up slowly on to his knees, using his other hand. He thought he was going to vomit. His head was throbbing, and he wanted to wipe his face.

"Your hands," Fleming said. "Come on, your hands. Are you stupid or what?"

Fleming was going to put handcuffs on him. They were going to bring him to the barracks. The crowd was still booing, but they were moving away, back down the hill. They couldn't bring him to the barracks just for pulling down recruiting posters.

Posters were being torn down all over the town. What

would Margaret do? He was kneeling, leaning on one hand, and he almost fell over as Fleming grabbed his two hands and pushed the handcuffs around his wrists. He swallowed and stopped himself from vomiting. Rogers was lighting a cigarette.

"Stand up. Come on. We don't want to stay here all night."

They held him by the arms and marched him along down the Railway Bridge. He wanted to lie down. If he could lie down he wouldn't vomit. He licked his lips. He thought his nose was bleeding.

"You're two sneaky cowards," a voice from the crowd shouted, "hiding in behind the wall, like snakes in the grass. Cowards."

"Prendergast got away on ye," someone else shouted.

Fleming stopped and began to kick Michael. He moved to avoid the kicks and he broke out into a cold sweat. His stomach churned and he couldn't stop the stream of vomit. He tried to move sideways towards the wall to get away from them while he was vomiting but Rogers kept a grip of his arm.

"Ogh. Is he drunk?" Fleming asked, jumping back away from him.

"No. I'm not drunk," he said. He was breathing heavily. There was a cold sweat on his face, and he knew he needed to vomit a second time.

He vomited again. There was vomit on his boots and he wanted to wipe his face, but he had the handcuffs on and Rogers was holding his arm.

"Ogh," Fleming said. "Will you look at the mess he's after making?"

Rogers laughed. "I think he's finished. Are you finished?"

"I think so," Michael said.

His head was throbbing as they walked past the Hollow

and the bottom of Slaney Street. His throat was sore and there were bits of vomit in his mouth. He saw some of the men going up Slaney Street and more of them crossing the bridge. It was probably better if they went home. There was no use in letting the RIC catch too many people. If he hadn't been so stupid he wouldn't have got caught. If he had started to run sooner, like Martin did, he'd have got away, too. He felt angry with himself because he had stopped to greet the RIC and that was why they had caught him. He knew that he was a terrible fool.

They were walking him along past the cotton tree and across the road towards the Bridge Inn. What would Walshe say when he heard what had happened? And Fennelly? The lights were on inside the Bridge Inn, and he remembered nights he had been in there without a worry in the world, having a drink with other IRB men. He would be a terrible liability to the movement now. What would Margaret say? How would she hear? She always waited up until he came home. They came to the top of Slaney Place. The lights were on in the Abbey Square. Maybe the Sergeant would decide to let him home after a while. They often arrested people on Saturday nights for being drunk and then let them home when everything had quietened down.

"I wonder when will the Sergeant send us out to Red Pat's Cross to shoot the dog?" Rogers asked Fleming as they came in to the Abbey Square.

"Not tomorrow. Tomorrow is Sunday. He wouldn't order us to shoot a dog on a Sunday," Rogers said.

They were under the trees in the Abbey Square. He could hear the river rushing along. There had been heavy rain for days, and it had stopped just in time for the Feis. He remembered stories about Manning beating up people in the barracks. He hoped Manning wasn't on duty.

"Would you not let me go home," he said, wondering

why he hadn't thought of asking before. "I wasn't doing anything. I have a wife and four children at home."

He felt them tightening their grip on his arms.

"You should have thought of that before you pulled down the posters," Fleming said.

Rogers laughed. "He wants to go home," he said.

They were coming close to the barracks. The sight of the bars in front of the windows made his heart sink. If they put him in a cell he might break up the place trying to get out.

The big front door of the barracks was open, and he heard another door banging somewhere upstairs. Sergeant Jones lived above the barracks with his wife and some of his children. Rogers and Fleming stopped in the hall and looked up the stairs. The timber creaked as Sergeant Jones, a big, tall man, came down.

"You caught someone," he said. "That's good. This will teach the Sinn Féiners a lesson. They strut around the town, thinking they own the place." He came down the stairs and stood in front of Michael. "Oh, it's Mr Carty. Mr Carty from Bohreen Hill," he jeered.

"Could I not go home? I was only on the road," he said. "I have a wife and four children at home, Sergeant. There was a crowd of us on the road. Could I go home?"

"He wants to go home," Rogers said with a jeering laugh.

The sergeant shook his head. "It's not up to us to let you out. It's nothing to do with us," he said, continuing to shake his head as if he thought Michael might be too stupid to understand the words. "We'll inform the military authorities that we caught you pulling down recruiting posters, and they'll decide what to do with you. It's a serious matter, very serious – interfering with the war effort. Five years, ten years, I don't know." He looked towards Reilly. "Take the handcuffs off him, search him and bring him to the cells."

*

She stood at the sink peeling potatoes for the dinner. Mr Fennelly had said that he would go to the barracks with her at around noon. They could bring Michael his dinner and maybe they would be allowed to see him. She dug deep into a potato to gouge out an eye. She was trying to force herself not to be angry with Michael. At times she thought he was completely wrong to have gone near the posters in the first place. But although she had gone over it in her mind, again and again, she couldn't come to a conclusion about what had happened. How could he have taken such a risk and left her here on her own? But he didn't think that he was going to be caught. It didn't seem to him that there was any risk involved. Recruiting posters were being pulled down everywhere. She kept imagining the darkness on the Railway Hill, and wishing that he would run faster, get away from the RIC men, as if she could go back to the night before and change what had happened. She didn't know how she was going to manage with no wages if he was kept in jail. Philip and Aidan took it well when she told them what had happened, but Cormac had cried and shouted that he wanted his daddy. He had been very upset before he went to Mass.

She pushed her hair back from her face. She knew she shouldn't be blaming Michael for what had happened. It wasn't his fault. It was the RIC and the British who should get out of Ireland for good, and leave the Irish people in peace. She cut the potato in half and rinsed it in the basin of water. She shouldn't be feeling sorry for herself. It was much worse for Michael, locked up in a cell in the RIC barracks. It was wrong of her to be angry with him.

She cut away the rotten half of a potato, and began to peel the rest of it. The house was quiet. The baby was in the corner, playing. It was Dan Hogan and Jim who had told her what had happened. She couldn't believe it when she heard it first. It was dark at the front door and the wind was howling through Dohertys' trees.

"We didn't want you waiting here until late in the night wondering where he was," Dan Hogan had said, following her into the kitchen.

"Sit down," she said. Her heart was thumping.

Jim was leaning against the banisters at the bottom of the stairs. He looked very shaken. "I was talking to him in the Hollow. It never occurred to me that the RIC might be around or I'd have told him to leave the posters until some other time," he said, as if it was all his fault.

"I'll make tea," she said. "I'd say they'll let him home in a while. They often keep people in the barracks for a few hours. People who get drunk." She knew that her voice sounded strong, but as she stoked up the range she was shaking. Sometimes they beat up people in the RIC barracks. She hoped he'd be all right. He shouldn't have gone near the posters. "I'd say he'll be home soon," she said as she cut slices of bread and took out the rhubarb tart that was supposed to be kept for Sunday. She prayed to God to let Michael walk in the door. How could he have been so foolish?

"He'll probably be charged under the Defence of the Realm Act, like Hegarty and Bolger," Dan said when they were sitting at the table drinking the tea. Jim was upset by what had happened, but she thought that Dan was trying to hide his excitement. Some people loved a fight.

"It's not that serious, is it?"

Neither of them answered her and then she heard someone at the front gate. She was sure that it was Michael. They had let him out and this was all a false alarm. Jim's cup was rattling against the saucer as she got up and ran out into the hall. Dan followed her with the oil-lamp. She would tell Michael never to touch the recruiting posters again. She didn't care if all the men in Enniscorthy joined the British

Army as long as she had Michael safely home with her. But when she opened the front door Séamus Walsh and Mr Fennelly were walking up the path. They had come to see was she all right.

Dan was delighted to see them. Séamus Walsh sat in Michael's chair at the head of the table. They all seemed elated as they talked with contempt about the RIC.

"They're like snakes in the grass," Séamus Walsh said.

"They may have won this battle," Mr Fennelly said. "They may win many battles. But we will win the war."

"I hope they won't keep Michael for too long," she said.

She was holding the handle of the kettle, waiting for it to boil. They seemed to have forgotten she was there.

"I know it's a big shock for you, but this is good publicity for the movement," Séamus Walsh said, turning to face her.

"Yes," she said. She had seen Séamus Walsh on the street and at Mass, but she had never been speaking to him before. His people were big farmers out in Caim, and he owned a pub near the bridge.

"The RIC will look bad, hiding in behind a wall trying to catch people out, and Michael will be a real hero," Dan Hogan said.

"That's good," she said but in her mind she was blaming Dan. He was a coward not to have gone up to help with the posters, and all the other men were cowards, too. They called themselves Fenians but they were no good. Michael was the only one of them with any courage.

"We all think very highly of Michael. You could depend your life on him," Mr Fennelly was saying. His voice was soft. His eyes were sparkling behind his glasses. "Michael would never cause trouble between people, nor look to be promoted above anyone else." His hands were joined, as if in prayer, and resting on the table. "He's completely devoted to the movement. If every Irishman had his commitment and his character this country would have been freed years ago. The movement needs more men like Michael."

She knew she shouldn't feel angry. Mr Fennelly was praising Michael, but he was talking as if the movement owned him, and as if she and the boys had no rights. How were they going to manage with no wages?

"Michael may have a poor job," Mr Fennelly continued slowly, "just following a horse for the railway – but it's people like him we need."

"He may be only following a horse for the railway," she said angrily, "but it would be great if he could go out and do his work instead of lying in the RIC barracks. Maybe, as you say Mr Fennelly, Michael has a poor job, but he's a devoted father to the boys. They'll miss him. I'll miss him too." She had thought that in a free Ireland people wouldn't look down on other people. Mr Fennelly had no right to come in to the house and insult Michael's work. It occurred to her that he didn't know she came from a well-off family. Dan Hogan and Séamus Walsh would know that.

"I suppose you'll miss him," Mr Fennelly said, scratching the fingers of his right hand. "But unfortunately the family often has to suffer because of the struggle. The struggle must come first."

His voice was calm, and his calmness made her even angrier.

"Why should Michael be the only one to put the struggle before himself? Why were there not some other people up there helping him, putting the struggle before themselves?" She couldn't keep the anger out of her voice although she knew she sounded just like her mother.

There was silence for a while and then Dan Hogan cleared his throat and scraped his chair backwards along the floor. Jim was pursing his lips and looking down at the table.

"We should have been up there helping him," Séamus

Walsh said quietly. "We'll do everything we can to help him now. We'll get him a good solicitor."

"Yes," Mr Fennelly said. "He's one of us."

"And, of course, there's nothing wrong with following a horse for the railway," Séamus Walsh said. "Michael does an honest day's work."

"Yes. Yes," Mr Fennelly said, scratching at his little finger. "Of course."

"It will be very hard on the boys," Séamus Walsh said, "but maybe it will be a help to them to know that their father will be thought of as an Irish patriot by all decent Irishmen."

She was sorry she had spoken so angrily. They had come to help her. They were on her side. If Michael was here he would have been embarrassed at her speaking like that to Mr Fennelly. How could he consider her feelings when he had devoted himself to freeing Ireland from British rule?

"I'm sure it's a terrible shock for you, Margaret," Jim said.

"It is," she said. Jim had suffered for years in an English jail and he never made a fuss about it.

"Time in jail is part of the struggle," he said. "It's not easy, but we all have to be prepared to play our part and to make sacrifices."

"I know, Jim," she said. She had grown very fond of him. He visited the house often, and the children loved him. Cormac went in to Hogans' every day after school to see him. "It will be hard to explain to the boys," she said.

She poured tea for them. She was ashamed of herself for giving out in front of them. It sounded as if she was against the fight for Irish freedom, and she wasn't. They were so tough and determined. Maybe it was because she was a woman that she got downhearted so easily. She wouldn't mention to them that she was ashamed of Michael being in the RIC barracks but it was usually only thieves or drunkards who were brought there. She knew she should be proud of him for standing up to the British, and she was, but she was ashamed, too.

"There was silence in the bar when word came in," Séamus Walsh said. "Everyone is very fond of Michael. The whole town will be on your side."

"That's great," she said but she was thinking about listening to her mother and Julianne giving out.

They stayed with her late into the night. They were good company, and she calmed down after a while. Jim told great stories about his time in England. Sometimes it seemed as if they had forgotten the news they had brought to her, and they would be laughing at something when she would remember that Michael was in the barracks. She would think of him lying on his own in the cell, or maybe he was being questioned by the RIC. In 1798 they had arrested Anthony Perry and tortured him so badly that he betrayed his comrades. She couldn't bear to think about that, and she would listen to the men for a while. Times had changed, she kept telling herself, and Michael wasn't a leader in the movement. He wasn't important enough to be tortured. Maybe they wouldn't keep him in for too long. He would have enjoyed this night, of all nights, at home, when these four men, whom he thought so highly of, were in the house. She talked for a long time to Séamus Walsh who knew her mother's people and the Bourkes of Marshalstown. His face was a strange shape, almost square, and he had a moustache.

"We shouldn't have kept you up until this hour," he said when they heard the cathedral bell ringing out four o'clock.

"I was glad of the company," she said.

"You could call to the barracks in the morning and ask them what they're going to do," Mr Fennelly said as he stood up to leave. "I'll go with you if you like. I'll call here after eleven Mass. You could bring him his dinner."

She had been surprised when Mr Fennelly said that,

because he hadn't looked at her even once during the night. She peeled the last potato and brought the pot of potatoes over to the range. She wanted to have the dinner ready when Mr Fennelly arrived, and not delay him.

The baby, still in his nightclothes, was talking to himself, as he played with the blocks that Jim had bought for him. He didn't understand what had happened. It hadn't been easy to tell the others. Cormac hadn't said much in the beginning but when he came downstairs he had cried for his daddy. They had all been asleep when she came home from Mass, and she had delayed in the kitchen, putting off going up to them. They lay very still in bed and said nothing when she told them. Cormac was lying across the bed, and had almost pushed Aidan out on to the floor.

"You know how wrong it is for Irishmen to be joining the British Army. It's not right to have posters in an Irish town, luring Irish men off to fight Britain's evil wars," she said. "Your father is always ready to stand up for what is right, and that's why he tore down the posters." She wanted them to be able to hold their heads high in the town, and not go cowering around expecting people to think badly of them.

Philip sat up in bed and nodded at her, but the other two didn't move.

"Your father wants the British out of Ireland so that this country can be a good place for us all to live in," she continued. "What he did was absolutely right."

"But why are they blaming him? That's not fair," Philip said. "He's not the only one who pulls down recruiting posters. They're being pulled down everywhere."

"They caught him. They're sneaky cowards," she said.

Aidan sat up and shook his head scornfully. "They're stupid. They caught Hegarty and Bolger," he said, "but they let Prendergast walk out of the house."

"They're vicious, too," Philip said. "Everybody knows how vicious—"

She interrupted him. She didn't want them thinking about how the RIC could hurt their father. "You know that your father is not like other people who are brought to the barracks," she said. "People who don't know how to behave and make a show of themselves on the street. Thieves. Drunkards. Your father is an Irish patriot, and he's in the barracks because of his love for his country."

"We know that," Philip said.

"Of course we do," Aidan said, pushing Cormac out of his way, and moving into the middle of the bed.

The baby was waking up, making a long singing noise in the other bedroom.

"But when will daddy be coming home?" Cormac asked. "Will he not be here for the Feis?"

"This is more important than the Feis," Philip said.

"That's right," she said, going into the other bedroom for the baby who had started to cry.

They came downstairs after a while, and Philip and Aidan seemed to be vying with one another, each trying to be more contemptuous of the RIC. They reminded her of Mr Fennelly and Dan Hogan – they seemed excited by what had happened. She was glad that they were proud of what their father had done, and she stopped herself from pointing out the downside of it to them. They would be able to hold their own when they went out to Mass. Cormac sat and listened, but he didn't say anything. He was too young to understand history or politics. He didn't go upstairs with the others to get ready for Mass. She had gone out to the clothes line and he came after her.

"Will daddy be out when the ground dries up?" He looked angrily at her, but his voice sounded as if he was about to cry.

175

"I don't know when he'll be out," she said. "It probably won't be too long."

"We promised Jim that when the ground dries up we'd bring him down the banks to show him where we swim in the river. Will he be back when the ground dries up?"

"I don't know when he'll be out, Cormac," she said. "It will probably be soon."

"I want daddy." He started to cry. "Go to the barracks and get him for me. Even if there won't be Irish freedom you go to the barracks and tell them that he'll put back up the poster. Wouldn't it be all right if he put it back up?"

"No," she said. "It wouldn't. There's going to have to be a trial."

"Try," he said. "Go over to the barracks and try. Say he's sorry."

"No. There's no use," she said. He came with her back into the kitchen.

"Will they hang him?"

"No. No," she said. "They couldn't do that to him. There will have to be a trial. He's in jail because he loves his country, but he'll probably be home soon. Of course they won't hang him. Go upstairs and get ready for Mass."

"No," he said. He stamped his foot. He was crying. "No."

"Go upstairs and get ready for Mass, Cormac," she said. "Be a good boy."

"No. I won't go to Mass," he cried.

Philip and Aidan came down the stairs.

"The twenty-to bell is gone," Philip said. "We'll be late if we don't go soon."

"Go back upstairs and bring down Cormac's coat," she said to Philip. "Stop crying, Cormac," she said. "You're a big boy. You've to go to Mass now with your brothers." She took the towel from the sink to wipe his face. "Stop crying. I'll wipe your face."

"No. No. Go away from me. No. No," he screamed, stamping his foot. He snatched the towel from her as she reached out to wipe his face. He threw it on the floor.

"You're very bold," she said. She caught his hand and she slapped him a few times. "Calm down, Cormac. Stop shouting." She gripped his arms. "Your daddy is in the barracks, and he'd be very cross with you for behaving like that. He'll be home soon. Put on your coat and go to Mass." She put her arms around him. "Are you sorry?" she said. "Are you sorry for being bold?"

He kept on sobbing.

"You're sorry for being bold," she said, "and you're a good boy. You're going to be very good and put on your coat and go off to Mass with your brothers. We'll forget all about you being bold. Philip will mind you. Be very good for Philip."

"I want my daddy," he said, gripping her skirt.

"Here's Philip with your coat," she said. She took his hands from her skirt and put on his coat. "You're after making your first Holy Communion. It would be a mortal sin to miss Mass on a Sunday."

"I want daddy." He was sobbing.

She buttoned up his coat. "Stop saying that," she said, pleading with him as she bent down to wipe his face with the towel.

"You've stopped crying now," she said brightly when there was a pause for an instant in his crying. "You're a very good boy. Cheer up, now."

He cried again as Philip caught his hand. She wiped his face again and turned firmly away. If she looked at him he might run to her. He had to go to Sunday Mass. He was usually so good, and she never had to be cross with him.

She lifted the kettle to pour boiling water on the potatoes. It was nearly eleven o'clock. They would be home from Mass soon. She dried her hands and began to stir the porridge for breakfast. She set the table. The baby came over to her.

"Do you want a bottle? Will I get you a bottle?"

"Bottle," he said.

She heard the boys at the gate. "The boys are coming home," she said to the baby. "Do you hear them at the gate? Aidan will play with you."

"Aidan," he repeated.

"And Cormac and Philip," she said.

He repeated the names after her, and pointed and laughed as the boys came in to the kitchen. She put the porridge into bowls for them. Cormac came over and stood beside her at the range. He was smiling. She was glad that he wasn't sulking.

"Word has spread through the town," Philip said. "Everybody was asking us. We told them all about it."

They seemed excited, as if the attention was keeping them buoyed up.

"B…b-b-b…b-b-b…" Cormac began, looking up at her.

Aidan interrupted. "Everybody thinks that the RIC was wrong to hide behind the wall. People are really angry about that," he said.

She put the bowls of porridge on the table. Philip and Aidan sat down but Cormac stayed standing close to her. "B…b…b-b," he began.

"They all gathered around us at the side of the Cathedral yard," Philip said. "Even Brother Quirke stood there listening to what we had to say."

"B-b-b…b-b-b…" Cormac was blinking his eyes, looking up at her, trying desperately to get the word out.

"Ned Earle said that Father Rossiter would bring him down Holy Communion to the barracks," Philip said.

"Let Cormac talk," she said. "What did you want to say, Cormac?"

"B-b-b-b…" he began. His face was almost alight with excitement but he wasn't able to finish the word.

"He started talking like that when we were coming down the Irish Street," Philip said.

"Stay quiet, Philip," she said.

"B-b-b…b-b," Cormac was staring at her as if he was imploring her to help him to move on from where he was stuck.

"Say it, Cormac. Go on. Say it," she said. "Calm down. Take a deep breath and say whatever it is you want to say."

"B-b-b-b…b-b…." he continued, and then he uttered the 'b' with a desperate emphasis and the rest of the sentence followed like an avalanche. "B-enny Murphy asked me about him." He smiled with relief when he said it.

"Did he? Benny Murphy from Court Street," she said.

He nodded at her and smiled.

"Why did they pick on him? That's what everybody is asking," Philip said. "The RIC are big bullies. Those posters are never left up, anywhere in the town."

"Wh-wh-wh-wh-wh…" Cormac began.

"Say it, Cormac. Go on. Say it," she said.

"Wh-wh-wh…wh…" His face was almost alive with excitement but he wasn't able to finish the word.

"What happened him? Did someone upset him? I told you to mind him," she said, her voice turning into a wail. If he got a stutter he would be beaten in school for not being able to talk properly, or he would be left sitting at the back of the class and treated as if he was stupid. "Were you not minding him?"

"We were minding him," Philip said. "We sat beside him at Mass."

"Nothing happened him. He was with us," Aidan said. "I don't know what he's talking like that for."

"Wh-wh-wh-wh…" Cormac kept trying to talk,

breathing strangely and blowing out of his mouth. He was very anxious to talk but he wasn't able to. "Wh-wh-wh…" He kept looking at her as if he was asking her to help him to start the word.

There was a knock on the door. It was hardly Mr Fennelly arriving so early. She didn't have the dinner ready. It might be one of the neighbours calling to enquire about Michael. Or maybe it was Kitty. Kitty would call as soon as she heard the news.

"Wh… wh-wh-wh-when will Jim be d-d-down?"

It was hard to believe that he had wanted to ask something so simple. "After dinner," she said as she went to answer the door.

The baby started to cry and came after her.

"Hold the baby, Aidan," she said. "Don't let him come out in to the hall after me."

She got a terrible shock when she opened the door. It was Sergeant Jones from the RIC barracks.

"Mrs Carty?" He spoke loudly. "Michael Carty's wife?"

She held on to the latch. "Yes." Her voice was just a whisper. What had he done to Michael? Why was he coming to the door like this? "What's wrong? Is everything all right?"

"Am I at the right house? Number three, Bohreen Hill? You're Mrs Carty?" His face was expressionless. She couldn't tell whether he was going to give her good or bad news.

"Yes," she said, forcing herself to speak more loudly.

"You know your husband was arrested?"

"Yes," she said. "For no good reason."

His face reddened. "The military authorities and the court will decide whether the reason is good or not," he said. "I came to tell you that your husband was charged this morning and has been moved to Waterford Jail."

"Waterford," she repeated.

"The prisoner is on his way to Waterford now."

180

The baby was still crying in the kitchen. The Sergeant seemed to be waiting for her to say something. She held the latch and moved the door. She wished he would go. She couldn't think of anything to say. Michael was gone to Waterford Jail.

"I always come to tell the family," he said, putting his hands on his chest, and stroking the collar of his uniform with his thumbs. He seemed to be admiring himself. He hesitated again, then turned and went down the path.

She closed the door and leaned back against the wall. Aidan came out holding the baby who was screaming and struggling to get into her arms. She took him and carried him into the kitchen. How could Michael have left her with all this despair and confusion?

"D-d-d-d-d..." Cormac began, coming over to stand beside her.

The baby was still screaming. "Stop crying, Michael," she said. "You're getting too big for all this crying."

He smiled at her through his tears.

"We'll get your blocks for you to play with," she said. "We'll build you a castle, but stop crying. Get Michael the blocks, Aidan."

"D-d-d-d-d..." Cormac said.

"Say it Cormac," she said.

"D-d-d-d-addy's gone to W-w-w-w-waterford." Cormac smiled as if he was pleased that his daddy was in jail.

Chapter 11

He walked towards the corner of the cemented path, staying the regulation five paces behind the new prisoner. There were guards with bayonets drawn, standing against the wall on each side of the exercise yard. It was late afternoon but the sun was still beating down. He could hear children shouting as they played in the street outside. The stables and store houses were in front of him as he turned towards the pump. He was roasting with the heat, and dying for a drink, but another prisoner stopped off before him. Only one prisoner at a time was allowed at the pump. He walked along in the shade under the high cell block. Exercise time was the best part of the day in the jail, and the hour was nearly up.

They were keeping up a good brisk pace as they came once more out of the shade and into the heat. He was watching the pump. There was no one there. He gestured at a guard who nodded. He pumped its handle a few times, and when the water began to gush out he bent down and drank and splashed the water all over his face with his hands. The flow of water was weakening, and he gulped down the last few trickles. He thought of going down the Banks on a summer evening and wading into the cold river. He was here in the jail for more than a month now, and he still didn't know when he was going to get home. Some days he was full of despair, sure that he would be sentenced to years in jail, but other days he thought that he would probably be let out after his trial if only they would hurry up and hold the trial. The charge against him wasn't very serious, Séamus Walsh had said when he came to visit him. Fennelly had got a Mr Buggy, a solicitor in Waterford, to defend him. Most magistrates, decent Irishmen, would refuse to find him guilty, Walsh had said, but the military authorities were trying to delay his trial in order to make sure he spent as long as possible in jail. They had moved him to Waterford because they knew that they would have no chance of getting him convicted in Enniscorthy. It was just the sort of crooked thing you would expect the British to do.

He waited for his place in the line, and walked again around the yard. After a while the whistle blew, and the line of prisoners moved towards the side door to go back to the cells. He took one last deep breath before facing the stench of the jail. He followed the new prisoner up the stone stairs. The new prisoner was in Brogan's cell. He was small and he looked very young. He had made a terrible fuss when he was brought in, banging on the door, pleading with the guards to let him out. They had gone in after a while and beaten him up. Michael had shouted in at him several times since morning but he hadn't answered. Brogan, the young fellow who had been in that cell, had been sentenced to life imprisonment for manslaughter and transferred to Mountjoy Jail in Dublin. Brogan wasn't the full shilling, but still the sentence had shocked Michael. He had been thinking about it on and off all day. What would Brogan do when he realized that he was going to have to spend years in jail? He had expected a very short sentence. He had said that he was going to be charged with larceny, and that there was very little evidence against him. He never told Michael that he had committed such a serious crime.

He went into his cell – cell 31A. Caulfield, the guard who had told him about Brogan's sentence, locked him in. He sat at the table facing the wall under the high window. He was sorry that he had finished his library book, *A Tale of Two Cities*. Some days while he was reading it he had become so absorbed that he had forgotten he was in the jail. The books would be changed in the morning. Tonight he would re-read the Gospel according to Saint John which was a permanent fixture in the cell, like the tin plate, mug, spoon and pot. He took up the tin plate and ran his finger along the rust on its rim. There was no sense in comparing himself to Brogan. What had happened to Brogan couldn't happen to him.

The new prisoner was moving around. He seemed to be dragging the table or the stool across the floor. He'd get into terrible trouble and be beaten up again if he did things like that.

"I don't think you should move the table," Michael shouted. "What's your name?"

But there was no answer. The new prisoner didn't want to talk. Michael missed Brogan although Brogan had often got on his nerves. Brogan insisted on having the same conversation several times a day.

"I'm Joseph Brogan from Cappoquin, County Waterford," he would shout through the cell wall. "What's your name? Where are you from?"

Sometimes Michael wouldn't answer.

"Carty," Brogan would shout angrily. "Answer me. I'm Joseph Brogan from Cappoquin, County Waterford. What's your name? Where are you from?"

"I'm Michael Carty from Enniscorthy," Michael would say to keep Brogan quiet.

"You're from Enniscorthy, are you? You're Michael Carty from Enniscorthy," Brogan would say. "I'm Joseph Brogan from Cappoquin, County Waterford. Joseph Brogan from Cappoquin, County Waterford," he would repeat as if he was afraid he was going to forget who he was. There was often a boastful tone in his voice. He usually sounded very proud of himself although Michael knew now that Brogan had very little to be proud of.

He turned around on the stool to face the door. Sometimes when he looked at the wall for too long he thought that the cell was going to close in on him, that it was even smaller than it was. He pressed his hand against the cold jagged white-washed stone beside him. He had probably lost his job at the railway, but other people had sacrificed even more. People had given their lives for the cause of Irish freedom. He would get casual work, a day here and a day there, in places around the town.

He fingered the rust around the handle of the tin mug. He should have asked Margaret about his job when she came to visit but he couldn't bring himself to mention it in front of the guards. She had been nervous. The guards were listening to her, and it seemed as if at times she was talking to them as well as to him.

He hadn't expected a woman to visit the jail. He had received a letter from Margaret, and he was waiting every day for another letter, but when he was told there was a visitor he thought it would be Jim or Walsh or Fennelly. The guard had gripped his arm tightly as they went across the exercise yard. The visiting room was off a passageway at the front of the jail. She was sitting at a table. There was a guard standing behind her.

She turned her head. "Hello, Michael," she said. Her head and her face looked terribly small.

He had stopped at the door, not able to believe his eyes. He wanted to touch her. "Margaret," he said.

The guard pushed him. There was another guard sitting writing at the centre of the table which stretched almost the length of the room. The guard pushed him again, and pointed at a chair at the head of the table.

He sat down. "You shouldn't have gone to all this trouble," he said. "It's too much of a journey."

"I wanted to see you," she said.

He thought she was going to cry. He didn't know what he would do if she cried.

"I'm all right. It's not too bad here. I've got used to it now," he said. "It's great to see you."

"You look pale," she said.

"I'm looking forward to coming home."

She was smiling, leaning forward on the table. He was thinking how lovely she was, but then the guard who had been writing looked over at her and grinned jeeringly. She became very upset as if she suddenly understood what a terrible place a jail was. Closing her eyes and grimacing, she moved back in the chair and crossed her arms, her fingers gripping her shoulders, which were shaking. The jeering guard scratched the pen along the page. Michael wanted to box him and knock the leer off his face.

"How did you get here?"

"By train," she said nervously.

He knew he should talk, talk about anything, just keep talking to bring her back to herself, but he didn't know what to say. He certainly didn't want to talk about the jail in front of the guards. He had decided that he was never going to tell anyone about his time in jail. When he got out of here he would put all this behind him, and pretend that it had never happened.

"Any news at home? How are the boys?"

"They're not too bad. They miss you. Cormac misses you," she said.

"Did Aidan's team win the hurling match?"

"They did. Jim went up to see it. He said that Aidan played very well."

"I was thinking about that match," he said. "Aidan is a great hurler."

"Philip came first in his class in the summer exams," she said.

"Did he? Any other news?" He changed the subject immediately. He didn't want to talk about Philip. If he got a long sentence Philip would have to leave school and get work as a messenger boy.

"Any news around the town?" He hoped Margaret realized that any names she mentioned would be written down and passed on to the RIC in Enniscorthy.

"Tom Lambert took another bad turn," she said. "He won't last long more."

"How are the women managing to mind him?"

The guard was writing down the name, but it was safe enough to mention the Lamberts because it was no secret that their house was a hotbed of Republicanism.

"They're finding it very hard." Her voice was a little louder as if she was trying to force herself to be strong, but her eyes kept flickering towards the guard to see was he still jeering at her. "Tom doesn't know he's dying," she said. "He talks about getting better and going out again along the Scrub Road for a walk. I go down and sit with them for a while in the evenings after I put the baby to bed," she continued, sitting up straight and moving her arms slowly down on to the table. She was getting stronger. "Tom finds it very hard to talk but he always asks about you. Everybody is asking for you, all the people of the town. Someone from every house on the Irish Street, and the Island Road. I wouldn't say people would be half as concerned about me. Father Rossiter called to the house."

There was silence. He thought of asking had she heard anything from the railway, but he didn't want the guards to know that he had probably lost his job. Maybe Kelly would hold the job for him for a few weeks, like he did that time when he had bronchitis, but he hardly would. He could ask her how she was managing for money, but he wouldn't mention that either in front of the guards. The guard behind him coughed.

"My cousin Anna," Margaret said, folding her arms, "is going off to Broadstairs next month. Julianne is taking it badly, but Anna has her heart set on entering the convent of the Faithful Companions of Jesus."

He already knew about Julianne's daughter, Anna, who was going to enter a Convent. "The order has three houses in Ireland, Laurel Hill, Bruff and Newtownbarry where Anna went to school, but their novitiate is in Broadstairs in Kent," she continued.

He could see that she was making a big effort to keep a conversation going in front of the guards and that was why she was telling him things that he knew already.

"Anna will have her beautiful long hair cut off," she said. "Julianne never wanted her to become a nun. She was hoping against hope that Anna would change her mind." She spoke slowly and carefully, and he admired how posh she sounded but he wished she would talk to him like she would if they were at home. He wanted to touch her, and have an ordinary talk with her, ask her more about the boys. He wanted to talk to her about Aidan and hurling. Aidan had been talking about giving up hurling although everybody said that if he kept it up he would make it on to the county team.

When the visit was over one of the guards brought him back across the exercise yard. He remembered the stink of stale urine which hit him when he went back into the cell block. He couldn't remember Margaret's face. Sometimes he could see her eyes, but never her whole face. He sat very still, facing the wall of jagged stone, and tried to picture her face.

Maybe she would come to see him again, but he would be going home soon. It was hard to imagine what it would be like to be at home again. He would be free to walk outside in the fresh air whenever he wanted to. He could half-picture fields, green, yellow, brown fields, stretching off in the distance, and dark borders of trees around each field. The fields in Kilbride were small. There were thistles in the top half of the field above Murphys' house. There was a stone wall, and long wet grass. In a way he loved Kilbride. He had had to tell the children stories about it. They had insisted that he tell them stories about his childhood, and he had told them happy ones. He never mentioned Father Roche. They presumed he had been evicted and he let them believe the lie.

A guard tramped on the passage outside. Every so often a guard walked up and down the passage and looked through the iron bars of the spyhole at each prisoner.

"Put the table back beside the wall. Move it back. And the stool too," the guard shouted at the new prisoner. "Over by the wall. Don't move the furniture. And look at the spyhole when you hear me coming."

The new prisoner was having difficulty getting used to the rules and regulations. Michael had found it hard too when he arrived first. He sat on the stool and looked towards the spyhole. If you kept all the rules you stayed out of trouble. If you didn't look at them when they came to the spyhole they would shout at you. Some of the guards were awful, others weren't too bad. The elderly guard with the big face and the double chin nodded in at him.

He was hungry. He took up the tin plate. He should start reading the Gospel according to Saint John again. He had grown to love it even though he wasn't sure what the beginning of it meant.

The food trolley began to rattle at the end of the passage. It was suppertime. He took up his plate and mug. The guards were shouting as they gave out the supper. The doors were being unlocked and then banged closed. It would be skilly and bread again. There was the same smell from all food served in the jail, but he was hungry. There was never enough food.

"Shove out your mug and your plate." The guards were shouting at the new prisoner. Michael stood up and moved across the cell. He stood close to the bed, a little back from the door, in view of the spyhole. A guard banged the keys against the door as he opened it. Michael handed out his mug and plate and waited for them to give him his food. He took the skilly and brown bread, and sat on the stool at the table. The spoon in the cell was full of teeth marks, and had been gnawed into a strange shape by previous prisoners. He forced himself to eat slowly. There was plenty of time. After supper the sun shone through the high window of the cell for about half an hour. He liked to sit on the bed and look at the sunlight, and the shadow of the window-bars on the roof of the cell.

He was surprised to hear a guard marching down the passageway. They usually stayed away for about half an hour after supper. He got a fright when he realized that it was his cell door that was being opened. He stood up and faced the door. "A visit," the guard said.

He followed the guard along the passageway and down two flights of stone steps.

"It's your solicitor," the guard said as they went across the top of the exercise yard.

Buggy was standing at the centre of the table in the visiting room, taking papers and a notebook out of a case. He was small and almost completely bald. He was wearing a dark suit. He looked about sixty years of age.

"Michael Carty," he said. He had a round pleasant face. He held out his hand across the table and Michael shook it.

"I'm Patrick Buggy. Mr Fennelly from Enniscorthy asked me to represent you. Is that all right?"

"Yes," Michael said.

Buggy sat down and leafed through the papers on the table in front of him. "Sit down," he said. "I've finally got a date set for your trial – next Wednesday," Buggy said.

"That's great," Michael said.

Buggy shrugged and grimaced, looking doubtful. "There are two charges against you," he said.

"Two?" Michael said. "I thought it was only pulling down the recruiting posters."

"You didn't admit pulling down the recruiting posters, as far as I can see," Buggy said. "You didn't make a statement, did you?"

"No," Michael said.

"Good. The second charge is being in possession of a revolver on a railway bridge," Buggy said.

"But it's not a crime to have a revolver," Michael said. "They can ask questions about it, but it's not against the law."

Buggy looked down. "Regulation 33 of the Defence of the Realm Act," he said, reading from one of the pages in front of him. "It's an offence to be near a railway bridge while in possession of a firearm. You were on the railway bridge, weren't you?"

"I was on the road," Michael said. "It's a road as well as a railway bridge. They're just trying to catch me out." The National Volunteers often marched on the Railway Bridge, carrying arms. They didn't charge them under the Defence of the Realm Act.

"Regulation 33 of the Defence of the Realm Act," Buggy said quietly. "You were on a Railway Bridge?"

"Yes," Michael said.

"However, as you say, the railway bridge is in the town of

Enniscorthy, isn't it? It's used regularly by all the people of the town?"

Michael nodded.

"I'll be arguing that you had every right to be in possession of a revolver on the railway bridge, because the railway bridge is also the King's Highway," Buggy said.

"It's terrible to hear an Irish road, built by Irish people, being called the King's Highway," Michael said.

Buggy sighed and shook his head. He put his two hands on the table. "The King's Highway," he repeated slowly. "I'll be using their language and their laws to try to get you out of jail. I don't want you to say anything in the court. Do you understand?"

Michael nodded.

"I won't put you in the stand, but the magistrates will be watching you. Try to look quiet and respectable. That's what I'm going to say about you – that you're a respectable married man with children. How many children?"

"Four," Michael said.

Buggy tidied the papers and reached out to put them in the case. "Have you any questions?"

"Is it very serious?" Michael asked. "Does the second charge make it much more serious?"

"It's serious," Buggy said, putting his papers into the case. "All court appearances are serious."

"Do you think I'll be let out?"

"It's hard to know," Buggy said. "If it was in Dublin you'd be let off. But Waterford is a Redmondite city. It would be easier to talk to Dublin magistrates. It's hard to know. But I'll be doing my best for you."

The guard came in for him. He sat on the stool in his cell and ate the last piece of brown bread. He didn't know what to think now. It wasn't in any way certain that he would be let out after his trial. The second charge against him made things much worse. He stood up and walked up and down the cell. He gripped the iron bars of the spyhole. He didn't know how he would put in a winter in the jail.

*

The carriage stopped. The guard on the seat opposite opened the door and let down the steps. Michael was handcuffed to the guard Waters. He waited for Waters to stand and, staying close to him so that the handcuff wouldn't dig into his flesh, he followed him across the carriage and down the steps on to the road. The courthouse was a big stone building, built back in from the street, with a wall and railings around it. Waters led him along by the side of the courthouse, under a chestnut tree which was swaying in the wind.

They went in through a small red back door. His head felt apart from the rest of his body. He had been sick for the last few days, and he wasn't completely better yet. He prayed to God to have him set free. He kept his head down as he followed Waters into the courtroom. He hated people seeing him being led along like an animal. Waters led him up two timber steps into the dock, and he stood between the guards. The magistrates were sitting in a row on a raised-up platform close to him.

A man, whom he thought was the court clerk, stood up and read out his name from a big book, and asked him was that him and was that his address. He answered, and he couldn't believe how low and hoarse his voice was. The clerk was whispering and showing something to one of the magistrates. Beams of light were shining across the courtroom. He looked up towards the row of long windows on the wall opposite. Some RIC men were gathered behind the stepped seats at the back of the court. He recognized Rogers who was in a group in the corner, having come to the court to give evidence against him.

"The prisoner is charged with pulling down recruiting posters." The clerk had gone back to his table and was reading out of the book. "And with being in possession of a firearm while in the vicinity of a railway bridge, contravening Regulation 33 of the Defence of the Realm Act."

Waters moved to sit down, and Michael sat beside him on a long narrow form. He looked up into the court. There were groups of people in the seats. He was delighted to see Séamus Walsh and Jim sitting near the front of the court. They saluted him. James Dempsey, Margaret's brother, was up at the back, near the RIC men. He didn't know what James Dempsey was doing there. Joe Walker, a reporter with the *Echo*, was sitting in the front row, scribbling into his notebook. The whole town would be reading about this in next week's paper.

"I now call on Head-Constable O'Connor of Waterford to prosecute," the clerk said.

A tall thin RIC man stood up at the far table. Michael saw Buggy at a table near him.

O'Connor began to speak. "These are two very serious charges before your worships," he said. "The prisoner's action in tearing down recruiting posters was calculated to be prejudicial to recruiting and to the defence of the realm. On the second charge, railways are important to the defence of the realm which is why nobody is allowed in the vicinity of a railway bridge while in possession of any class of a firearm."

One of the magistrates coughed and raised his hand. "If I might ask a question," he said.

"Mr McDonald," the clerk said.

"Was the accused given the option of being tried in Enniscorthy?" McDonald asked.

"No," the head constable said, shrugging and jutting out

his chin as if he didn't care what anybody thought about him.

Buggy stood up. "Mr Carty ought to have been given that choice. Accused ought to be tried in the place in which he is found. It might be as well for your worships to know why this case has come before you here in the city of Waterford. This is but the backwash of what the authorities know the rest of the country would refuse to do. Mr Carty would be guaranteed a fair trial in his home town of Enniscorthy. If he were moved to Dublin the juries there, composed of men of all creeds, and of all shades of political thought, would refuse to do the bidding of the authorities in this preposterous case. The military authorities now ask the magistrates of the city of Waterford to do what no one else would do."

"The accused is in Waterford Jail since the end of May. Is that correct, Constable O'Connor?" McDonald asked.

"Yes," the constable said

"Five petty session courts were allowed to pass, and no attempt was made to bring Mr Carty before them. Is that fair, in your opinion?" McDonald asked.

"I have no opinion on that matter, sir," O'Connor said.

"I have an opinion on the matter, Your Worships," Buggy said, pushing back his chair and standing up again. "It is an absolute violation of the Petition of Rights to keep a man in jail for five weeks notwithstanding the fact that a weekly court was being held in the city."

"Mr Buggy is complaining about the delay, Your Worships," Constable O'Connor said. "Perhaps he would now let us continue with the case. I have some evidence to show your worships – the pieces of the poster which the prisoner tore down, and the revolver which was in his possession on the Railway Bridge."

He handed the pieces of the poster and the revolver to the clerk who laid them in front of the magistrates.

"Constable Rogers will now give evidence," O'Connor said.

Rogers came down from the back of the court and bowed towards the magistrates. The clerk went over and Rogers wrote something into a book.

"At 9.15 on 22nd May, Constable Fleming and I were sent out on special duty," Rogers began. "We concealed ourselves behind a wall on the right hand side of the road leading out of the town."

As soon as Rogers used the word "concealed" Michael knew that someone had written a statement for him and that Rogers had learned it off by heart.

"When Constable Fleming and I approached the prisoner he turned and said 'Goodnight'. He did not realize that we were RIC men. Unfortunately we failed to apprehend the other suspect who disappeared among the crowd of men. The prisoner was found to be in possession of a revolver on the Railway Bridge."

"The Railway Bridge where you claim this incident took place, Constable Rogers," Buggy said. "This Railway Bridge is on the King's Highway between the town of Enniscorthy and the Island Road, is it not?"

Rogers opened his mouth, and looked to the right and the left.

"Constable Rogers, I've asked you a very simple question," Buggy said. "Is the Railway Bridge on the King's Highway?"

Rogers hesitated, as if he wasn't sure what the right answer was. "Yes," he said doubtfully after a while.

O'Connor stood up. "The prosecution case is now concluded."

Rogers went up to the back of the court. Michael was horrified to see James Dempsey putting out his hand to shake hands with Rogers.

The clerk gestured to Mr Buggy who stood up.

"Your Worships," he said, "there are two charges against the prisoner. Pulling down recruiting posters, which there is no clear proof that the prisoner did, couldn't be calculated to seriously interfere with the defence of the realm. The second charge would be serious if the prisoner had been in possession of a revolver while on a railway line, but he was, as Constable Rogers has told us, on the King's Highway. The charge is ridiculous and preposterous. The prisoner is a respectable married man with four children. Mr James Dempsey, a most highly regarded Enniscorthy merchant, will shortly testify to that effect. The military authorities knew that they had no case which would get a guilty verdict so they didn't charge the prisoner for five weeks. If the military authorities continue with actions such as this, an end will be put to all civil freedom."

Buggy sat down. Michael was delighted with the excellent case he had made.

"Mr James Dempsey will now give evidence," the clerk said.

Margaret must have persuaded him to do this. He would hardly have volunteered.

James came down to the front of the court and nodded gravely several times at the magistrates as if he knew them and held them in very high regard. He had put on a lot of weight over the years, and he looked heavy and serious and solemn. The clerk spoke to him and James wrote in the book which the clerk put in front of him. Then he faced the magistrates.

"Your worships, I have known Mr Michael Carty for twenty years or more." He bowed towards Michael as he said his name. He spoke slowly. His accent was slightly posh, and there was a certain haughtiness about James. "Since he first came to Enniscorthy to work for the railway he has made deliveries to my premises in the town. I have always found him to be reliable, courteous, obliging, responsible and honest. I cannot imagine that he would wish to in any way interfere with the defence of the realm." He paused. He seemed to love standing there talking. "I am pleased to have this opportunity to speak to your worships of my high regard for Mr Carty." He hesitated before bowing once more at the magistrates and leaving the stand. One or two of the magistrates were nodding. They seemed very impressed by James Dempsey.

"The case is now concluded," the clerk said as James walked up to his seat.

Michael was astonished at James's performance in the court. It was very nice of him to come to Waterford to speak in his favour even if he didn't mean a word of what he said. The magistrates were standing up and going out through a door on the other side of the court.

"They'll hardly take too long," Waters said to the other guard.

He would know shortly what was going to happen to him. People began to whisper in the court. Some of the RIC men went outside, letting the door of the courtroom bang. He didn't feel that he was there in the court although he knew he was sitting in the dock. He felt he was back up in the cell in the jail but the light from the court was all around him up there. He made himself look around the court and try to face up to whatever was going to happen. Séamus Walsh and Jim nodded their heads at him as if to say that they thought he would get off. Joe Walker from the *Echo* was still writing into his notebook.

The magistrates were coming back. Everyone stood up.

"Having considered the evidence," one of the magistrates said, "we find the prisoner guilty on the first charge of pulling down a recruiting poster, and not guilty on the second charge of being in possession of a firearm on a railway bridge. Accordingly we have decided that the revolver and ammunition are to be forfeited, the prisoner is to be fined a guinea, and is to be imprisoned until this court rises."

"What?" Michael said. "When is that? When does the court rise?"

"Come on," Waters said. "It will be four or five o'clock when the court rises and you can go home then. We'll have to stay here with you. We'll stay in the courthouse. There's no use in going back up to the jail. Where do you live?"

"Enniscorthy," Michael said.

"You'll be able to go home on the train," Waters said.

Chapter 12

People pressed their way slowly out the doors of the cathedral, and then walked briskly across the yard. He stood near the side door, watching out for Dan Hogan. It was bitterly cold. Dan had said that he would bring the horse and cart from the leatherworks to collect Jim. Jim was sick, and they couldn't expect Mrs Byrne to look after him in the lodgings any longer. Margaret was going to turn the parlour into a bedroom for him.

The wind was shaking the bare branches of the trees in the cathedral yard. They walked among the crowd down the street.

"I'll come for you straight away after the dinner," Dan said. "I hope it's not going to rain. It's terrible bad weather to be moving a sick man."

"Tom Byrne said he'd be there to help us," Michael said.

Dan went on into the Market Square and Michael turned down Irish Street. He told himself to walk straight home, not to go down the Island Road, past James Dempsey's shop. The shop would be closed. He wouldn't find out anything walking past it. But still he turned down into Old Barracks. He got work on and off from James Dempsey since he lost his job in the railway. When there was a funeral or when the shop was busy, extra help was needed, and James sent down for him. He had been working there every day in the lead up to Christmas. Walking past the shop he might see someone in the yard or at the door, and find out about a funeral.

The river was full and loud as he came to the Island Road. He glanced up towards the wall where the RIC men had hidden the night they caught him pulling down the recruiting posters. He was always trying to forget that incident. It would have meant nothing at all if he hadn't lost his job over it. He walked down past Dempseys' big three-storied house which looked damp and grey in the cold. There was no one around.

The boys came around the corner of Irish Street on their way to ten Mass.

"Mmmmammy is l-l-l-lighting the f-f-f-fire in the p-p-parlour for Jim," Cormac said, standing right in front of him and looking up at him The stutter was terrible. "I'm g-g-g-going to s-s-s-sit in the p-p-p-parlour with my b-b-b-book and mm-m-mind him," he said.

He went into the house.

"Was there a big crowd at Mass?" Margaret lifted the frying pan as she turned around from the range. She asked him that question every Sunday morning.

"It was packed out." He stood beside her at the range to warm himself. He touched her arm. He loved more than ever to be near her since the time he spent in jail.

"Who said Mass?"

"Father Cummins," he said.

She put an egg and some fried bread on a plate for him. Julianne had brought them eggs from Marshalstown, and they had some money this week. He had worked for three days while James Dempsey had been stocktaking. Margaret's mother had been very good to them, and Jim gave them whatever he had left over from his wages.

He sat at the table. She poured tea for him, and stood beside him cutting slices of bread from a brown loaf.

"Dan says he'll come down straight after dinner," he said.

She put the bread on a plate in front of him. "I'll light the fire before dinner to have the room warm for him." She went over to the sink and began to peel potatoes.

He wondered did she mind taking Jim in. They had no choice. They couldn't expect Mrs Byrne to mind him and there was no place else for him to go. She said she didn't mind. Nothing could be as bad as worrying about someone in jail.

"It's cold to be moving him," she said. She didn't turn around to look at him. "You'll have to bring one of the blankets to cover him. But at least it's not raining."

The cat jumped up on the window ledge and stared in at them through the glass.

*

He sat at the front of the cart with his elbow on the ledge. The sun had broken through the cloud, but it was low in the sky and there was no heat from it. The clatter of the cart and the clop of the horse's hooves sounded loudly in his head. He missed working for the railway, going around the town on the horse and cart. He didn't like being stuck in Dempseys' shop and yard.

"Jim got a hard knock. We'll miss him in the works," Dan said, reining in the horse to turn the corner at the top of Bohreen Hill.

"He loved working with ye," Michael said. "He loved the company."

"He was great fun. He seemed to like everyone," Dan said. "He talked and laughed a lot. Some days all the joviality came easily to him, but other days there'd be an expression on his face, and he'd hesitate, and you'd think that maybe he'd rather not be talking at all. But he'd make himself, and those were the days when he'd be the funniest of all. But some days he would be quiet all day. My father always said that it was the jail, the solitary confinement, catching up with him. He was very quiet the day he got the bad turn," Dan said. They had told Michael this before. Every time he met someone from the leatherworks they told him about this.

"I was putting wood in the stove when he stumbled past me to go to the door. There was a strange stare in his eyes. He fumbled for a while for the twine to pull the door open. We called to ask was he all right but he didn't answer. Whatever way the bad turn was affecting him, God help him, he seemed to need air badly. He wanted to be outside."

They went along the Nunnery Road past the Presentation Convent. Dan tethered the horse to the iron bar jutting out of Byrnes' house.

Mrs Byrne came to the front door. She was a big tall woman with grey hair pulled loosely into a bun at the back of her neck.

"Come on in," she said. "We've finished the dinner and we're waiting for you."

She stood in the middle of the parlour. Stephen Bolger was sitting in an armchair beside a big fire.

"Stephen packed everything up for you, didn't he, Jim?" Mrs Byrne said gently.

They had dressed Jim and put him sitting on the couch in behind the door. He had fallen over on to his bad arm. He was gripping the arm of the couch with his good arm and trying to hold his head up. He smiled a crooked smile, one side of his mouth opening but the other side staying shut. He was pale. Doctor Power had said that nothing could be done for him, that he might last for a year but that was all.

"His clothes are in the case," Mrs Byrne said, pointing at a small brown case tied with a leather strap which was beside the china cabinet inside the door. "His books are in a box in the hall."

"How are you, Jim? I think you're looking a bit better," Dan said.

Jim kept smiling. He said something but it was hard to know what he was saying.

"Will you try to walk, Jim?" Dan asked. "I'll catch one arm and Michael will catch the other."

"I don't think he'll be able to walk, Dan," Mrs Byrne said, moving to stand beside them. "We had to carry him down the stairs and in here. It would be better if they carried you, wouldn't it, Jim?"

Michael and Dan knelt down, one on each side of Jim. They put their arms under his thighs and caught hands, like two adults carrying a child.

"That's the way the men carried him downstairs," Mrs Byrne said.

"Are you all right, Jim?" Dan asked.

"I'll help you." Tom Byrne came into the parlour. "I was out in the back kitchen. I didn't hear ye coming in."

They heaved Jim up between them. As they moved towards the door he slumped heavily forward, but Tom Byrne caught his shoulders and tried to pull him back.

Mrs Byrne was standing back in the hallway to leave room for them. "I hope that hall-stand is not going to get in your way," she said. "We should have moved it before you started."

"I'd say we'll be all right," Michael said. He moved slowly sideways, leading the way. The doorway was too narrow, and Tom Byrne had to let go of Jim and wait behind in the parlour. Jim's head lolled sideways. Mrs Byrne tried to straighten him up. "Mind him," she said. "Mind his head. Don't hit him off the hall-stand."

They carried him down the hall and out through the

front door. Tom Byrne ran out after them to help lift him on to the cart. Jim kept smiling but they could see that he was finding the move very hard.

"He might be better lying down," Mrs Byrne said. "You have a pillow there, and cover him up with the blanket."

Michael and Dan knelt on either side of Jim, and pulled him into the middle of the cart.

Stephen Bolger had followed them out to the door.

"Go back inside, Stephen," Mrs Byrne said. "If that cold goes down on to your chest you'll get a terrible dose."

"Won't you all come down to see him?" Michael said, turning back to face them. "Margaret said to be sure to say that."

"We will, of course," Mrs Byrne said. She was crying.

"He'll be as right as rain in a few weeks," Tom Byrne said, touching her arm. "He'll be grand."

"I know. I know," she said. "But I'm going to miss him. I always get too fond of lodgers. I hate to see them go." The tears were streaming down her face. "Goodbye, Jim," she said. "I'll come down to see you."

*

The light was beginning to fade. He stood up from the armchair at the fire and lit the oil lamp. Jim seemed to have dozed off again. He kept falling over to one side in the bed and someone had to lift him back up. Cormac was sitting beside the bed reading a book.

He closed the shutters and went into the kitchen. Aidan and Philip were at the table doing their lessons. Margaret was sorting clothes at the range.

"Jim was delighted that the Lamberts called to see him," he said.

"It will keep his spirits up to have visitors," she said. "Kitty said she'd call down tonight."

"I'll be going out, going up to the history lecture in Antwerp later," he said. "I'll ask some of the men to come to visit him." He thought he might go and sit in Redmonds' pub for a while after the lecture but he didn't mention that. They had little enough money and he shouldn't spend any of it on drink.

"What's the lecture about tonight?" Philip asked.

"I'd say it will be about the Plantation of Ulster." He sat down at the table opposite the two boys. Aidan kept writing but Philip looked up at him. "Last week it was about the Battle of Kinsale, the Treaty of Mellifont and the Flight of the Earls," he said. "O'Neill and O'Donnell were tired of the oppression and the struggle. They led their followers on board ship in Lough Swilly, and set sail for Europe, never again to return to their native country."

"It's hard to imagine how they just left, turned their backs on it all and went away," Philip said.

"They had suffered so badly, and they had lost," Michael said. "It was too much to bear. They wanted a normal ordinary life, but we shouldn't blame them for leaving. They had played their part."

They heard Cormac laughing in the parlour.

"Jim must be after waking up now," Margaret said. "He didn't stay asleep long."

"They're playing the game with their hands again," Michael said, smiling. He stood up, and turned around to the baby.

"Do you want to come inside to play a game with us?"

The baby stretched out his arms, and Michael lifted him up. He carried him into the parlour and put him sitting on the side of the bed.

Cormac's hand was on top of Jim's paralyzed hand which was flat on the blanket. Michael put his hand next, then took the baby's pudgy little hand and laid it on his. The baby looked very serious as if he was concentrating on the game. He seemed to have to make a big effort not to let his hand slip back towards himself. Jim put his good hand next, then Cormac spread his hand on top, next Michael, and finally the baby stretched out his little hand, almost falling over as he did so.

"It's a tower," Michael said. "It's a castle."

They all watched one another then, and watched the hands, waiting to see who would be the first to pull out a hand and break the castle down, but at the same time not wanting the castle to be broken down. Small children loved this game. Michael had always thought that he couldn't remember his mother but Jim had told him that she used to play this game with them when they were small, and now the touch of other hands on his brought back to him a hazy memory of the touch of his mother's hands. He thought he could now remember his mother's presence in the house in Kilbride, too. But maybe he was only imagining memories since Jim had talked to him about their mother.

The baby's hand had almost slipped off the top of the tower, Cormac was moving his hand to make them think that he was going to break down the tower, but it was Jim who pulled his good hand out first. Cormac quickly pulled out his two hands, and the baby roared laughing as the tower collapsed. They all laughed. Jim made a strange low chesty sound. His laugh was different since he had the bad turn.

"Again," the baby shouted.

*

Martin Webster and Joe Morrissey were putting out the chairs for Brother Browne's history lecture when he arrived in Antwerp. The fire had gone down low, and the big front room was freezing. There were some men standing at the window talking. Martin asked him about Jim, and they all stopped talking to listen. People all over the town were asking about Jim.

"It was so sudden," a man said. "I was talking to him on Christmas Eve and he seemed to be in great form."

"Himself and Stephen Bolger spent Christmas Day with us," Michael said, "and we didn't notice anything different about him."

"How long is he home now?" Martin Webster asked.

"A little more than a year," Michael said.

He went over to fix the fire. More men were arriving for the lecture. He put a block of wood at the back of the grate, and he used the tongs to pick out big pieces of coal to cover the dying embers at the front. When he turned around Brother Browne was walking up the room with the big notebook full of history notes under his arm. He stopped to talk to some of the men. He was the Superior in the Christian Brothers. He had a big face and dark eyes with very bushy eyebrows. He would probably talk on and on tonight for hours and hours. There would be questions and a discussion afterwards. Michael knew suddenly that he couldn't listen to it. He would have to get out of Antwerp. He couldn't stay. He took a step away from the fire. He was going to go up now, straight away, and sit at the counter in Redmond's pub. He couldn't bear to listen to a history lecture, not tonight of all nights, after moving Jim. He walked over towards the window. He would have to get out quickly before the lecture started. He didn't want to offend Brother Browne. He circled around a group of men and walked down between the chairs and the wall. He hoped no one would stop him and start talking to him. He glanced up as he walked along the back of the room. Some of the men were sitting down waiting for the lecture to start, the others were still standing in groups talking but he didn't think anyone had noticed him. The floor-boards creaked as he went out the door. He ran down the stairs. He couldn't believe his luck that there was nobody coming upstairs.

He felt guilty as he went out into Mary Street but still he was delighted to have got away. He thought of a prisoner escaping as he walked up Slaney Street in the cold although he knew that it wouldn't be as easy as that to get out of a jail. He was looking forward to sitting up at a bar counter and having a drink. The wet steps in Slaney Street were shining under the light of the street lamp. He crossed the road, and decided to go for a bit of a walk, up Church Street and down George's Street, before going in to the pub.

He walked along by Dwyer-Broe's. The big front doors of the Athenaeum were open, and the lights were on. He wondered was James Dempsey in there. James Dempsey, Margaret's brother, was a member of the Athenaeum. The Dempseys were still losing business because they had given him work after the court case. A few days before Christmas a neighbour of the Dempseys, Jack O'Toole, had died, and his funeral on the Island Road, which should have gone to James, went instead to Tom Bolger, the other undertaker in the town. Jack O'Toole had fought in the British Army during the Boer War, and his sons were off fighting in Flanders. Jack had been very bitter about the Split in the Volunteers and everybody knew that his family wouldn't let Dempseys bury him because Michael Carty who had pulled down the recruiting posters worked there. James didn't say a word about the funeral, but Willie Comerford who worked in the shop kept talking about it. Willie had talked a lot, too, when the RIC had cancelled the monthly fuel order in Dempseys a few days after James spoke up for Michael in the court.

He turned the corner and went up Church Street. The trees in the church grounds were creaking in the wind. Margaret had said that she didn't know how James had got the fuel order from the RIC in the first place. The RIC hadn't done business in the shop in her father's time. They normally dealt in the Protestant shops but James was a great businessman. It was Margaret who had asked James to go to the court case in Waterford. Walsh and Fennelly didn't think that James would agree to go because the RIC would pick on whoever did. Mr Buggy said he wanted a wealthy respectable merchant as a character witness, someone with no Republican connections.

"They all thought I was only wasting my time asking him," Margaret said. "I didn't like having to ask him but I didn't think he'd refuse. 'That will be grand,' he said. He made no fuss at all. He became very still like Julianne used to do years ago. He was probably imagining himself in the courtroom, impressing the magistrates. That's what James is like. He likes to win."

"He spoke very well. He gave such a good account of me that I hardly recognized myself," Michael said. He was very excited. It was his first night home from the jail.

"I hope the RIC won't pick on him," she said.

"He kept talking to them. He spent ages at the back of the court talking to that fool, Rogers."

"James wouldn't really care about Rogers," Margaret said. "James doesn't care about many people, but he likes to appear to be on good terms with everyone, and to get the better of them if he can."

He walked into George's Street which was deserted. The whole town was deserted. It was very cold. A few drops of rain fell. The children had been hoping for snow, and days off school. He turned into the Market Square, and went in to Benny Redmond's. There were four men from the country, sitting in a line along the side of the bar, and two others sitting back on the low seat near the fire. Lucy Redmond came out from the darkness of the back room.

"Hello, Michael." She spoke in a slow drawl. People around the town often imitated her, but Michael thought she was a lovely lady.

He sat on his own near the end of the counter.

"What can I get you, Michael?" She moved her fingers over the rolls of her hair. Her hair was always in rolls, around the front of her head, and along the sides.

"A bottle of stout," he said.

"A bottle of stout," she repeated smiling. Lucy was always very nice to him because she had been in Margaret's class in the Loreto Convent years ago. Neither Lucy nor Benny had ever referred to the recruiting posters or his time in jail. They wouldn't approve of things like that. They were very careful people.

"We were all very upset about your brother," Lucy said as she took the top off the bottle. "It was terrible, and we had all grown so fond of him."

"We moved him down to our house today," Michael said.

She stood in front of him, holding the bottle and the glass. "He was in here with us the night before he took the bad turn, and he seemed to be in great form," she said. "Isn't it frightening to think how quickly a person can go downhill? You'd want to be all the time at peace with God because you'd never know the day nor the hour when He'd call you." She put the bottle and the glass down on the counter in front of him.

One of the men at the side of the counter gestured to order another round, and she went over to serve them.

"Yes, men," she said, moving her fingers slowly over the rolls of her hair. She took up a cloth and wiped the counter.

He poured some of the stout into the glass. Jim would last another year maybe, but that was all, Doctor Power had said. People who had only known Jim for a short while were very upset about his sickness. He took a drink of the stout.

The fire was hissing behind him. He had known Jim since he was a child although he couldn't remember much about the early years in Kilbride and he had lost contact with him for a while. But it had been great when Jim came home. Jim and himself had talked a few times about the past. Jim had told stories about their mother. Once it had rained and rained every day for weeks in Kilbride. The hens got dropsy and had to be slaughtered. It was shortly before their mother died, and she must have been sick even then. She couldn't bear to stay in the yard or the house for the slaughter, Jim said.

"I remember her taking you by the hand. You were very small," he said. "She walked slowly up the lane. I stayed with my father. The yard was full of feathers for days afterwards."

Michael knew that he was foolish but he liked this story. Although he couldn't remember he was delighted that his mother had brought him with her. His mother must have loved him.

He had told Jim about their father's death and wake and funeral. He had told him, too, about how he had left Kilbride without saying a word. He didn't like talking about it, remembering it, but Jim wanted to know. Sometimes Michael remembered things that had happened but he didn't feel that he was the person they had happened to. He didn't feel he was the person who had been in Kilbride, or the person who had spent years working for the railway. Sometimes he didn't feel he was anybody at all. Margaret and the thought of Irish freedom brought him back to himself. Margaret loved remembering their life together. She talked sometimes with great joy about the good times they had had. He often felt uneasy when she would begin to remember, afraid that he might have forgotten what she remembered or that something bad might have happened to him in the story she was going to tell. "Do you remember the day?" or "Do you remember the time?" she would say. He would feel tense, as if her memory was going to exclude or hurt him, but it never did. She thought of their life together as happy and good. He tried to let himself be sucked in to her memories. He would smile and laugh as she talked but he was always glad when she moved on to talk about the present or the future.

Two men came in to the bar and Lucy Redmond served them. Benny Redmond came in and took off his coat, and Lucy went upstairs. Michael ordered another drink. He would have to make sure to leave before the lecture in Antwerp ended. Some of the men might come in to Redmonds' and he didn't want to draw attention to the fact that he hadn't been at the lecture. He had been out from home long enough. More than ever since he was in jail he loved going back home. There was no one like Margaret. His unjust imprisonment had turned her into a great Republican supporter.

More men came in to the pub. The pubs were always busy late on a Sunday night. He was delighted when he saw Joe Lambert coming in. Joe should have been at the lecture in Antwerp, too.

"I fell asleep at the fire after tea," he said, sitting on the stool beside Michael.

Doctor Power came up behind them. There was a stranger, a big tall middle-aged man, with him. The doctor ordered two whiskies.

"Sit down, Doctor," Benny said. "I'll bring you over the drinks."

Doctor Power and the stranger sat down near the door. Benny lifted the flap in the wooden counter and brought the drinks over to the two men.

"Do you see the man with Doctor Power?" Joe Lambert's voice was low under the hum of conversation in the bar.

"That's the new RIC Sergeant, McCrory, Jones's replacement. He's getting a drink on the house."

Michael glanced quickly around. Benny Redmond was shaking hands with the new sergeant who was standing up, smiling, looking as if he was a very nice person when there was no doubt that he was a thug just like the rest of the RIC. Another man came over from the counter and shook hands with the sergeant, too.

"A big welcome for a traitor," Joe Lambert said quietly.

"It's terrible," Michael said. "They're making a big fuss of him. He should be shunned in all decent company."

"It's very cold outside," Joe said loudly as Benny Redmond passed behind them.

It was as well not to let anyone know how strongly they felt.

"It is," Michael said.

He hoped his voice sounded calm but he felt very angry. It was terrible to see an RIC man, a representative of the Crown, a traitor, being welcomed to a rebel town like Enniscorthy. The sooner they had a Rising the better. He couldn't wait to see the flag of the Irish Republic fly over every building in the town.

Chapter 13

April 1916

It was pitch dark in the bedroom. Margaret had stayed awake. Michael was asleep beside her. The Rising was going to start at two o'clock in the morning. He had said that it wasn't worthwhile going to bed but she had persuaded him to try to get some sleep, promising to waken him in time. At last, after days of uncertainty, Dublin had been taken over by the Volunteers, and instructions had come from Pearse that the men in Enniscorthy were to rise, too. She was expecting another child. She hadn't said anything to Michael about it. They had been too preoccupied with talk of the Rising for her to mention it. She couldn't bear the thought of having another baby.

She got out of bed and fumbled on the dressing table for the matches. She lit the candle and looked at the clock.

"Michael," she said. "It's time to get up."

"All right," he said.

She went downstairs and lit the oil lamp in the kitchen. It was cold. She got her coat in the hall and put it on. The parlour door was open. It was always left open so that they would hear if Jim called them during the night. She went back into the kitchen and began to set the table. She was delighted about the Rising. The Lamberts would be overjoyed. They had been so bitter yesterday. They thought then that the time for a Rising had come and gone, that a

215

glorious opportunity had been squandered. Joan had been making a rhubarb tart when Margaret went into the kitchen. One of the uncles was sitting in a chair near the fire.

"We've just found out that it's all Eoin MacNéill's fault," Joan had said, turning around from the dresser. "The Rising, we were told, was supposed to start after the parade on Easter Sunday, but MacNéill put that notice in the *Sunday Independent* cancelling the parade."

Margaret thought of asking who had told them about Eoin MacNéill but she knew that they wouldn't tell her. They usually had all the Republican news but they would never say how they found it out.

"Wouldn't you be surprised at Eoin MacNeill?" Margaret said. "Wasn't it Eoin MacNéill, along with Douglas Hyde, who set up the Gaelic League?"

"I never had any time for John MacNeill," the uncle said.

She stirred the range. She took the delft from the dresser, and knives and spoons from the drawer. Michael was moving around upstairs. There had been so many rumours during the past week. Michael had been working for James during Holy Week, but business was slack after Easter and he had nothing to do. He went in and out to Lamberts where he heard all the news. Roger Casement had been captured on Banna Strand, trying to smuggle arms in from Germany, and word had spread that all the Volunteers were going to be arrested.

He came down the stairs. She could never get used to seeing him in a uniform. For an instant she wanted to go back to bed with him, but she told herself to stop.

"I'll make tea when the kettle boils," she said.

"Don't go to any trouble," he said. "I can't believe that this day has at last come." He sat down at the table.

"This is history," she said, cutting slices of bread. "You're going out to make history."

"Other people were beginning to lose hope," he said. "But after listening to Pearse speaking at the Emmet commemoration I knew that there would be a Rising. And do you remember what he said at O'Donovan Rossa's funeral? 'Life springs from death; and from the graves of patriot men and women spring living nations.'"

She didn't like him mentioning life springing from anywhere. She wondered had he guessed about the baby. "It was a great speech, the best speech I ever read," she said quickly. "'The Defenders of this Realm have worked well in secret and in the open.'" She sat up straight in the chair, looking at him as if she was trying to convince him with the oratory. "'They think that they have pacified Ireland. They think that they have pacified half of us and intimidated the other half. They think that they have foreseen everything, think that they have provided against everything; but the fools, the fools, the fools! – they have left us our Fenian dead, and while Ireland holds these graves, Ireland unfree shall never be at peace.'"

"It's a great speech," he said. "There should be clapping and cheering when you finish it."

She laughed. "We don't want to waken the children." She stood up and made tea.

"I hate leaving you with Jim," he said after a while. "Will you be able to manage?"

"I will, of course," she said. "The boys will help me."

"I'll go in and say goodbye to him."

He took up the candle and went into the parlour. She could hear him talking to Jim.

"You're after falling down. Will I help you?"

Jim had fallen sideways off the pillows. He couldn't get back up on his own, but he would always try, and frown and groan first when he couldn't manage, but then he would laugh at himself for not being able to move. He always tried to appear as if he was in very good humour. She wrapped the bread and went to the parlour door. Michael had put the candle down on the mantelpiece. Jim was lying straight in the middle of the pillows.

"We're going to get rid of them at last. This is our chance. We'll do it this time," Michael said.

A big broad smile came across half of Jim's face. One half of his mouth stayed closed, and the other half opened crookedly, far too wide. He said something.

"What?" Michael asked.

Jim's face twisted and he frowned as he made a big effort to speak clearly.

"Good luck," he said, trying to open his mouth wide.

She went into the room and stood beside Michael.

"We'll be praying for you," she said, "won't we, Jim?"

"Goodbye," Michael said.

He walked behind her out of the room. For an instant she wished she could go with him, join with the women in Cumann na mBan. It would be easier to fight in a Rising than to stay at home and carry a baby for months and then give birth to it.

*

The sky was full of stars. It was cold. He could hear the river rushing along as he turned up Irish Street. He tapped on Kehoes' window, and stood on the top step, waiting for Jimmy to come to the door. The pikes for the Rising, which were made by Cleary, the blacksmith in Templeshannon, were hidden in a cave at the side of a rock in Kehoes' backyard. Jimmy Kehoe opened the door, and Michael followed him into the kitchen. Several men were carrying pikes in from the yard. They were talking but Michael wasn't listening. He was thinking about Jim. Jim was probably going to die soon.

The men stood some of the pikes in the corner of the kitchen and put more of them lying against the banisters of the stairs.

Jimmy gave Michael a pike. "I can't believe that this day has at last come," he said. "After all the years."

There was a knock on the window and more men came into the kitchen.

"Take a pike each, lads, and go on," Jimmy said. "I'll stay here until all the pikes are given out."

The men talked in low voices as they walked up the Irish Street in the dark. Volunteers from the Duffry were coming down Main Street. There was a big crowd of Volunteers standing on the road outside the Athenaeum which was going to be their headquarters during the Rising. More men came into the street, but he could see no sign of Walshe or Fennelly.

"What's the delay?" a man asked. "Where's Fennelly?"

"It's not two o'clock yet," someone answered.

Captain Joe Morrissey began to walk around, telling the men to get into marching formation, six abreast on the street. Morrissey was a big tall young fellow from the Shannon who had come to the fore in the movement during the last few months.

"Move back a bit, lads," he said. "Back a bit further." He loved giving orders, even when orders weren't really necessary. He didn't seem to realize that some of the men resented him.

Michael rested the pike on the ground. He was standing near the footpath, a few rows back from the Athenaeum. Some women from Cumann na mBan were on the path outside Dwyer-Broes' shop. The women planned to set up a hospital for the wounded in the ballroom of the Athenaeum. The different duties to be carried out during the Rising had been assigned weeks before, and Michael had been told that he would be on patrol duty in John Street with Senan Murphy, a young Volunteer from Tomnalossett.

"Here's Walshe," someone said.

Walshe and Fennelly had come around the corner from Slaney Street. They walked past the men, going along the path to the Athenaeum. Every time Michael saw them he felt grateful to them for visiting him in the jail and arranging for Buggy to defend him. As they reached the front of the march Walshe handed something to Fennelly. Fennelly stopped on the path, and both he and Walshe began to laugh. Michael felt proud to be part of a movement which had such good leaders. He admired Walshe and Fennelly. They were fearless and decisive. As soon as they got the order from Pearse they started the Rising. Enniscorthy was in an important strategic position, Pearse had said. By taking over Enniscorthy they could block British reinforcements going from the port of Rosslare to Dublin.

"Walshe is after giving me the key. Walshe is a member of the Athenaeum." Fennelly was walking back down the path talking to the men. Michael had never seen him so excited. "We won't have to break down the door," he said, waving the big key on a loop of cord. He turned back to unlock the huge door.

A group of men came around the corner from Castle Hill, and Morrissey told them to go to the back of the march. Walshe asked the first row of men to come into the Athenaeum with him to light the lamps.

"Final instructions will be given inside," Fennelly shouted from the top step of the Athenaeum. "Those in charge of blocking and guarding approaches to the town, taking over the railway station and tearing up the railway lines are to go to the rink at the back of the building." He gestured over his shoulder into the hallway of the Athenaeum. "The group who are going to cut the telephone and telegraph wires will meet in the office. Those in charge of commandeering supplies and issuing instructions to shops and businesses are to go upstairs to the ballroom. Those patrolling the streets will go to the reading-room, and the men who are to lead the attack on the RIC barracks are to go out to the backyard."

The lights were coming on inside the building. Walshe came out on to the steps, and stood beside Fennelly. Morrissey gestured to the men who began to march in single file into the Athenaeum. Michael knew that this Thursday of Easter week 1916 was the most important day in his life. This was the day that past generations of Irish people had looked forward to, and that future generations would look back on, with pride. Irishmen were working together and rising up all over the country, and today he could play his part in ending the British presence in Ireland once and for all. When his turn came to move he lifted the heavy pike, and marched up the steps, looking towards Walshe and Fennelly who were standing to attention watching the men pass by. He felt at one with Walshe and Fennelly, and with all the Volunteers throughout the country, with Pearse, Mac Diarmada and the other leaders in Dublin. They had all dedicated themselves to the cause of Irish freedom. As he went into the Athenaeum he told himself that he would do his best to follow all instructions to further the cause.

He turned into the reading-room. There were four or five Volunteers there before him. He stood behind one of the armchairs. There was a high table near the window with newspapers on it, and all around the room there were glass presses full of books. He would love to be one of the class of people who had enough money to be members of the Athenaeum and sit here in the evenings reading books and newspapers.

More Volunteers crowded in to the room. Senan Murphy who was going to be on patrol duty with him stayed just inside the door. Morrissey came in after a while. He had sheets of paper in his hand. He went across the room, and stood at the fireplace with his elbow on the mantelpiece. There was very little noise even though the room was crowded, but Michael could feel the excitement all around him. The men answered "*anseo*" when Morrissey called out their names. There was no one absent.

"We're not expecting trouble," Morrisey said, folding up the lists of names. "We're going to close all the pubs. Most citizens will behave sensibly. All businesses and workplaces will be closed except the gas company and bakeries, so very few people will be going to work. Warn people about their behaviour. Tell those who want to join us to come down here to headquarters. March in the middle of the road. Leave the pikes behind you. Walshe says that they're too heavy. Make sure that people see you, and tell them what's happening."

Senan was waiting out in the hall. He had a rifle. Michael had Jim's revolver. He put the pike in the corner and they went outside into the dark. They went up Church Street and along Court Street under Letts' high trees. They marched in the middle of the road from Letts' gate at the town end of the street, past the lane leading down into the Folly, and along to the fountain at the end of the street.

"Nobody will come out until it gets bright," Senan said. "It's still the middle of the night."

They marched up and down in the dark. At the town end of the street the houses were two-storied with good slate roofs, but at the country end there was a row of small thatched cabins. There was nothing moving anywhere on the street. They stopped several times to talk to the two Volunteers who were patrolling Court Street. It was quiet in Court Street, too.

"I wouldn't say anyone here will be going to work," Senan said after a while. Senan worked behind the counter in the co-op. He passed through John Street every day on his way to work. "There's no one in John Street working for the gas company. There's no baker here either, is there?"

"I don't think so," Michael said, "but I wouldn't know this street as well as you."

"Most of the men from the town end of John Street work out in Bonds' mills. I wouldn't say they'll be too pleased when they hear about the Rising," Senan said.

"No," Michael said. Colonel Henry James Bond who owned the mill was in charge of the National Volunteers, and he encouraged men to enlist in the British Army. Henry James's brother, Freddie Bond, was off fighting in the war.

After a while a grey light replaced the darkness, but the stars were still in the sky. They could see the trees and the high wall around the workhouse. They turned towards Court Street and looked across at Vinegar Hill.

"We must be after walking up and down here hundreds of times," Senan said.

Michael took out the bread that he had brought with him and gave some of it to Senan. They marched down the street and got a drink from the fountain.

"There's only one star left in the sky," Michael said after a while. "It's nearly day."

They were close to Letts' gate again when they heard what sounded like gunfire in the distance. Crows flew in fright out of Letts' trees.

"The sound is coming from down near the river," Senan said. "I'd say it's the attack on the RIC barracks."

There were only about twenty RIC men in the town and they would have to surrender, sooner or later. Michael remembered the little cell at the back of the RIC barracks where he had spent the night after he was caught pulling down the recruiting posters. He remembered Rogers and Fleming dragging him across the Abbey Square and pushing him into the long room at the side of the barracks. He had been such a coward that night, and he would rather forget all about it. There was another volley of gunfire. A man leaned out of an upstairs window and looked at them. Doors opened along the street and people came out and stood together and walked a little bit towards the town. Some of them were dressed, but others had coats on over their nightclothes. A woman and some children came up from the Folly Lane. The woman stood in the middle of the street with her arms out, looking confused. The children stood around her.

"We'll go and tell them what's happening," Senan said.

The woman from the Folly came over to them. Michael had often seen her around the town. He had once seen her begging in the Market Square. Her face was full of wrinkles.

"What's wrong?" She came up close to Senan.

"Wait now. Wait now," Senan said, holding out his arms to keep her from coming too near him.

"We're having a Rising," Michael said to her.

The people from John Street came over to them. Michael could see that they were impressed by the Volunteer uniforms and Senan's rifle. There was more gunfire in the distance.

"We have declared an independent Irish Republic," Senan said. "We are having a Rising to end British rule in Ireland."

The people from John Street looked away towards Court Street and said nothing.

"They're having a Rising. A Rising," the woman from the Folly said. She sounded like a well-off woman agreeing with something very pleasant.

"You can't leave the town without a pass," Senan said. "You have to go to the Athenaeum to get a pass."

"All workplaces are closed except the gas company and

bakeries," Michael said. "Everyone is to stay inside. But people who want to join us can go to our headquarters in the Athenaeum."

"Join you? Are you mad or what?" A man asked. "You'll all end up in jail. An independent Irish Republic, my arse."

"We can't go to work? We won't get paid," another man said walking away. "Will youse pay us?" he turned back and shouted at them.

The other people shrugged and, shaking their heads disapprovingly, went back towards their houses.

"You're after having a Rising," the woman from the Folly repeated, smiling.

Michael wasn't sure if the woman understood what a Rising meant.

Two of her children had wandered off up towards Court Street. The others were standing looking up at her.

"It would be better to keep the children in off the street," Senan said. "There might be more shooting."

"I'll bring them home. I won't let them out again," she said. She grabbed one of the children by the arm and hit him three or four times on the head. "Go home," she shouted, looking to see were Senan and Michael pleased with her. "Go home. Don't you know I never let you out on the street?" The child cried and struggled to get away from her, but she kept hitting him.

"Come on," Senan said.

As they marched down the street they saw a very thin man wearing a big hat standing at the corner of the Folly Lane.

"That's the woman's husband. The woman who came up from the Folly," Senan said. "Tom Landers is his name. He goes on the batter and puts them all out on to the lane in the middle of the night. But when he's on the dry he doesn't let her leave the house. He gives her a terrible life."

No one came out from the cabins at the country end of the street.

"They must be all still in bed," Senan said.

They turned at the fountain and marched again towards Letts' gate. The Volunteers in Court Street were waiting to tell them what had happened.

"Two of the policemen were trying to get into the barracks," one of the Volunteers said. "Our lads started to stone the barracks, and the policemen had to hide in the Bank of Ireland. The RIC are shooting at us, and we're shooting back. I'd love to go down and shoot at some of them fellas."

"I hate that Sergeant," Senan said.

They continued their patrol of the street for several more hours. Things were quiet.

"The people are afraid of us," Aidan said. "They're keeping their front doors closed. All the doors in John Street are usually wide open."

Some people from the cabins came out after a while. Most of them said nothing but one man laughed jeeringly when they told him about the Rising.

"You're awful eejits," he said, shaking his head.

It had turned into a beautiful warm spring day. Children came out several times on to the street, and they sent them back inside. Women went to the fountain for water. It was well into the morning when a Volunteer told them to go down to the Athenaeum to get something to eat.

"I'll patrol here," he said. "We have plenty of food. A bread van from Wexford was held up, and some of the men went to the grocery shops to commandeer ham, sugar and tea. The women are serving the food in the rink, out at the back."

There were six or seven men sitting at a long table in the rink. One of the Lambert uncles, Joe, was talking to Jimmy

Kehoe. Peter Paul Gilligan was there, and Martin Webster. It was Gilligan who had brought the message from Pearse that Enniscorthy was to rise. He had gone to Dublin to the races, and hearing about the Rising, he managed to get into the GPO to Pearse. He had travelled back the whole way from Dublin to Enniscorthy on a bicycle. There must have been messengers like Gilligan sent to every town in the country.

"The shopkeepers were raging when we went to commandeer the food," Jimmy Kehoe was saying. He was sitting at the head of the table. "But they didn't say too much when they saw the guns. We woke Tom Kielthy up when we knocked on the door. He was in his pyjamas, with his hair all sticking out. Young Jerry Doyle who works behind the counter for Kielthy was with us. He was delighted with himself pointing the gun at Kielthy."

"You knocked on the door? That was the mistake you made," Joe Lambert said. "I'd kick the doors in."

"Kelly didn't say a word when we went into the railway station," Martin Webster said to Michael. "He was afraid when he saw the guns."

"How are things up in John Street?" Peter Paul Gilligan asked.

"It's very quiet," Senan said. "There are no shops up there."

The women put plates of meat in front of Senan and Michael.

"There's plenty of bread, plenty of everything," they said. They made fresh tea.

A Volunteer came to the door after a while. "Rogers, the RIC man is after getting injured," he said, grinning. "He was sitting on one of the beds in the barracks shooting out at us, but one of us shot him in the leg. Walshe says that we'll allow a car to bring him to hospital."

Rogers was so stupid that although he was inside the barracks he couldn't even stay out of the line of fire.

"It serves Rogers right. I'm delighted to hear it," Martin Webster said.

"Wasn't it Rogers who arrested you last summer, Michael?" Peter Paul Gilligan asked.

"It was," Michael said. "He arrested me and he came down to the court to give evidence against me. He learned a speech off by heart and he stood up in the court and said it. He said all sorts of things about me." He laughed.

A Cumann na mBan woman came into the rink. "Everyone is to go outside," she said. "We have the flag ready, and we're going to raise it at noon. We want everyone who is not engaged in an essential duty to come outside to salute the flag of the Republic."

They stood up and went outside. Michael was delighted that he was going to witness the tricolour being raised above the town. It seemed very bright outside on the street after the dark inside the Athenaeum. There were groups of Volunteers standing around. Fennelly was there, describing how they had felled trees and were using them to block the roads.

"The British will never get into the town," he said. "We have all the roads blocked off."

"Most of the British troops are out in France," a man said. "We needn't worry about them. What about Wexford? Did Wexford rise? And Gorey?"

"I don't know," Fennelly said, "but I'd say they will when they hear about us, or when they get a message from Pearse."

"The whole country must be up in arms by now," another man said.

Walshe came out on to the steps of the Athenaeum and told the men to get into rows ready to salute the flag. Michael stood with Aidan near Dwyer-Broes'. He had a good view of the roof of the Athenaeum.

"The roof is flat behind the parapet," Senan said. "The women will be safe enough."

Walshe went over to the footpath outside the National Bank, and looked up at the roof, waiting for the women to come out. Fennelly took out his revolver. They must have decided that it was Fennelly who would have the honour of firing the shots after the tricolour was raised. Three women in Cumann na mBan uniforms came out on to the roof. Michael recognized them – Una Brennan, Gretta Comerford and Marion Stokes. They were in the Gaelic League and he had often met them in Lambert's. They leaned over the parapet looking for the flag-holder which usually held the Union Jack, but today would hold the flag of the Irish Republic.

"It's right in the middle," Walshe called up to them. "Over a bit to your left where the parapet is at its highest. That's it. You have it."

The men were all looking up. There was dead silence as Gretta Comerford unfurled the flag from around the top of the flagstaff and held it high above the Athenaeum. Michael felt a lot of different emotions, quickly, one after another, as he looked up at the green, white and orange tricolour. He was delighted that they had taken over the town of Enniscorthy in the name of the Irish Republic. He was proud to belong to the Republican Brotherhood, and to a great race of people who had suffered British tyranny for seven hundred years, yet had never given up the fight. He felt love for Ireland, for Caitlín Ní hUalacháin.

Walsh had crossed the road and had gone up to the top step of the Athenaeum. Gretta Comerford settled the flagstaff into the flag-holder. The tricolour stood above the town.

"In the name of God," Walsh said, "salute the flag of the Republic."

Michael raised his hand to his forehead, keeping his eyes all the time on the tricolour. He was full of joy that he was present at this historic moment with Walsh and Fennelly, and all his comrades-in-arms. He felt a great affection for them all. He looked down to see them, standing around him on the street, and then he thought of Jim who was dying, and his father who was dead. They would have given everything to be here on this day.

A shot rang out in tribute to the flag. He felt anger and contempt towards all the Irishmen who were fighting for Britain in the war. He would fight and, if necessary, die for the cause of Ireland, although he didn't want to die. A second shot rang out, and a third.

He was standing on the street, looking up again at the flag, and then he was startled when he realized that the ceremony was over. There was a low hum of talk. The men were moving back into the Athenaeum. Senan had gone on ahead. He followed them, but he didn't feel he was there, even though he could see that he was walking up the steps and through the hall of the Athenaeum. But it seemed as if a huge part of him had left him, and had gone off somewhere, leaving him with no sense of himself or where he was.

The men were talking in the rink.

"That was great, wasn't it?" Senan said to him.

He nodded, and smiled. He felt as if he was nobody. He couldn't think of what to say. He was glad to be with all these people, and he was grateful to them for including him. He was very fond of them all.

"It's a pity Jim Carty is not well enough to be here," someone said.

Senan looked at him. "Jim. Your brother, Jim," he said. "It's a pity he's not here."

There was silence, and then he realized that they were waiting for him to acknowledge the mention of his brother.

"Yes, yes," he said.

But they had begun to talk about something else, and he knew that it had looked as if he didn't care about Jim.

"I went into Jim before I came out," he said, "and he wished us the best of luck."

But nobody was listening to him. They had moved on to something else. They were talking about how the train had been stopped at Edermine, and the people sent back to Wexford.

He was glad to go back up to John Street, and walk up and down with Senan. He came gradually back to himself as he walked up and down, and the rest of the day passed quickly. The Volunteers in Court Street waited for them every now and then and told them what was happening elsewhere. Father Kehoe from the Mission House had come to the Athenaeum to bless the men. He had said that he would offer up Mass for them every morning. He was the only one of the priests who was on their side. At least in '98 the priests were on the side of the people.

They heard that the Court House where the National Volunteers stored their arms had been taken over by Morrissey and some of the men. There wasn't even a shot fired because there was no one there. The castle was taken over, too, and the Bennetts told to leave.

"They gave no trouble at all," the Volunteer said. "Walsh went into them. Walsh is good at talking to people. The Bennetts just did what they were told."

When it was getting dark, Morrissey arrived into the street with two young fellows whom Michael had never seen before. They didn't have Volunteer uniforms but had big "Irish Republican Police" armbands.

"We have two new recruits here. They came in from

Courtnacuddy to join us and we're delighted to welcome them," Morrissey said. He sounded different, not like himself. He sounded charming, like Walsh did sometimes. "The two of you can go and get some sleep now," he said smiling. "The new recruits will take over."

There were more new recruits in the hallway of the Athenaeum. They all looked young, and they were making a lot of noise. They had no uniforms, and some of them looked very tough. Fennelly came out and called one of them into the reading-room.

"I don't know who they are," the Cumann na mBan woman said as she poured tea for Michael. "But we have to welcome all new converts to the cause. Some of them came in from the country barefoot, and we had to commandeer boots for them. The shops had a very poor selection. We took anything that was any good. The shopkeepers weren't too pleased. We commandeered bedding, too, and we have beds ready upstairs in the ballroom. It's important that everyone gets a night's sleep."

Michael was tired and he went to bed early. He was elated when he woke up the next morning, and remembered that they had held the town now for more than twenty-four hours. He wondered how things were going in Dublin, and in the rest of the country.

"It's Friday now and it's four full days since Pearse took over Dublin," Senan said when they were having their breakfast in the rink. "The British are under terrible pressure in Flanders. They'll never manage to take Ireland back."

Morrissey came into the rink and gave "Irish Republican Police" armbands to all those on patrol duty. He told them that the shops would be allowed to open later on in the morning.

"The shopkeepers will only be allowed to sell limited quantities of certain items," he said. "Walshe thinks that there might be shortages after a while because the town is completely cut off from the outside world. The shops will be allowed to open, but not the pubs. We can't have people drinking, and we have issued a proclamation to them warning them about their behaviour."

Michael and Senan went up to John Street. They knocked on doors and spread the news that the shops and workplaces were open. Patrolling was easy on the Friday because they had had a good night's sleep, and the new recruits replaced them several times to let them down to the Athenaeum for food.

"The lads are commandeering motor cars and petrol," a Volunteer in Court Street told them. "But it's hard to drive the motors and when they stop it's hard to start them up again. There's one broken down in Church Street, and they're trying everything, but they can't get it to go."

A little girl was injured in the fighting, and Fennelly sent up a message that all children were to be kept in off the streets. Michael wondered how Margaret was managing. He didn't know who was patrolling Bohreen Hill. The boys would have to leave the house sometimes, to go down to the well for water, or maybe to go to the shops. It would be hard to keep them in the house all day when the weather was fine. But Margaret would keep them occupied. They could read or write or play cards. Cormac would sit and talk to Jim.

They saw Tom Landers, standing on the corner of the Folly Lane, grimacing and muttering to himself.

"I'd say he's raging that the pubs are closed," Senan said.

A motor car appeared speeding along past the workhouse coming towards the town.

"Is it our crowd who are driving it? We'll have to check who it is," Senan said as the car swerved into the street. "Or should we just get in out of the way?"

The brakes screeched, and the motor stopped. As they

walked towards it they realized that it was Martin Webster who was driving, his elbow resting on the open window of the car. He had a big smile on his face. There was a Volunteer sitting on the front seat beside him.

"Where did you get the car?" Senan asked.

"We called to Madeira House," Martin said. "Bunting himself answered the door. When he saw that we had guns he gave no trouble. 'You want my motor,' he said." Martin imitated Mr Bunting's deep voice and posh accent. "He showed us how to start it. I hope I'll be able to start it up again. Driving is not as easy as it looks. I don't know how old Bunting does it. Do you want to have a go?"

Senan shook his head.

"No," Michael said. He wondered were they commandeering all the motor cars in the town. He could imagine the row Margaret's mother would create if they took James Dempsey's new motor. But James would probably be like Bunting, and hand it over.

"We're going back in to help with the house-to-house searches for arms," Martin Webster said. "We asked the citizens of the town to hand in their guns, but of course very few of them did. We'll search the streets in the centre of the town first. I'd say it will be tomorrow before we get to John Street. We're going to take over Ferns tomorrow, too."

He sped off in the motor. It was hard to believe that they were taking over so easily. All the years of waiting and planning were paying off. If things were going as well as this in Dublin and in the other towns the British would never manage to take the country back.

It was dark when they went back down to the Athenaeum. There were dogs barking in Church Street, and Michael remembered the stories of 1798. After the first battle of Enniscorthy, pigs and dogs had roamed the burnt-out, smoke-filled streets of the town, feeding on the bodies of the dead. This time was so different. After centuries of struggle they had managed to topple the rotten edifice of British rule with very little trouble. He walked up the steps and into the Athenaeum. This Rising was going to be a success.

Chapter 14

All the talk in the Athenaeum the next morning was about the attack on Ferns. Some of the men were smoking out in the backyard, and Michael stood with them.

"After we take Ferns," one of the men said, "we're going on to attack Carnew. That will bring us into County Wicklow. We're doing very well here but it's about time for us to break out of Enniscorthy and join with people in the rest of the country."

"We're going by motor to Ferns if we can get enough motors to start," Martin Webster said. "We have a lot of support out there. We should be able to take over without much trouble."

The door behind them banged and Jimmy Kehoe came into the yard from the hall.

"I was on night patrol up the Shannon," he said, "and there's a rumour that the town is about to be bombarded, that there are five thousand British troops ready to swoop on us. They're saying that Wexford town is swarming with soldiers, and that the British attack will begin this evening."

"Was there not a Rising in Wexford?" Senan asked.

"I don't think so," Jimmy Kehoe said. "You wouldn't really expect a Rising in Wexford town. They're all Redmondites down there."

"There couldn't be five thousand British troops in

Wexford," Martin said. "The British troops are out in France."

"I know," Jimmy Kehoe said, "but it's very hard to get the people of the Shannon to believe that."

The rumours had spread to John Street. Even though it was very early in the morning several women came out to ask was the office in the Athenaeum open. They wanted to get passes to go out the country.

"I don't want to be here when the town is bombarded," a woman with a baby said. She looked very young, as if she wasn't long married. "The British army will be coming soon. I'm going home to my mother, out to Clonroche."

"The British army are over in France, Missis," Senan said. "You're very foolish to believe all those rumours. There's no chance of the British army coming here. We're taking over the whole country. We're after taking over Dublin. We sent a detachment out to Ferns this morning."

"Anyone with any sense will leave here," the woman said, walking away from them.

The street was busy like it had been on Friday. The men went to work. The women went down town, and some of them complained about the shortages of food in the shops.

"When the British Army comes youse will all be arrested," a woman said to them, as she swept the dirt from her hallway out on to the street. She left her door wide open. Most of the doors were left wide open all the morning. Michael couldn't understand why the people didn't close their doors if they were so sure that the town was going to be bombarded.

"It's very hard to get people to believe in us even though we've been in charge now for more than two days," he said.

"The people of John Street will only believe in whatever the Bonds want them to believe in," Senan said. "The Bonds don't believe in risings or in an independent Irish Republic."

They went down to the Athenaeum at noon and were delighted to hear that Ferns had been taken without any difficulty.

"The Rising is going very well," Senan said. "It's stupid of people to believe those rumours."

Fennelly and Morrissey were in the rink, sitting together at the side of the table.

"When the RIC in Ferns heard we were coming they left. We took over the barracks and the Post Office," Fennelly said.

"It was as simple as that," Morrissey said, flicking his thumb against his finger. "The RIC here are very quiet. They're afraid of their lives of us." He laughed excitedly.

"We're going to take over the Church Institute and the Bank of Ireland later on today," Fennelly said. "We need to control all buildings close to the Athenaeum. We have to be able to protect our headquarters."

They went back up to John Street and patrolled until nightfall. The rink was crowded later that night when Walsh came in. They didn't recognize him at first. There was only one oil lamp in the corner and it was dark. He looked tired and drawn. His face seemed to have got thinner over the few days of the Rising.

"I only have a minute," he said. He gripped the back of a chair. "I came in to tell you that there's a Peace Committee after being set up. Father Fitzhenry and Canon Lyster, the Protestant rector, are in charge of it."

"A Peace Committee?" Joe Lambert said, scratching his chair along the floor and turning to face Walsh.

Walsh nodded. "I didn't want rumours spreading about it so I came in to tell you. Some members of the Urban Council, and some of the town's merchants are on it with Father Fitzhenry and Lyster. Tommy Druhan, the grocer, is on it, and James Dempsey, the undertaker. Henry Buttle and

Jeffrey Bond are on it too. They're telling us that the British Army is on its way here to take back the town. They want us to surrender."

"Surrender?" Jimmy Kehoe said. "What do they think we are, a crowd of women?"

"Of course there's no question of us surrendering," Walsh said. "We've been waiting for years for this chance to rise, but I want to keep you informed. The Peace Committee are sitting inside with us talking about negotiating terms for surrender in order to save the town from bombardment. They say they're anxious to avoid destruction of property and loss of life. They want to go to Wexford to meet Colonel French of the British Army, and negotiate terms for surrender."

"Are they mad or what?" Joe Lambert said. "Those merchants are raging that we commandeered things from them. I wouldn't believe a word they'd say. What are you wasting your time talking to them for?"

"We can't refuse to meet them," Walsh said. "We'll meet anyone who wants to see us. We met a delegation of soldiers' wives this morning. Their allowances hadn't come to the Post Office, and we typed up orders directing the shopkeepers to give them food to the value of their pensions. We're doing our best to run the town in an orderly manner. I'll have to go back to the office now but I wanted to let you know what was happening."

The men gave out angrily about the Peace Committee. Michael was embarrassed that James Dempsey, Margaret's brother, was on it.

"I hate those merchants," Jimmy Kehoe said.

"They're talking about negotiating with the British," Joe Lambert said. "You couldn't negotiate with the British. The British can't tell the truth. They're only able to tell lies."

More men came in. They were angry, too, when they

heard about the Peace Committee. Michael wasn't surprised that the merchants were trying to throw a spanner in the works. Centuries of foreign rule had warped some Irishmen and made them forget their duty to their country. He didn't think that Walsh and Fennelly should spend too long talking to the merchants.

"And Father Fitzhenry," Joe Lambert was saying. "At least in '98 the clergy were on the side of the people. But the priests will probably condemn us from the altar at Mass tomorrow morning."

"Fennelly says that even if they do we're not to walk out," Martin Webster said. "God is on our side and it doesn't matter what anyone else thinks."

"We'd better not go to Communion," someone said. "There's every chance we might be refused at the altar."

Joe Morrissey came in to the rink after a while and called out the names for the different Masses in the morning. Michael's name was on the first list. He was to go with about twenty others to early Mass in the Cathedral the following morning. Morrissey said he would come up to the ballroom and call them.

Michael woke early, sure that he was in the bed in his father's house in Kilbride. He opened his eyes, expecting to see the little window and the rough uneven walls. Then he realized that he must have been having some sort of a dream. He was lying on a mattress in the ballroom of the Athenaeum. He lay very still trying to remember the dream, but he couldn't.

He got up as soon as Morrissey called them and stood on the steps of the Athenaeum waiting for the others. It was windy and the sky was grey. There were crows on the roof of the National Bank. When everyone was ready they marched through the Market Square and up Main Street. The town was deserted apart from a few people walking down from the Duffry to Mass.

"I wonder are there British troops in Wexford," Senan said.

"Maybe there are," Jimmy Kehoe said. "The sooner the real fighting starts the better."

They went in the side door of the cathedral. The men knelt together near the bottom of the side aisle behind Father Fitzhenry's confession box. They were early. Michael sat up after a while and watched the people genuflecting and getting into their seats. He recognized Nurse Casey walking up the side aisle, but kneeling in the middle of the cathedral, behind one of the pillars. Casey was the nurse who had attended to Margaret when the children were being born. She sat up after a while and folded her arms.

The paint was flaking off the wall above the confession box beside him. He stood up when the bell rang. He couldn't see the altar from the side aisle but he recognized Father Bolger's voice. He knelt down and offered up the Mass for the success of the Rising. Someone started to cough and he looked over at Casey. All through the night when women were in pain giving birth Casey would tell them long stories criticizing priests and doctors and the respectable men in the town. The stories were scandalous, Margaret said. You wouldn't know whether to believe them or not, but they were great because they took your mind off the pain. Most men were no good, Casey would say, and they were all full of their own importance, but she wasn't one bit afraid of any of them. She had told them what she thought about them. Casey's voice would get louder and angrier as she repeated what she had said.

They stood up for the Gospel and he told himself that he should be trying to pray. It was Low Sunday, the first Sunday after Easter. The Gospel was probably about the

Resurrection. He should be thinking about Christ rising from the dead. "Life springs from death," Pearse had said, "and from the graves of patriot men and women spring living nations." He heard the altar boys saying '*Laus tibi, Christe*' and he knew that the Gospel was over. The sermon would be next if there was going to be a sermon. There was a pause, and he heard Father Bolger's voice starting the Credo. The men looked at one another, relieved. There wasn't going to be a sermon condemning the Rising.

They sat down for the offertory. He looked over again at Casey. She was a huge big woman with broad shoulders. She looked so fierce. The children were afraid of her. During the nights when babies were being born she would come down to the kitchen for things, and he would stand up to try to help her, but she would crossly bustle around. He would ask was Margaret all right, and Casey would frown and say that there was a long way to go. He was always afraid that Margaret would die giving birth. Casey was probably nervous, too, but after the baby was born she would get into great form. A few days after the birth, early in the morning, she would come to the house and he would go with her and the baby to the cathedral for the christening. He would stand at the door of the bedroom afterwards and watch her giving the baby back to Margaret. Margaret would smile, and Casey would laugh, and they would both be delighted, touching the little baby's face and laughing, because it was a miracle, the birth of a baby.

He knelt down. The bells began to ring for the consecration, and suddenly he wanted to go home. He wanted to sit at the table with Margaret and the boys. He wanted to go into the parlour to talk to Jim. He didn't ever want to leave them again. He looked up even though he knew he wouldn't be able to see the host being turned into the Body of Christ. He wanted it to be an ordinary Sunday and when Mass was over he would walk down the hill, turn down into Irish Street and go home. He bowed his head because the bell had stopped ringing. He wanted to go home but he wanted to fight in the Rising, too, and the Rising was going well. Maybe the real fighting was going to start soon. You couldn't have everything. Margaret and the boys would be there waiting for him whenever he went back home.

There was a lot of coughing around him. People went up to Communion. Casey went up the middle aisle and walked flat-footed back down the side. She knelt with her head in her hands. She never wanted him to come upstairs with her when they came back from having the baby christened. She would always tell him to do something as they went into the house. She would say she needed boiling water, or tell him to make sure that the range was hot. He would rush to do whatever she said, and then go upstairs to look in because it was the best moment of all. There was no need to worry any more. It had all turned out all right. Margaret was smiling, getting ready to feed the baby.

"Have you the boiling water?"

Casey would speak roughly to him as if he was an intruder in the house, as if the birth of the baby had been nothing to do with him. But it had. If it wasn't for him in the first place there would be no baby. Casey could say and do what she liked, but she couldn't change the fact that it was he who had started the baby. It had all started with him.

When Mass was over they marched down Main Street and through the Market Square back to the Athenaeum. There was no news about the Peace Committee. Michael couldn't understand how anybody would want to negotiate with the British. He couldn't imagine anything worse than meeting a Colonel in the British army. He went on patrol in John Street with Senan. It was the first day that he was nervous, thinking that maybe the bombardment was going to start. He realized that he should have been nervous the other days as well. Some of them might be killed. He stopped and watched Senan examining a motor which had been commandeered and had broken down near the Folly Lane. People went to Mass.

After a while they saw Martin Webster talking to the Volunteers in Court Street. They waited for him at Letts' gate. He looked very agitated. He walked towards them with his head back and his arms out from his side.

"A deputation from Arklow has arrived at the Athenaeum," he said. "They came in a motor with a white flag. They're saying that Dublin is after surrendering, and that the Rising is over." He was shaking his head as if he didn't believe what he was telling them.

"Dublin is after surrendering?" Michael said. "I don't believe that. Pearse and Mac Diarmada would never surrender."

"Dublin was bombarded. The city was in flames," Martin said. "They surrendered to avoid any unnecessary loss of life."

"But what about the rest of the country?" Senan asked.

"There was never any Rising in the rest of the country," Martin said. "There was just us, and Dublin."

"If the British Army is outside the town," Senan said, "why haven't they attacked us? What are they waiting for?"

"Colonel Henry James Bond of the National Volunteers is with the British Army," Martin said. "He doesn't want any of his property in the town destroyed. Jeffrey Bond is on the Peace Committee. They're negotiating with the British Army."

Martin went down to tell the news to the men on the Mill Park Road. Michael and Senan continued to patrol.

"I can't believe it," Senan said. "Those bloody Bonds are

destroying everything. Everyone will be sneering and jeering at us if we have to surrender."

Putting up with sneering and jeering would be one of the easiest parts. Michael didn't mention handcuffs or long days and nights in jail to Senan. Senan had never been arrested and he didn't know what it was like.

"And the leaders," Senan said. "Pearse and Mac Diarmada, Walsh and Fennelly. What will happen to them?"

"It's better not to think about it," Michael said.

If they surrendered the leaders would be executed. The British would love a chance to destroy the best of all Irishmen.

They stopped several times to talk to the Volunteers in Court Street. In the middle of the afternoon Martin Webster came up to them again.

"The Peace Committee are trying to arrange for two of our men to be brought to Dublin under military escort to meet Pearse," he said. "We won't agree to surrender unless we are ordered to by Pearse, our Commandant-General. They say that they won't be able to get the British to delay bombardment for much longer."

Michael found it hard to keep going after hearing such bad news. They had lost again. He was despondent although, in a way, he had never expected anything else. It was stupid to have expected this time to be different.

"I don't think our men should go to Dublin," Senan said. "The British Army might bring them outside the town and shoot them."

It was late afternoon and the sun was casting a shadow halfway across the street. Some people were standing in their doorways and others were sitting on window sills. They were talking quietly to one another and watching Michael and Senan marching up and down. A tall woman dressed in good clothes came to the door of the biggest house on the street.

Her next-door neighbour walked down the street to talk to her.

"Even when we were doing well the people here didn't believe in us," Senan said. "I'm sure they're delighted to hear the bad news about us now. They almost adore the Bonds but they've no time for us. I was coming home from work one evening when Freddie Bond came into John Street. I never saw such a commotion. The children ran into the houses to say that he had arrived and people came rushing out to see him. The young fellows followed him down the street. They all wanted to be able to say that they had been talking to Freddie Bond."

"And he'd only be pretending to like them," Michael said. "At the back of it all the Bonds would have no time for anyone Irish."

It began to get cold and the people went inside. It was dark when they saw Joe Morrissey coming up Court Street.

"Doyle and Etchingham have gone under military escort to Dublin to talk to Pearse," he said. "They're saying that Pearse has surrendered unconditionally. Walsh says that we'll continue to guard all entrances to the town, but we're calling off the foot patrol for the moment. You can come down to the Athenaeum."

They walked down Court Street with Morrissey. There seemed to be no doubt that the Rising in Dublin was over.

"When did they leave for Dublin?" Senan asked.

"A few hours ago. It will be late when they get back," Morrissey said. "Walshe and Fennelly are trying to get the Peace Committee to negotiate conditions for us if we have to surrender. We'll agree to the arrest of the leaders but we want the rank and file to be let go free."

They turned around the corner at the Church Institute. Groups of men were standing on Castle Street, and on the steps of the Athenaeum.

"I think we should take our guns and disperse. Get out of the town into the countryside and continue the fight from there," Joe Lambert was saying.

They stood on the street. A woman had pulled back the curtain and was looking out the top window of a house on Castle Hill. Martin Webster walked over towards the house and stared up at her. She dropped the curtain and disappeared from view.

Joe Lambert had gone over to a different group of men and was making the case again for continuing the fight from the countryside. Michael agreed with him. It would be better to keep on fighting than to hand the leaders over for execution. It would be better to fight on than to face years in jail.

They went inside after a while. Some of the men went upstairs to the ballroom, others went into the rink. Everyone seemed to believe that Pearse had surrendered. Michael and Senan sat at the end of the long table. Men huddled in groups, talking intensely in low voices. They went in and out to the hallway of the Athenaeum to see was there any news. Michael stood on the top step for a while, looking up and down the street. Fennelly came out of the reading-room and stood beside him. Fennelly who was always so well turned-out looked dirty and dishevelled.

"This waiting for news is terrible," Michael said.

"I'd rather wait," Fennelly said. "At least while we're waiting we can have some hope."

If the news was bad Fennelly would be shot or hanged.

"Maybe it's not true about Pearse," Michael said. "Maybe things won't end too badly."

Fennelly shrugged. "Whatever way this ends, and it may end with my death, I know that there was nothing else I could have done," he said. His Kerry accent was more pronounced than usual. "My whole life has led up to this moment and if my life is going to end because of it there's no use in me trying to avoid it."

Peter Paul Gilligan came to the door of the office and called Fennelly. Michael stood for a while on his own looking out onto Castle Street. He couldn't bear to think of Fennelly being executed, and Walsh, too, and the leaders in Dublin. He went back into the rink. Joe Morrissey and some of the other young fellows were there. Joe had put his head down on the table and they thought that he had fallen asleep.

"Joe," someone said, to see was he awake, but he didn't answer.

It was well into the night when Doyle and Etchingham got back. Martin Webster came into the rink with the news. Dublin had surrendered, he said. Pearse was in Arbour Hill prison and he had ordered them to surrender, too. The men came down from the ballroom and everyone crowded in to the rink. Michael moved in against the side wall to make room for the crowd. Father Kehoe from the Mission House was at the top of the room talking to Doyle and Etchingham who looked dazed as if the meeting with Pearse had taken a lot out of them. Walsh and Fennelly came in, but Michael couldn't believe it when he saw Jimmy Druhan and James Dempsey from the Peace Committee following them. Why would they think they had a right to attend a meeting of the Volunteers? Some of the men made a hissing noise when they saw the two merchants but when Walsh stood up on a form at the top of the room the hissing stopped.

Walsh read out Pearse's order. "It's not a trick. Doyle and Etchingham met Pearse in Arbour Hill prison," he said looking around at the two men. "They can vouch for this being Pearse's signature." He held Pearse's letter up for everyone to see.

"I think we should go out into the open countryside and continue the fight from there," Joe Lambert shouted. He was standing beside the table in the middle of the crowded room. He looked around him as if to infer that he had the support of all the men. "Why should we hand ourselves over to the RIC? We can inflict plenty of damage on them by continuing the fight from the hills."

"We're soldiers," Walsh said. "We obey orders. We have been ordered to surrender."

James Dempsey coughed and moved forward looking up at Walsh on the form. "It's only the leaders who will have to hand themselves over," he said. His voice was low. He seemed nervous. Michael hoped that James wouldn't make a show of himself by sounding pro-British. "We've been negotiating with the British army," James continued. "We have arranged that the leaders will be arrested but that everyone else can go to their homes." He didn't seem to realize that he should be ashamed of having negotiated with the British Army.

There was snarling from the back of the room. The men pushed forward as if they wanted to get near to James and attack him.

Fennelly stood up on the form beside Walsh. "None of us wants to surrender," he said. "We're keen to put up a fight but if the town is bombarded innocent civilians will be killed. Innocent Irish people."

"We have to obey Pearse's order," Walsh said.

Michael expected some of the men to continue with Joe Lambert's argument but no one said anything.

"The leaders will surrender. Everyone else will go home," Walsh said after a few seconds' silence. "But this is not the end of the fight. This is only the beginning. The fight for freedom will continue until an independent Irish Republic has been set up."

"The British today have superior fire power," Fennelly said. "Might is on their side, and that is why we must surrender. But right is on our side and right will triumph in the end."

"Now we will ask Father Kehoe to bless us," Walsh said.

Michael bowed his head and made the sign of the cross. He prayed for Walsh and Fennelly, and for Doyle and Etchingham, who would probably be sentenced to death.

"In the name of the Father and of the Son, and of the Holy Ghost. Amen." Father Kehoe moved across the top of the room sprinkling holy water over the men.

"Get home as quickly as you can, and lie low," Walsh said as the men began to leave. "Be ready for the fight when it starts again."

Some of the men stopped to shake hands with Walsh and Fennelly. Everyone was quiet. It was unbearable to think of the fate that was in store for these men who had been such dear friends and comrades. Walsh and Fennelly, Doyle and Etchingham, were facing the gallows or the firing squad. And as Michael moved towards the top of the room he couldn't believe it when he realized that Joe Morrissey was staying behind, too. Morrissey was too young to face execution. He should go home but he had a high rank in the Volunteers, and had played a commanding role during the Rising. He would have to stay with the leaders and hand himself over. And then the full enormity of what they had done struck Michael. They had held the town of Enniscorthy for four days, and humiliated the British Empire. He himself and the ordinary men would walk away scot free but the British would get their revenge.

He shook Morrissey's hand. He couldn't believe how strong and elated Morrissey seemed. The older leaders seemed a little more subdued as if they understood better what was facing them.

"Goodbye, Michael," Morrissey said, gripping Michael's hand tightly.

"Goodbye, Joe," Michael said. "Good luck."

*

They sat in the parlour talking to Jim. She knew she should tell Michael about the baby but she might cry if she started to talk about it, and how could she cry about a thing like that when Walsh and Fennelly and young Joe Morrissey were facing a death sentence?

"We went up to the Market Square on Saturday," she said. "I wanted the boys to see the tricolour above the Athenaeum. All the shops were open but the town was quiet. There was just one horse and cart in the Market Square. It would usually be very busy on a Saturday."

"It was quiet because nobody could get in from the country," he said. "The roads were blocked off. There was no trouble anywhere. Maybe it was because there was no drink. One of the pubs opened in Slaney Street, but Walsh went down and confiscated the keys."

It was mid-morning. They were expecting the RIC to come any minute to arrest him but he didn't seem to be thinking about the hard times which lay ahead. He was full of excitement and pride about the Rising.

"What time is it? I'm surprised they haven't come for me before now," he said. "They know me well. They arrested me before."

They had thought for a while that only the leaders would be arrested but Mrs Donnelly had called shortly after the boys went to school to say that some of the men from the Shannon had been picked up.

"The Lamberts are waiting for them to come for Joe," she said, "and then it will be Michael's turn. Will I take the child for you? You wouldn't want to have a child under your feet."

The baby went off with her. They were angry after she

left, angry with themselves for believing that the British would let anyone go free after the Rising.

"I feel stupid," Michael had said. "I should have known not to trust them."

"I'm sure everyone believed them," she said. "We're Irish and we tell the truth. We expect other people to do the same."

Jim grimaced when he heard the news.

"We'll beat the British in the end," Michael said. "We may have to suffer a lot but it will be worth it when we win."

She was impressed by his courage in the face of arrest and imprisonment. He talked cheerfully about the Rising and told them stories about all the things that had happened.

"We commandeered petrol from all over the town," he said. "We made a mistake by taking more than a dozen cans of it from Baroness Grey down in Brownswood, but Walsh said to bring some of it back. The steward's wife was sick and a motor car might have to be sent to Dublin."

She knew she should tell him about the baby before he went to jail.

"I'll make your dinner. We shouldn't let the RIC rule our lives. We should try to do all the ordinary things while we're waiting," she said.

She went out into the kitchen and put the kettle on the range to boil. She filled the basin with potatoes from the sack in the corner. From the parlour she could hear Michael talking to Jim, and every now and again, Jim's low wheezy laugh. She could call Michael and he would come out to the kitchen to her. She had been overjoyed to see him in the middle of the night. She hadn't expected him to come home. People had been saying that the town was going to be bombarded and that all the Shinners would be arrested up in the Athenaeum. He sat on the bed and talked to her for a while and then they had made love.

She went to the sink and began to peel the potatoes. The black and white cat was walking along the wall at the end of the yard. She heard a noise from the front of the house. It sounded like boots crunching on gravel, and then there was a thud. She stopped and stood completely still.

"Come out, Carty, with your hands up." The voice was rough.

"No," she said. She could feel her heart beating. It was the RIC. She ran towards the parlour.

Michael had pushed back the chair and was standing up. He made a little sound and then he stood still.

"Come out, Carty, or we'll break down the door." The voice was ignorant but there was a delighted tone to it, too.

Michael moved towards the parlour door.

"Your coat," she said, rushing back to the kitchen to get his coat. "Your coat is at the bottom of the stairs." She was whispering, afraid that they would hear her.

"Come out, Carty."

"Put on your coat," she said, following him to the front door.

She helped him to put it on, and then he opened the door. "Go back in," he said to her. "Don't let them see you."

She moved back and looked in at Jim who had covered his face with his good hand.

"Leave the door open, Carty. Keep your hands up until you get down here."

He was walking down the path and she could see some RIC men standing at the gate pointing guns at him. One of them was slouched over the rounded top of the wall.

She wanted to open the door wide and stand and watch them, show them that she supported Michael in his fight to free their country, but suddenly her stomach lurched, and she was much too hot. She was going to vomit. She ran out into the kitchen and through the yard to the lavatory. She vomited and a cold sweat came out on her face. She got down on her knees and after a while she vomited more. She could feel the cold of the stone on her legs. She was shivering. Michael was gone. She felt weak and her head was aching. The baby was making her sick.

Chapter 15

She woke suddenly, and knew immediately that everything had changed. Michael was not in bed with her, he was in jail, and one after another the leaders of the Rising were being taken out and shot. Philip was moving around in the other bedroom, getting ready to go over to the railway station. The newspapers arrived from Dublin on the early train, and people gathered at the station every morning to see who the British had executed the day before.

She pulled up the bedcovers around her. She had been awake during the night, worrying in case Michael would come to any harm. They would hardly execute him. He hadn't been one of the leaders but the recruiting posters might be a black mark against him now. They might keep him in jail for a long time. The only thing to do was to pray, to believe that God would look after them.

She shivered and hunched up her shoulders under the bedcovers. Philip went downstairs and closed the front door. Everybody in Enniscorthy was worried about Walsh and Fennelly who were in danger of being executed. The Peace Committee had asked for clemency for them because there had been no loss of life during the Enniscorthy Rising. She couldn't keep Séamus Walsh's face out of her mind. She had prayed during the night for God to spare Walsh, and Fennelly, too. She got very slowly out of bed. If she moved slowly in the mornings she didn't feel sick.

She put on her clothes and pulled back the curtains. She stood buttoning her cardigan, looking out at the field behind the house. A rabbit ran across the grass and disappeared into some bushes near the far ditch. It was as if 1798 had come back to Ireland again. She had never imagined that she would live through such terrible times, but maybe God would answer the prayers of the Irish people and end the executions now. It was three days since a young man from Cork, named Thomas Kent, had been taken out and shot.

She put her nightdress under the pillow and pulled up the covers on the bed. It was easy to keep the bed tidy with Michael gone. She missed him terribly. She wondered did he know about the executions. She had written to him but he mightn't have got the letter. He had been brought first to Waterford Jail and then transferred to Richmond Barracks in Dublin. She was proud of him and of what they were all going through for the cause of Irish freedom.

She went downstairs and looked in on Jim who was still asleep. Early morning sunlight was flickering at the top of the kitchen window. She opened the bread bin. There was plenty of bread left for the breakfast, and she would bake more later on. Her mother had brought her flour and wheatmeal from the shop. John had sent in potatoes from Tomanoole, and there were sausages in the safe for the dinner. She would draw Jim's pension later in the Post Office, and pay the rent on the house. She was luckier than some women whose husbands had been arrested. Her family were well-off.

She picked up books that the boys had left on the kitchen table and put them on the dresser. Cormac's Rising copybook was open. He was writing down everything he could find out about the dead leaders. Thirteen men had been executed. She turned the pages of the copybook. She had imagined each man on his own in his cell during the hours before his execution, and then pictured him walking out at dawn into the yard and standing alone waiting for the shots that would end his life. She had gone through it time after time in her head.

The executions had started on the Wednesday, two days after Michael was arrested. No one could believe what the British were doing. There was nothing else being talked about. Most people had been against the Rising when it was going on, but as they heard, day after day, of more and more executions, they were turning against the British and becoming Republican supporters.

She took down crockery and began to set the table for breakfast. On Wednesday the third of May, at dawn, the British had brought Pádraig Pearse, Tom Clarke and Thomas MacDonagh out into the yard of Kilmainham Jail to face a firing-squad. The following day, they had executed the poet Joseph Plunkett, along with Michael O'Hanrahan, Edward Daly and Willie Pearse. They had picked out Willie Pearse because he was Pádraig's young brother. He hadn't been one of the leaders. There was no good reason to execute him.

She set the table with plates and bowls and cups. She took the bread from the bread bin and began to cut it and lay it out on the big bread plate. Her mother had been very much against the Rising when it was going on but the execution of Willie Pearse had turned her into a Republican supporter. She said that she would never forgive the British for murdering a widow's two sons. She had come to the house on her own, without Julianne.

"May the men who shot Willie Pearse burn in hell for all eternity," she had said. She was sitting in the armchair at the range. "I'll never forgive them for murdering a widow's two sons."

"We'll have to try to forgive the British in time," Margaret said. She would never let her talk be too full of hatred in front of the children. Aidan and Cormac had just come in from school. Philip had stayed in late to do extra Latin.

"I won't ever forgive them," her mother answered.

Aidan took the bread out of the bread bin and a knife from the dresser drawer.

"We have to try to forgive our enemies whatever they do on us," Margaret said. "God will give us the grace to forgive, and we know that the seven men are gone straight to Heaven."

Her mother shook her head. "You can forgive the British if you like but I won't," she said. "You're very saintly, like your father. I don't know how I ever got mixed up with ye because I'm not a bit like ye. I can't get the thought of poor Mrs Pearse out of my head. That's the sort I am. Does anybody else feel like me? I've had a hard enough life myself, but I can't imagine how any woman could survive a blow like that. Poor Mrs Pearse must be gone out of her mind with grief, thinking of her two fine sons dead." She started to cry. She folded her arms and pressed them close to her chest.

"It's terrible. I think it's terrible, too," Margaret said. She was sitting beside Cormac at the table. Cormac was watching his grandmother crying.

"Do you want bread?" Aidan asked Cormac, pointing the bread knife at him. "Go out to the safe and bring in the butter."

"And they're after murdering three poets," Margaret said. She began to cry, too. "Pearse, MacDonagh and Plunkett, the three of them were poets, and it's a worse crime to murder a poet than to murder—"

"It's not worse to murder a poet," Aidan interrupted. He was cutting the bread. "It's wrong for them to murder any of us," he said, putting the bread knife down on the table. "It doesn't matter whether we're poets or not."

"I know all the executions are wrong," she said, "but …"

"Don't start talking nonsense about poets," her mother said. "I'm bad enough without having to listen to that. Don't you know I hate talk about poetry. It's the same as people making a big fuss about singing. I had a bad enough life with your father listening to that sort of talk." She frowned and shook her head. "Your father was good in some ways, and you think he was great, but he was a fool, too. The greatest clown of a fellow would come into the bar and your father would be nice to him all night hoping that he would sing a song. I was left sitting inside on my own. I hate all that poetry and singing. It's Mrs Pearse I feel sorry for. Her two sons are dead. Is nobody else like me?"

Her mother was waiting for an answer but Margaret didn't know what to say. She felt blank for a while. She watched Cormac coming back in from the yard with the butter dish. He sat at the table and turned the pages of his Rising copybook. The clock was ticking. Aidan buttered the bread and gave some to Cormac.

"I have two sons of my own," her mother said, "and I don't know how any woman could get over the death of her two sons."

"It's terrible," Margaret said. "Everything is destroyed."

She stood up and tidied away the boys' school bags. Everything was different. She longed for the carefree time before it all started. She hadn't appreciated how good those times were. But it was wrong to give in to the grief. She should pray and she should work. Her mother had brought early rhubarb from the shop. She got the wooden board and the good knife and began to cut the leaves off the stalks of rhubarb. Aidan went out to the yard to bring in fuel for the range. He banged the scuttle against the back door. The birds were twittering outside. She couldn't believe that some things were continuing as normal. It seemed wrong that the birds would keep on singing as if nothing had happened. The wind was blowing, too, and the sun was shining but the men were dead. Nothing could ever be worthwhile again after these executions. Three poets had been murdered by the British. Her mother was right. Poetry was no use. Why would anyone sing? Tears rolled down her face and she wiped them away with the back of her hand.

Aidan was scraping the shovel against the stone floor of the shed as he filled the scuttle.

"Are you running short of fuel?" Her mother spoke in a low monotone.

"There's still some there," Margaret said. She hated discussing the details of their poverty. Suddenly she was exhausted and she sat down, leaving the rhubarb and the leaves on the table. She didn't know how she was going to give birth to an infant and take care of it.

"I'll get James to send you over some fuel next week," her mother said in the same low voice as if she was trying to make up for having shouted so loudly a while before. "I'll wait until some day when Nancy is gone out. I don't like her knowing that we're giving you things. She might think she could start giving things out of the shop to her family."

Margaret tried to smile at her mother to show gratitude, but she couldn't get her face to move. She was astonished at her mother's capacity to fight that old fight against Nancy even in the midst of this terrible grief. None of the old things mattered to Margaret. She watched Aidan carrying the fuel back in to the kitchen, but she didn't care what anyone did. Pearse, MacDonagh and Plunkett had been shot dead. Willie Pearse was dead. The British were murdering the leaders of her nation. They were trying to destroy the Irish people.

"E-E-E-E-Edward D-D-D-Daly is r-r-r-related to T-T-Tom C-C-C-Clarke, and th-the t-t-t-two of th-them were sh-sh-sh-sh-sh-shot," Cormac said.

"What did Cormac say?" Her mother refused to try to understand the stuttering. She made Margaret repeat everything that Cormac said.

"He said that Edward Daly is related to Tom Clarke."

"Is he? I don't think so," her mother said. "Tom Clarke spent years in America. He should never have come home when you think about what's after happening to him now." She shuddered. "But I don't think he's related to Edward Daly."

"Cormac is usually right," Margaret said. "Cormac knows all about the leaders."

She looked at Cormac. He was smiling at her, and she knew then that there was one thing that hadn't changed. She still loved Cormac. Everything else was different after the executions but she still loved Cormac. Brother O'Sullivan beat him every day because of the terrible stutter.

"Show me that copybook, Cormac," her mother was saying, taking her reading-glasses out of her handbag. "Joseph Plunkett got married in the chapel in Kilmainham Jail just before he was shot. Have you got that written down?"

"He has," Margaret said. "He knows all about the Rising."

"To G-G.-G-G-Grace G-G-G-G-G-Gifford," Cormac said, smiling.

On Friday the British had executed Major John McBride.

"He wasn't a major in the British Army," Philip told Cormac. "He fought with the Irish Brigade in the Boer War against the British, and that was where he got the title of Major."

"He was married to Maud Gonne," Margaret said. "The poet William Butler Yeats was in love with Maud Gonne but she married McBride."

Cormac turned to a new page in his copybook. "Major John McBride," he wrote in his beautiful handwriting.

After the execution of McBride it had seemed as if the British were going to stop. Nothing happened for two days, but then on Monday they had executed four more men, none of whom Margaret had ever heard of before, but whose names now she would never forget. On Monday the eighth of May, Eamonn Ceannt, Con Colbert, Michael Mallin and Seán Heuston were brought before a firing squad and shot. She sometimes agreed with her mother. God, in His infinite mercy, might forgive the British for what they were doing but no Irish person ever could. On Tuesday they had picked on Thomas Kent from Cork. There had been no executions since Tuesday. Maybe God would answer their prayers and the Enniscorthy men would be spared.

She put the plate of bread in the middle of the table. Jim began to cough feebly and she went into the parlour to him. He had fallen down off the pillows and she lifted him back up.

"I'll get your breakfast in a minute," she said. "It's a lovely day."

He smiled, trying to keep the bad side of his mouth from twisting downwards.

She went into the kitchen and finished setting the table. A shaft of light shone down the stairs from the landing window. She stood still and blessed herself when she heard Philip opening the front door. He came into the kitchen and stopped at the bottom of the stairs. He was holding his hands out as if he had let something fall. He opened his mouth to speak but he didn't say anything.

"Who?" Her voice came out as a whisper.

"James Connolly," he said. He looked pale and shocked.

"They couldn't have. There must be a mistake," she said.

"They carried him out on a stretcher and then they tied him into a chair." He shrugged.

"They couldn't have," she said. "Even the British couldn't have done that."

"They did," he said, gripping the banisters of the stairs. "It was on the newspaper. They used a rope to keep him sitting up straight so that they could shoot him. I suppose they wanted to aim at his heart, or maybe his head. I knew that they would have to shoot him at some time but I thought they'd wait until he got better."

She sat down. Aidan was coming down the stairs.

"James Connolly," Philip said to him.

She couldn't believe what the British had done. She pictured Connolly falling forward, slumping down over the rope, and she started to cry. Everyone loved James Connolly. She had read all about him. He had led the working people of Dublin when they faced starvation during the Lock-out in 1913.

"Wh-wh-wh-wh-wh…" Cormac was coming down the stairs. Little Michael came slowly after him, cautious, holding on to the banisters, making sure he didn't fall. She made herself stop crying.

"James Connolly," Philip said to Cormac.

Cormac looked towards the table. "Wh wh-wh-ere's m-my R-R-R-R-ising c-c-c—"

"It's on the dresser," she said.

He pushed some of the crockery into the middle of the table. He got the copybook and his pen and ink from the dresser. "J-J-J-J-James C-C-C-C-C…C-C-Connolly," he said, looking at her and smiling.

"James Connolly," she said and tears flowed down her face again when she said the name. "They're after murdering James Connolly. But he's gone straight to Heaven. Lord, have mercy on him." She made the sign of the Cross.

"And Sean Mac Diarmada," Philip said, moving towards her. "They shot Sean Mac Diarmada, too."

She moved back in the chair and held her hands up in front of her, as if she was protecting herself from attack. Tears were streaming down her face. Had God abandoned the Irish people? How could God have allowed Mac Diarmada to be shot? She pictured him limping out into the cold dawn to face the firing squad.

"No. No," she said.

The baby started to cry. He came across the kitchen to her. God shouldn't have let this happen. God should have withered the hands of the soldiers holding guns ready to shoot Mac Diarmada. The Irish people needed a sign that God was on their side. She was sobbing. The baby was screaming, holding his arms out for her to lift him up. The Irish people had sided with God against the British throughout the centuries. God should not do this to them now.

The baby was screaming. She put her arm around him.

"Will I go in and tell uncle Jim what they're after doing?" Philip asked.

"Yes," she said.

Aidan went over to the range and spooned out the porridge into bowls.

She made herself stop crying. "You're all right," she said to the baby, lifting him up on to her knee. "Don't be crying." She warmed his little feet with her hands but he kept on crying.

"Hand me over his cardigan from the range," she said to Aidan. "I'll dress him properly when you're gone to school."

As she put the baby's arms into the sleeves of the cardigan she was ashamed of her pride and arrogance in giving out to God. God had given her so many blessings. How could she talk like that to Him, and blame Him for what the British were doing? Lucifer had been sent down to hell because of his pride. She had committed the sin of pride, too. She was so proud that she thought she knew what God should do. God was not responsible for the evil that men did. God had given people free will, and He let the British do evil if they wanted to. She would go to confession and ask God to forgive her for questioning Him. God's plan for the world was good. Sometimes ordinary mortals couldn't see any goodness in the unfolding of it but it was a sin to question the goodness of God. She was glad that she hadn't said anything out loud. At least the boys didn't know the way she had been thinking.

The baby had stopped crying. Philip came back in and sat at the table. "We'll say a prayer for Connolly and Mac Diarmada," she said. "And we'll ask God to console us in our grief."

She put the baby down on the chair beside her and turned around towards Cormac. He never said prayers out loud because of the stutter but she always made sure to include him when they were praying. He blessed himself, and, bowing his head, joined his hands. She said the 'Our Father' first, asking God to forgive her for her pride, and then she prayed for Connolly and Mac Diarmada.

"Eternal rest grant unto them, O Lord, and may perpetual light shine upon them. May they rest in peace," she prayed.

"Amen," Aidan and Philip said.

Cormac blessed himself quickly and took up his pen again. He smiled. "S-S-S-Sean M-M-M-M-M-Mac D-D-D-Diarmada," he said, dipping the pen into the ink bottle, and writing the name across the top of a page.

*

There was a barbed wire fence around the exercise field. Any prisoner who went near the barbed wire would be shot, the camp commander said at roll-call every morning. Exercise-time was over, and Michael walked up from the field with Frank Donaghy. The sky was grey and it looked like rain. It seemed to rain a lot in Wales. He was in the camp in Frongoch for almost six months now, and it had rained nearly every day. His boots squelched through the wet grass and the mud. There was mud everywhere in the camp. It was windy and cold.

"Did you ever read *Come Rack, Come Rope*?" Donaghy asked. Donaghy was the camp librarian.

"No," Michael said.

"I'll give it to you today when I open the library," Donaghy said. "I'd say you'll enjoy it. It's about the Penal days in England." Donaghy was seventy years of age. He was tall with bright blue eyes and thick grey hair. He was a journalist from Dublin and he had fought with Pearse in the GPO.

They came to the rows of huts. The young lads had gone on ahead to the camp dining hall, and there was shouting and laughter in the distance.

"There must be a letter from some girl," Donaghy said.

Letters were given out before dinner. The lads roared laughing as they read letters from girls out loud to one another. It was good to hear laughter after all the sadness. For a while it had seemed as if they were all going to lose their minds with grief. Fifteen of the leaders had been executed in May, and Roger Casement was hanged in August. More than a hundred others, including the Enniscorthy leaders, had been sentenced to death but those sentences had been commuted to life imprisonment in jails in England. The rank and file were here in the camp in Frongoch.

"I had a very interesting talk with Michael Collins this morning," Donaghy said as they walked along the path which they had called Pearse Street after the dead leader. "We've sworn a lot of the young lads into the IRB. We're drawing up plans for continuing the fight when we go home."

"We'd want to be well-organized when we get out of here," Michael said, glancing towards the hut where one of the prisoners, Ernie Barron from Dublin, had lost his mind. They had taken care of him for a while in the hut until the authorities moved him to a lunatic asylum.

The men were standing around the camp dining hall, waiting for their dinner. He was hungry. The food in Frongoch had been terrible at first but it had improved when they were allowed to buy extra provisions with money that was flowing in from supporters in Ireland. The mood in the country had changed, it was said. Everyone had been sickened by the executions. Huge numbers of people were attending anniversary Masses for the dead leaders, and money was pouring in to help the prisoners' dependants. More and more people now wanted an independent Irish republic. Margaret had written to him to say that Enniscorthy had changed. Even her mother had become a Republican. Margaret had said in that letter, too, that she was expecting another baby.

"I'll see is there a letter for either of us," Donaghy said.

He went into the camp dining hall. Michael stayed outside. There were two armed guards slouching against the wall near the high arched gateway of the camp. It was cold, but the prisoners weren't supposed to go inside until the dinner was ready. He stood looking down towards South Camp where he had been detained when he first came to Frongoch. South Camp had been closed a few weeks before as the prisoners were being gradually released. There were often rumours that the whole camp was going to be closed down and everyone sent home. He tried not to think too much about going home because he expected them to hold on to him until the very end. He had a police record since the time of the recruiting posters. The camp wasn't as bad as Waterford Jail. There were classes and books, and good company.

The young lads who were near the door of the dining hall had gathered around in a circle and they began to shout and cheer. He went over to see what was happening. Michael Collins and Martin Webster were having a boxing match. Collins seemed to have the upper hand. He stretched forward and hit Webster a box on the chest, knocking him back. The men cheered. Michael looked around to see had Donaghy come back out of the dining hall, but he hadn't. Donaghy had been a great sportsman in his youth and he loved boxing and wrestling. It was great to see such spirit, he said, when the young lads organized contests. They would need courage and ruthlessness to free Ireland. There was a loud roar, and a cheer. Webster had straightened himself up and was punching wildly but not making contact with Collins who each time moved skillfully out of the way.

"Come on, Collins," someone shouted.

"Come on, Martin. Up Enniscorthy," Tom Butler shouted from the other side of the fight.

"Come on, Martin," Michael shouted. It would be great to see a young lad from Enniscorthy beating Collins who was from Cork and who had worked for a while in London.

"There's a letter for you." Donaghy was behind him. "There's nothing for me." He pushed his way in to get a good view of the fight. He started to shout immediately. "Come on Collins," he roared.

Michael moved back from the fight to open the envelope. It was Margaret's writing. Inside, there was just a single page, with writing back and front.

My dear Michael,

Jim has died, RIP. He was very low over the last few days and Father Bolger came last evening and anointed him. We sat up all night with him. He said your name several times during the night and passed away peacefully at nine o'clock this morning. Philip and I were with him at the time. Mrs Donnelly, Joe Byrne and the Lamberts have been very good. I don't know what I would have done without them. The neighbours are coming in and out to the wake. My mother is here with us. Nurse Casey calls to me every day even though there is no need for her yet. James is coming over shortly to tell us about the funeral arrangements.

We miss you terribly, particularly at this time. We know that you would want to be here with us but we are proud of what you are doing for the cause of Irish freedom.

All my love,
Margaret.

He folded the letter and put it back into the envelope. It wasn't a shock, he told himself. He had known that Jim was going to die. The men were roaring and cheering behind him. The wind was cold. Donaghy's voice was loud above the din.

"Come on. Finish him off," Donaghy roared.

He moved down the slope, away from the noise. The sky was dark and angry. The guards at the camp gate were standing up straight now looking up towards the fight. He could see the high distillery chimney and the tower of South Camp. He wished he had been in the house when Jim died, sitting beside the bed in the parlour with Margaret. He wished he was there now for the wake. It would be a big wake. Neighbours from the Irish Street and the Island Road would come in the morning, and then word would spread through the town that Jim had died. People would be talking about it in all the shops and on the streets, and after dinner they would come to the wake from other parts of the town.

A sudden gust of wind almost tore the letter out of his hand and the cap off his head. He gripped the letter tightly with one hand, and held his cap down with the other. He walked up, and around the side of the dining hall to where there was more shelter. The boxing match was still going on and the men were shouting. He thought of people who would definitely go to Jim's wake. Joe Brooks would walk down from the top of the Shannon to the wake, and a lot of people from the Duffry would come, too. All the men from Hogans' Shoemakers and the men who stood at the bottom of Slaney Street on summer nights. It would be good for the boys to see that the family was well-regarded in the town even though they didn't have any money. Lucy Redmond from the pub would come to the house.

Maybe he could ask to be let home for the burial. He might get there in time for the funeral Mass. A man from Dublin had been let home to his mother's burial. He took the letter out of the envelope. It was dated Friday. Today was Tuesday. Jim had died on Friday, and had probably been buried on Monday. It was too late to go home for the funeral. The funeral was over. The shopkeepers would have closed their shops when the hearse was passing by. Hogans' Shoemakers where Jim had worked was probably closed for the whole day. People would have said, "It's terrible that Michael is not here when his only brother is being buried. The British have a lot to answer for."

The wind seemed to have died down. There were drops of rain falling. He folded the letter and the envelope and put them into his pocket. He was never going to see his only brother again in this world, but they would be re-united in Heaven. He would go and tell Donaghy. Donaghy was the person he wanted to tell, although Donaghy, being from Dublin, had never known Jim. He walked around the corner of the dining hall.

Donaghy was watching the boxing match. "Come on, Michael Collins," he was shouting, leaning forward and raising his clenched fist into the air. "Yes, Michael Collins," he roared.

Michael moved over near him. "Frank," he said, but his voice was drowned out by a loud cheer. Webster and Collins were close together now, and punching hard.

He went into the dining hall although the bell for the dinner hadn't yet rung. There were men sitting at some of the tables. The insurance men were talking quietly at the table in the corner where he usually sat. The insurance men were from all over Ireland, some were from Enniscorthy, and they were planning to set up the first Irish-based insurance company, to compete with the English ones and stop Irish money leaving the country for England. Michael went past them, and down to the end of the table. Senan Murphy was there with Desmond O'Farrell, the poet.

"I'm going to lose my mind," O'Farrell was saying to Senan. He groaned and twisted his face into a frown. "They're boxing out there again and I have to listen to that terrible shouting and cheering," he said. His face was very red. "All I want is a bit of peace and quiet. I'd love a full week away somewhere on my own. There's shouting and roaring here from early morning until late at night. Wouldn't you think they'd sit down and read a book? Michael Collins is the ringleader of them. I can't bear Michael Collins."

"It's all only a bit of fun," Senan said, looking up to acknowledge that Michael was there.

Michael sat down opposite the two men.

"Fun? It's not a bit funny," O'Farrell was saying. "I was trying to work out a line of a poem this morning. I was thinking about it from the time I woke up, and all the time while I was eating my breakfast it was going through my mind. I sat down to write it when I heard a big thud behind me. It was Collins and some other fellow wrestling on the floor of the hut." His eyes were rheumy behind his glasses. He looked as if he was going to cry. Donaghy was always advising him not to antagonise the young lads by giving out about them.

"You won't lose your mind," Senan said, laughing. "There's no fear of that."

"I'd rather be in solitary confinement. It would be easier on me than being here," O'Farrell was saying.

Michael took the letter out of his pocket. "Jim died last Friday." He heard the words but he didn't feel that he was saying them.

"Jim. Your brother," Senan said. "I'm sorry. Lord, have mercy on him."

"Your brother," O'Farrell said, adjusting his glasses. "I'm sorry for your trouble." He shook Michael's hand.

"Michael's brother was in England, and then he came home," Senan said to O'Farrell. "He was in the IRB. He spent years in jail."

Michael could hear everything they were saying, but he was thinking about the wake. He would leave the wake-room for a while and go into Margaret in the kitchen.

"Did you tell everyone else about it, Michael?" Senan asked.

"No. No. I'm only after getting the letter," he said.

"I'll tell them," Senan said. "All the people from Enniscorthy would want to know that."

Senan stood up and went down to the insurance men. A sudden gust of wind rattled the windows of the dining hall.

"I wouldn't have been giving out about the boxing match if I had known that you had heard bad news," O'Farrell said. "I'm sorry."

"It doesn't matter," Michael said. "I've been expecting to hear the news. He hasn't been well since Christmas." He could hear his own voice out in front of him. He knew that he must be making up the words and saying them, but the voice seemed separate from him.

"I'm sure it's a shock to you all the same," O'Farrell was saying. He made the sign of the Cross. "Death is always a shock," he said.

Michael nodded. The dinner bell rang. Rain began to pelt noisily down on to the roof of the dining hall. He looked down towards the insurance men. Senan was telling Tom Wilson about Jim. Wilson stood up and walked around the table.

"I'm sorry to hear about Jim," he said, shaking Michael's hand and sitting down beside him. "Senan is just after telling me."

The men were rushing in out of the rain. More of the insurance men came down to sympathize with him. He knew the insurance men well because they held their meetings in hut twenty-two. It was the quietest hut, and Michael went there in the evenings with Donaghy and O'Farrell to read. He turned around in the chair to shake hands with the men.

Donaghy came in and Wilson stood up to give him the seat beside Michael.

"I'm sorry for your trouble, Michael," Donaghy said. "Aidan told me about your brother."

Some of the Enniscorthy men came over to sympathize with him. Several men from Belfast came over, too. There were five or six men in a line waiting to sympathize with him like people waiting in the aisles of the cathedral in

Enniscorthy at a funeral. Philip and Aidan would have helped him to carry the coffin. They were old enough now to do things like that.

Rain was beating down on the roof of the dining hall. Donaghy and O'Farrell were talking quietly to one another across the table. He was shaking hands with Tom McEldowney from Belfast when he saw James Ryan coming over and standing at the end of the line of men waiting to sympathize with him. He didn't know Ryan well. They met in the evenings in hut twenty-two. Ryan, a final year medical student, studied his medical books in the corner and talked mainly to the insurance men. Everyone had great respect for him because he had looked after the wounded Connolly in the GPO. O'Farrell talked often about those last few hours with Pearse and Connolly in the GPO.

A big gale of wind rattled the windows of the dining hall so that he could only barely hear what the men were saying to him.

"I'm sorry for your trouble."

The GPO was on fire, and British shells were pounding the street. Connolly, badly wounded, was laid out on a stretcher. Ryan stayed at his side. The British had brought Connolly out at dawn into the yard of Kilmainham Jail, tied him to a chair and shot him. Ryan had looked after Connolly during those last few hours in the GPO. If he never did anything else for his whole lifetime it was enough for him to have done that.

"I didn't know your brother, but I'm sorry to hear your bad news," James Ryan said.

"Thank you," Michael said, shaking Ryan's hand.

Ryan walked away from him. He was an amazing young fellow. He didn't seem to have been touched by what had happened. He studied his medical books every evening and was going to do his final exams to be a doctor when he went home.

Chairs were being scraped against the floor of the dining hall as the men stood to go up for their dinner. He turned his chair back around towards the table.

"Stay where you are," Donaghy said to him. "You look very shocked. I'll bring you down your dinner."

Chapter 16

The train chugged slowly out of Ferns station. He looked out the window at the white mist rising up from the fields. It was Christmas Eve and he was going home. Frongoch had been closed down. It was damp and cold, the bleak mid-winter. There had been snow on the mountains of Wales, and on the Wicklow mountains, too, but the land around Enniscorthy was flat and low-lying. The trees and the bushes looked black and dead. The train trundled along past a big two-storied house with a slate roof. The boys would probably be at the station to meet him. Word had been sent to Enniscorthy that the men were coming home. He would see the new baby, a girl, born on the fifteenth of December. He didn't expect Margaret to come out so soon after the birth of the baby but he couldn't wait to walk up the path and into the house to her.

"We'd want to stand up soon. There's no use in missing our stop," Senan said. Senan was sitting beside him. Martin Webster and Jimmy Kehoe were in the seat opposite.

"I'd say there will be a big crowd at the station to meet us," Martin said, clearing the steam off the window with the back of his hand.

"It's dark all day," Senan said. "You'd think it was night-time."

It had been dark when they got off the boat in Dublin. It was a Sunday and Jim Ryan who knew the city well had brought them to Mass in the Pro-Cathedral. It was dark still as, exhausted, they stood waiting in Westland Row Station for the Wexford train. The red brick of the station reminded him of Enniscorthy. He fell asleep when the train began to move, and slept until they stopped in Arklow. He couldn't wait to reach home.

"Look," Jimmy Kehoe said, pointing towards the window at the other side of the train. "The river Slaney. We didn't think we'd see it again so soon."

The river was full and dark, flowing close to the tracks for a while and then circling into the countryside.

Tom Sinnott stood up in the compartment next to them. "We're nearly there. Come on, lads," he said.

Senan stood up and began to hand down the bags from the baggage rack. The train lurched and Michael staggered backwards before grabbing the bar at the top of the seat and straightening himself up. He could still feel the movement of the sea. It had been a rough crossing and he had been seasick. He took his bag from Senan. He went out into the aisle and stood among the crowd of men. They had been quiet for most of the train journey but now they were talking loudly and laughing.

"I'm starving. I wonder what's for the dinner," someone said.

"It will hardly be as bad as Frongoch," Martin Webster said. "Do you remember the herrings with their guts in them?"

They all groaned and laughed. The whistle blew and the train began to slow down. Michael couldn't believe that he was home. They passed the outhouses at the edge of the station where he used to work. He held on tightly to the bar of the seat as the train began to slow down. They came to the platform which sloped upwards at first and then ran along at the same height as the body of the train. They passed the signal box. There were people standing on the platform waving and moving in towards the train. He was looking out for the boys. He recognized Martin Webster's mother and father.

"There's your mother, Martin," someone shouted.

"I know," Martin said. "I might have been away for a few months but I'm still able to recognize my own mother."

The train stopped but then chugged on again and Michael was thrown sideways although he was still gripping the bar of the seat. The platform was crowded with people. And then he saw Margaret. She had a warm hat on, and she was looking into the train, looking for him. There were people in her way and she couldn't see him although he was directly in front of her. He let go of the bar and waved at her but still she didn't see him. "O, Lord," he said to himself, overjoyed because soon he would be with her. "I'm here. I'm here," he wanted to shout although there would have been no hope of her hearing him above the noise of the train. He saw Philip and Aidan. They were at the front of the crowd and they had already seen him. They waved and turned back to tell Margaret. But the train moved on past her and he was facing the station door when it stopped.

The men were pushing back along the aisle. He would be with her in a minute. He moved out of the carriage, and waited for his turn to get out the door. He stepped down from the train. Philip and Aidan were there in front of him.

"Philip. Aidan." He shouted to make his voice heard above the noise of the steam which was rushing out of the engine.

"Hello," they answered. They had been pushing forward to see him but now they stepped back, as if not knowing how to respond to his great delight at seeing them.

He moved out on to the platform to make way for the other men getting off the train, and to find her. The platform was crowded. Everyone was shouting. He saw her. The two little ones were with her.

"Michael," she said. She was smiling. She held out her hand to shake his.

"Margaret." He took her hand in his. She had gloves on. "How are you? Are you all right? It's very cold for you to be standing there so soon after the baby." He had to shout to be heard above the noise of the train. "I didn't expect you to come out."

"It's great to have you home," she said.

The boys were watching them but then they all turned to look down to the far end of the platform where there was a great commotion and loud shrieking.

"I'm going down there to see what's going on," Aidan said.

Philip followed him.

Tom Wilson came over. His wife was with him. "The young lads are showing off the souvenirs they made in Frongoch but I'm going to go home. It's too cold to be standing around," he said, rubbing his hands together. "I'll see you after Christmas."

"How is the baby?" Mrs Walsh asked Margaret.

"She's grand, thank God," Margaret said.

"You'd want to take care of yourself, now," Mrs Walsh said. "Take it easy. Take a rest every chance you get."

The platform was crowded. He had never seen Enniscorthy station so busy in all the years he had worked there. Joan Lambert came over and shook his hand.

"It was terrible about Jim," she said. "Terrible that you weren't there."

"You were very good to him," Michael said.

The guard was banging closed the doors of the train. Steam was hissing loudly out of the engine. Some people were going out the side door of the station and others were moving towards the main door.

Cormac pulled Margaret's arm. "W-w-w-we'll g-g-g-go h-h-h-home," he said. "It's c-c-c-c-old."

"Cormac," Michael said. "How are you?"

"N-n-not t-t-t-oo b-b-b-bad," Cormac said, smiling. "I h-h-h-have the R-R-Rising c-c-copybook to sh-sh-sh-show you."

"That's great," he said. "You told me about it in your letter."

He bent down to speak to little Michael but the child turned away and hid his face in Margaret's coat.

"Say hello to your daddy," Margaret said. But the child kept his head buried in her coat. "He's not very friendly sometimes but he'll get used to you in a while," she said. "Will we go? Philip and Aidan will come home when they're ready."

They moved slowly among the crowd out the station-door. Several people shouted hello to him and welcomed him home. They walked through the Railway Square. It was around noon, but the sky was dark and seemed to be low, down close to the town. Cormac ran across in front of Margaret and caught his hand.

"You're my d-d-d-d-daddy," he said.

Michael laughed. "I am," he said.

They said Happy Christmas and Many Happy Returns to the people going up the Shannon. There were people in front of them and more behind them, all with the men coming home from Frongoch.

"W-w-w-we h-h-h-have a t-t-t-turkey f-f-f-for Ch-Ch-Ch-Christmas," Cormac said as they walked past Buttles'.

"John brought us in a turkey from Tomanoole," Margaret said. "We haven't much for the dinner today but we'll have the turkey tomorrow."

"I might get work after Christmas," he said.

"Yes," she said. "James might need someone to help in the shop or the yard. He's always busy with funerals in January and February."

"Jim," he said. "You buried Jim."

"Yes," she said. Her eyes filled up with tears.

"I'll have to go out to his grave," he said. "After dinner, maybe."

They were going up past Farrells', coming on to the bridge. It was ten-to-one by the cathedral clock. The river was full and rushing loudly towards the bridge. It was perishing cold. People were heading up Slaney Street. Cormac was still catching his hand but little Michael hadn't looked at him yet. They turned up past Antwerp. He looked at the walls of the Maltings from where he had pulled down the recruiting posters.

"Everything went all right with the new baby," he said.

"Yes, thank God," she said. "You thought of a lovely name for her. I was delighted when I got your letter."

"Maeve," he said. "An Irish name. I wanted her to have an Irish name. When we were passing through the railway stations in Wales we were surprised to hear all the people speaking Welsh. Even some of the guards in the camp spoke Welsh."

"Did they? You'd be amazed that the English would let them," she said.

"You would," he said. "They're so near England. You'd think the English would be after stamping out the Welsh language. Look what they did to us."

They walked down into the Island Road. There were beautiful white swans on the bank of the island. The houses looked cold and damp although there was smoke coming from every chimney. The street was deserted. A dog barked in the distance. It was dinner time on a Sunday, he reminded himself, Christmas Eve, 1916, and he was home from jail.

James Dempsey's shop was closed.

"My mother is going to come after dinner to see you," Margaret said.

They walked to the end of the road and across the bottom of Irish Street. When they turned into Bohreen Hill Cormac ran on ahead and little Michael followed him.

"Mrs Donnolly is sitting in with the baby," Margaret said.

They walked up towards the gate.

"I can't believe I'm home," he said. He put his hand on her shoulder.

She walked ahead of him up the narrow path. He could see through the window that the parlour fire was lighting. The whole house would be warm. Margaret was treating his homecoming as a special occasion.

Mrs Donnelly came to the front door. "You're home, Michael," she said. "You got here for Christmas. It was a long haul."

"It was," he said. "And it's not over yet."

They went inside and closed the door. He put his bag down beside the dresser and took off his coat and cap. "The baby slept all the time," Mrs Donnelly said, putting on her coat, "but I think she's stirring now. I looked in on her a minute ago. I'll go home now and leave ye."

They followed her into the hall. Margaret opened the door.

"Happy Christmas," Mrs Donnelly said.

"Many happy returns," they replied.

He stood behind Margaret at the door watching Mrs Donnelly walking down the path. He wondered who had carried Jim's coffin out of the house and down the path. It would have been awkward to get a coffin out of the parlour and through the narrow hall.

The baby began to cry as Margaret was closing the front door.

"She's awake," Margaret said. "I'd say she's hungry."

He followed her into the parlour. The cradle was against the wall where Jim's bed had been. Margaret moved the blankets down a little so that he could see the baby. She had stopped crying but he thought that she would probably start roaring again soon. Her eyes were screwed-up, closed, but she was moving and opening her mouth. He could see dark hair around her bonnet.

"Isn't she amazing," he said. "A new baby is such a miracle."

Margaret laughed. The baby began to cry.

"She's lovely," he said.

"She's hungry," Margaret said.

"I don't know who she's like," he said. "Maybe it's too early to say."

"Everyone says she's like my mother. I'll put on the dinner and then I'll feed her."

"Will I take her up?"

"Do, if you like. I'll be back into her in a few minutes."

The baby's eyes were open and she was roaring. He reached carefully into the cradle. He wanted to take the blankets out, too, to keep her warm, and he knew that he would have to be very careful with her head. Babies weren't able to support their own heads. He lifted her out of the cradle, keeping his arm under her head. The blankets were all over the place. She stopped crying as soon as he took her up. He sat down in the armchair at the fire.

"Hello Maeve," he said, wrapping the blankets snugly around her.

He thought she was pleased that someone had lifted her up. She was awake but she didn't cry. She blinked her eyes and moved her mouth. He sat in the armchair at the fire, holding her in his arms.

"Hello, Maeve," he said again, touching her little face.

He heard a noise at the gate and he looked towards the window. Philip and Aidan were coming up the path. The Christmas candle was on the window ledge waiting to be lit.